GW01161820

The Code

By Caroline Corfield

Caroline Corfield.

Published 2022

Special Thanks to my mother-in-law, husband, daughters and friends.

A list of characters is at the end of the book for reference

9 781739 929848

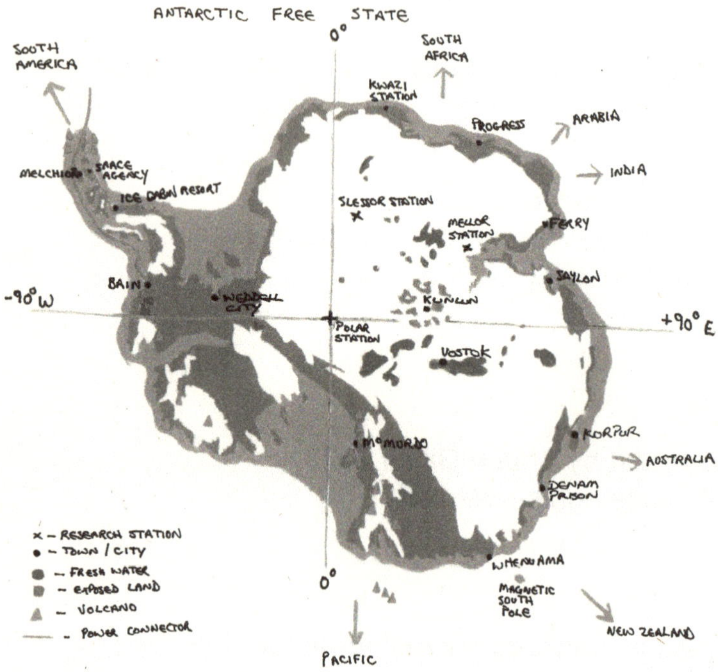
ANTARCTIC FREE STATE
0°
SOUTH AMERICA
SOUTH AFRICA
KWAZI STATION
PROGRESS
ARABIA
INDIA
MELCHIOR
SPACE AGENCY
ICE DAWN RESORT
SLESSOR STATION
MELLOR STATION
FERRY
SAYLON
BAIN
-90° W
WEDDELL CITY
KUNLUN
POLAR STATION
+90° E
VOSTOK
KORPUR
AUSTRALIA
McMURDO
DENAM PRISON
WHENUAMA
MAGNETIC SOUTH POLE
NEW ZEALAND
0°
PACIFIC
× – RESEARCH STATION
• – TOWN / CITY
– FRESH WATER
– EXPOSED LAND
– VOLCANO
– POWER CONNECTOR

Chapter One - Progress

The tower's heat transferred through to its spiralling gantry: he could feel the temperature as he climbed, even through his survival suit. His aim was the manual controls in order to turn the wheel one full turn to the right. There was no automatic over-ride and no system-monitoring of the controls, so it would take some time to track down the alteration but the change would alter the processing mix, creating the need to flare and that would increase the release of pollutants.

When people could finally realise how bad these plants were for the planet then there'd be no more need to show them like this, he thought, justifying his actions, with the secure foundation of the fanatic. Never once had he questioned where the information had come from or the money that had brought him to the town of Progress. For him the end required whatever means came to hand.

But before he could finish the turn, he felt something hit his jawline, just above the edge of his survival suit. There was a dulling ache in his jawbone. His arms weakened. He willed them to comply but felt them slacken anyway. There was panic in his head but no feeling of increased heart beats in his chest. He didn't know why, but he knew he was going to fall, and it would probably kill him. He watched himself let go of the wheel handle, then the gantry. Feeling the air on his face, he fell, fifteen metres to the frozen ground, amongst the snaking pipes of the Ethylene Plant. There was the intense pain of his broken bones even as he struggled to take one last breath.

A lithe, dark figure climbed over the pipes carefully. It stooped where he had fallen, then stood up and slinked away.

An hour later, Detective Ray McCarthy clambered over the pipework, some of which was cold or cool and some of which was so hot, steam wisps left their surface, visible in the light from the floodlights. She was careful with every pipe regardless. At the same point as the figure had stopped earlier she crouched down amongst them. Strong shadows, thrown by the floodlights, made it difficult to see exactly what was there, but Ray already knew it was a body. Otherwise she wouldn't have been there. It was late evening, she'd have been at home, watching the tennis, with a beer, with her flatmate, in the warmth. All the opposite things to what was happening now.

Pulling down her visor, she examined the body, using its optical zoom and built-in lights. Whoever this was, had fallen; from one of the distillation columns, probably. She'd get someone to check them. There were broken bones. The survival suit was badged with the plant's operator logo and a name, Pat Gallway. The loose fit on the body suggested it wouldn't be a surprise to find that Pat was still alive and missing a work's survival suit. She called for someone to come over, get up and check the whole gantry for evidence.

She took several still photos to accompany the video footage that had been collecting automatically since she arrived at the body. Standing slowly, she waved for the body to be recovered. Clambering carefully back across the various temperatures of pipework, she spotted the foreman for the day shift was waiting. Somebody would have the foreman's name already: she was legendary for not remembering the small shit.

“Pat Gallway, you know him?” she asked.

“Sure, bit of a bum, but you take what you can get, especially since so many leave in the winter. Is that him?”

“I doubt it. Do you have an address for Mr Gallway?”

“Yeah, he stays in the company apartment block, on Five and Hydrogen.”

“So he’s temporary?”

“Not so much, can't save a deposit, least long enough to put it down on a place and not a bar top.”

If it hadn’t been for the small puncture mark above the chin edge of the survival suit she might almost have fallen, as it were, for the idea this was a drunken accident. Because murder was almost unheard of in Progress. Industrial accidents less so.

"Thanks. There’s a good chance whoever it turns out to be, was up the gantry. What’s up there?”

“Manual safety valves.”

“You might want to check them once the guys have finished.”

"Thanks."

She was back in her office. The police station overlooked the shopping complex and leisure park on Omega Road. She'd purposefully chosen an office away from the front of the station building as the light coming through the glass of the complex was so bright it was hard to concentrate. It even caused the energy saving to kick in on the street lighting, turning it off.

Between the complex, the flares from the Ethylene plant she'd just come from, and the greenhouses on the other side of town by the airport, the whole of Progress was lit up. You'd hardly believe it was winter at all. Not until late at night when the complex closed, the energy saving kicked in for real and the greenhouses turned down, then, like something that crept off the sea, the darkness overwhelmed most of the town, although she always felt sorry for the workers in the company accommodation which faced the various chemical plants. There the lights were always on and when there was flaring, which had been often lately, the site was reminiscent of old-time descriptions of hell.

She was waiting at her desk to hear if Pat Gallway was at home, and if he wasn't, what they'd found in his room. In the meantime, the body from the plant had been taken to pathology, and she was waiting to hear about the puncture mark and if there was a chance to identify the body through records. She was also waiting for an opportune moment to head home, because she knew these things were not going to turn up on her desk soon.

Winter took its time, the hours seemed to stretch in the dark and everybody seemed to move slower. Ray just wanted to catch the end of the tennis, but nobody here understood that. Everyone in the office was hooked on the Olympics, especially as it was the first time a team from the Antarctic Free State was competing. And one of their own was there, James Wylie out of Weddell City Police was in the shooting. If you mentioned sport, that was pretty much all you got to hear about. She kept her mouth shut about the tennis.

The following morning, driving along Airport Road she could see the amount of snow that had fallen, and the teams working round the clock to keep the roads clear of the fresh stuff, leaving just enough to give traffic a grip. The lights were twinkling on the fresh snow, and the wind coming in off the sea kept it moving about on the road's compacted snow surface. She took her time, because that was how you stayed alive in the winter.

Progress wasn't big, fifteen thousand permanent residents, a strip of habitation strung out along the coast. A long way to the west was an area of greenhouses, Kwazi Station, serviced by ships in the winter and by road from Progress in the summer. Working there in the winter was a long shift. A long way to the east was the summer ferry port to Saylon. In the winter Progress hunkered down and got on with its job of making stuff for the AFS and Ray knew in the winter those long ways were in reality no ways. Her murderer was going to still be in Progress: the airport and harbour master were already on the watch for anything untoward.

Getting to her desk she sat with her police canteen coffee. There was a paper report waiting. The dry bones of the pathology report: the pictures would be in the digital version. She fired up the computer, and had a look.

As suspected, Pat Gallway's details did not match the body. Nobody local did either. A request had gone to central records in Weddell City last night, which would mean a result just before lunch, she thought. The plant foreman had emailed to say a safety valve had been tampered with, but not critically.

Putting in for warrants to search Pat's finances and phone records, she checked the uniformed's report on the search of his room. Cleaned out, like he'd moved on. The reasons were beginning to stack up for finding this Pat Gallway.

She continued to read the full pathology report. Sometimes things stuck in her head, but more often the words seemed to simply flow through her mind and leave nothing behind. Well, that wasn't strictly true, they must leave something behind, because she knew things afterwards but she didn't go to some mental filing cabinet and look them up. Information seemed to live in her head in a more ethereal way, and she was buggered if she knew how it worked, but happy that it did.

The puncture mark had been noted. The wound site examined. The drug was Tubocurarine with traces of Pancuronium. She looked them up. The first you could make from a plant, apparently, available in South America. How convenient, she thought. The second was used in lethal injections. Plenty of states in the sub-continent that did that. The death penalty had become popular again across the world after the carnage wreaked by the Carrington level coronal mass ejections. Nearly thirty years ago now, she recalled, it would take some time for the world to regain the luxuries of the past, including the idea of reformative rather than retributive justice.

The plant was a climbing vine, a liana. She knew a lot of biological specimens were making their way into the AFS, both officially and unofficially. The climate was changing in Antarctica, faster than elsewhere in the world, and new species had been turning up by natural means on the shores for some time. Now there was an official policy to take plants and species under threat of extinction in the northern polar regions to conserve them. Unofficially, a lot more was turning up; house plants, rare plants as a kind of exotic currency and crucially for her, the raw materials for illegal drugs.

It was hard to catch the illegal greenhouses, they had thermal insulation that would put the latest buildings to shame. Hermetically sealed, no light escaped, no heat, nothing that could be detected. They used battery power, but again well camouflaged. The spotter planes went up once a month and surveyed the hinterland of Progress, occasionally they got lucky and caught an operation with an air leak, or a lapse in routine. She reckoned in this case though, the drugs had probably come into the AFS preprepared. As she read on, the reason for both became apparent: the Tubocurarine took five minutes to act but the lethal injection drug was nearly instant. Clearly it was also more expensive or harder to come by.

She'd decided on a trip out to the company apartment block on Five Lane and Hydrogen Road. An H shaped building, matched by a twin at other end of the Pharmaceutical district, on One Lane and Hydrogen

Road. The founding fathers of Progress had spent little time on the street names, considering it to be an indulgence. Pat's three storey apartment block was the last building in town if you didn't count the Salt Plant on the shore side of Hydrogen Road.

Entering the air lock into a spacious common space, she saw chairs and tables, dispensing machines, a bank of sat phones. It felt very institutional. There was no lift so she took the stairs and came out onto a long corridor, seeing the tape across the room door some way down it. She reckoned the block could house at least three hundred.

She'd seen worse hotel rooms; it was big, with a small en suite shower and toilet facility. The view was less enticing however; standing at the window, across the road and to her right, she saw the tangle of cooling columns, fracking towers and associated pipework of the whole chemical complex that included the Ethylene Plant. There was dust on the window sill, dark and sooty. A testament to the recent flaring events.

The room didn't smell clean, but it was empty. Maybe, she thought, something had been left that the uniformed officers had missed. Getting down on her hands and knees, using the lights of her visor, she checked under the bed. Against the leg there was a scrap of paper. Stretching over she found it was the corner of a receipt, the kind you get from taxi drivers, with the beginning of a telephone number, and it was the Vostok code. Crawling out from under the bed, she placed it in a small plastic bag.

The dark dust was everywhere. She pulled back the uncovered duvet and checked the mattress, free from evidence of drunken accidents, and there'd been no beer stains on the window sill or coffee table either. Pat Gallway was only getting more intriguing.

Her mobile buzzed, she pressed her visor comms.

“McCarthy.”

“Boss, you should get back, the Anti-corruption Team have turned up. The dead man is on some kind of list of theirs.”

“Damn. Right. Minutes. In minutes.”

She hung up. This was sounding very much like the tennis was not for her this year.

Chapter Two - Imported Greens

Enya Zhao, head of the Anti-corruption Team was down two men. James Wylie, who was off gallivanting with the Olympic team, which she was secretly very happy about, but tried not to show, and Glenn Murcheson, who had less of an excuse. She couldn't get more than mildly annoyed about Glenn since it was a holiday booked six months ago.

So, it was Chris Saraband and Eric Jordan that she met at the airport, where Anatoli Dale, their charter pilot, was waiting to fly them to Progress. Though she and Anatoli were in a relationship, she preferred it if they didn't turn up to work together. Anatoli had proposed two years ago and she was aware she was putting off a number of decisions about his role with the Team.

The name of a dead body had come in last night and, once identified as Steve Jung, a key activist in the riskier reaches of the Green movement, it had triggered a call to her. He was a name of interest on her list of people with connections to Thierry Vonne, the new junior senator for Lomonosov. Thierry was a Green activist too, and he'd been meeting Rafael Dupont.

Rafael was on another list entirely. Not of interest, but of deep suspicion. Most of her job was teasing out the spider webs of connections within the political class of the AFS. Some would be relatively innocent groups with a common goal, and others would be groupings of mutually beneficial and often very profitable arrangements, that went beyond the usual nepotism inherent in such a small population.

Her job, as she saw it, was to weed out those who saw only self advantage in their roles, nepotism could come later. Rafael Dupont was widely known to have presidential ambitions and she didn't think anyone believed it was because he thought he would do a good job. It was the power he was after. The chance to make executive decisions for a country with the hardest currency in the world, still trading in materials long since banned from production elsewhere, but still needed, with a surplus of energy and an increasing potential for development. A country rich in natural resources.

It was the ability to cream a lot of that off for himself which drove Rafael Dupont. Currently he was courting the growing Green movement. Like the Resistance before, it was attracting its share of nutters and zealots, but Enya noticed, fewer senators. Thierry Vonne was a noticeable exception, and the rumour was he'd got elected because of his openly Green opinions.

The link with Steve Jung was tenuous but that was how it always started, so she pulled at the thread, and here she was in Progress. They'd touched down mid-morning. The twilight was lighter here than in Weddell City, which was a full ten degrees further south than Progress. The town was still lit up though. Across from the airport she saw the glow from the massive greenhouses, and she'd already noticed the chemical manufacturing sites at the other end, when they'd come in to land.

A taxi had taken them all to the police headquarters and now they were waiting in an office, somewhat squashed in with two extra chairs added to the two for visitors that had been in the room. Enya looked again at her watch. It had been twenty minutes since someone had said

Detective McCarthy was on her way. She didn't think Progress was that big, or the traffic that bad. She was curious to find out what the delay was for.

Positioning herself to watch the coming and going in the outer office through the glass wall and door she saw Detective McCarthy coming. A small, compact woman, with short cropped hair, a mix of blonde and white, wearing her dark red survival suit shrugged to the waist. And she was carrying a mug of coffee.

The door swung open with a twang through the glass from the hinges and Enya watched the detective squeeze round to the working side of the desk.

"Hi. Sorry I'm late. Needed to check something out. What can I do for the Anti-corruption Team?"

Enya looked directly at her, since her gaze had been travelling across the four of them, trying to figure out, presumably, who she should apologise to the most.

"I'm Enya Zhao, this is Chris Saraband, and Eric Jordan, we're the team. This is Anatoli Dale, he's our transport. I was told you were on your way twenty minutes ago. I'm curious what you've checked out during that time?"

Enya had tried to keep her voice level, she didn't like people saying they were on their way when clearly they weren't. It was a lie. At the very least it was untrustworthy. She still wanted to get the measure of this McCarthy woman before deciding whether to work with her or remove her from the case. She could do with an extra pair of hands.

"I was back at Pat Gallway's flat. Found a bit of a taxi receipt from Vostok. Wanted to see if it generated any information."

"Who's Pat Gallway? I'm here because your dead guy is Steve Jung," said Enya.

Enya was eyeing the coffee mug. The detective seemed to be oblivious to social cues, but her tone was entirely matter-of-fact which Enya always appreciated.

She watched the detective put the mug down on the desk.

"*Your* dead guy was wearing Pat Gallway's clothes."

Enya caught the inflection on the 'your'. So Detective McCarthy expected the job to be given over to them wholesale. She didn't seem too cut up about it either. Enya was more tempted to add her as a temporary member as a result.

"Is there a bigger room to discuss this in, with coffees for all of us?" asked Enya pointedly.

She saw McCarthy look at her mug with a trace of guilt.

"Yes. Of course. Sorry. I'm not much for mundane details. Come with me."

Enya saw her pick up the mug and head out the door.

They all trooped out after her. Enya tapped Anatoli on the shoulder as she went past, asking him to find hotel rooms. She had decided there was sufficient reason to stay.

The conference room was more than big enough. They all sat at one end of the long table, where a wheeled whiteboard was situated to the side of a wall screen, and Enya saw McCarthy put up the receipt scrap to the whiteboard. The screen behind the whiteboard flickered into life, as Enya heard McCarthy tap a few things on a keyboard inset to the table. It showed the first picture from the pathology report, a close up of a puncture wound in a man's jaw, presumably Steve Jung.

“I'll go sort out coffee,” said McCarthy heading towards the door, “have a look through the report.”

The glass door swung shut.

“She's odd,” said Chris.

“Is she any good though?” asked Enya.

“She found the scrap, after uniform were supposed to have looked,” said Eric, whom Enya was finding, always gave people the benefit of the doubt until all doubt was extinguished.

“True,” mused Enya, busy reading the pathology report, “Tubocurarine and Pancuronium. Nice. They wanted him found at the site of his sabotage then. There's a message being sent here.”

“By who?” asked Chris.

“That's a job for our local detective. Our question is why?”

“So you bringing her onto the team?” asked Chris.

"With Wylie and Murcheson gone, do I have much of a choice?"

"Boss," Eric and Chris chimed together in mock anguish.

The door swung open as McCarthy and another officer brought in a flask and some mugs.

"There we go. What do you think?" said McCarthy, nodding at the screen.

"I think we're going to need you to join us for a while," said Enya.

"Oh," said McCarthy.

She sounded less disappointed than Enya had feared. Maybe it wouldn't be so bad after all, she thought.

"So McCarthy… What's your first name?"

"Ray."

"So Ray, what did you find out about the taxi receipt?"

"Nothing so far. The number is just one digit longer than the Vostok code. Got a pal in Vostok department going to see what they can find."

Enya had met some of the police department in Vostok two years ago. They had not inspired confidence, and the knowledge Ray had contacts there was not a positive point. Enya tried another angle.

"Got anywhere with the supply of Pancuronium?"

"I reckon it was supplied pre-mixed, rather than made up here. But I have feelers out for what the area's illegal greenhouses are up to. Usually it's recreational drugs, but who knows if they have a more dangerous sideline."

"Okay. I'd like you to continue to track down the supply, and track down this Pat Gallway, if he truly exists."

"I can get the foreman to come in and give our sketch artist a description."

"That would be helpful. Is there no photographic ID on record?"

"The company don't ask for it, so no. It puts a lot of their seasonal workers off," said Ray, in a manner that Enya identified as someone who knew which battles were worth fighting and that this policy wasn't one of them.

"Does it now?" asked Enya, for whom all battles were worth it. She wondered more about links between the management of the AFS Ethylene Plant and some of her lists.

"Steve Jung was tampering with the safety valves on the tower," said Ray, "the foreman said it would have led to automatic flaring, apparently the mix would have been dangerous to continue to process as a result. We get flares maybe every two months, but he said lately they'd had to do it nearly every week."

"I need dates for the flaring events. See if we can tie that back to Steve Jung arriving in Progress. Tell me what do you have on local Green activists?"

She saw Ray look at her with a quizzical smile.

"You're joking right?"

"Everywhere has them. You telling me Progress, with the chemical plants especially, doesn't?"

"If they're here they're keeping a very low profile. We get imported Greens, they don't stay long."

"I'll need what you've got on the imported ones then," said Enya, "Why'd they leave?"

"I'd hazard a guess at the high level of hostility by locals, towards any idea that would wreck local livelihoods," said Ray.

Enya noted the hint of sarcasm in Ray's tone. It annoyed her. The basic questions had to be asked, even if you could surmise the answers, sometimes your suppositions would be wrong.

"And this hostility, does it escalate to violence at all?"

"It's a small town, an atmosphere of hostility is enough. The last fight we had was a bar brawl with some navy and that was last year. Navy were confined to ships after that."

"I forgot this was the home port. I always expect it to be Saylon. What was the fight about?"

"Guess," said Ray.

"Okay." She paused. "I'd like to think the navy are clean in this case, but for thoroughness let's get the crew lists of all the ships in port for the last week. And I want the names of these imported Greens."

Enya turned to Chris and Eric, "You'll get to work on cross referencing these names with our lists. Something is bound to turn up. But first we go find our hotel."

She saw them pick up the bags they'd hauled around with them. She knew Anatoli would already have her bag with him.

"See you in two hours Ray," she said, with a smile that didn't usually generate a smile in return, and continued, "Back here. If you could arrange for us to keep the conference room for now."

Ray was gobsmacked, watching the team depart through the glass doors, across the office until they disappeared. She'd heard some of the rumours about the Anti-corruption Team's chief, but having experienced Enya Zhao in the flesh, nothing did justice to the woman. As for her team; the two guys reminded her immediately of competent and loyal huskies.

She'd been surprised to have been asked to stay on the case and to work with them, and was wondered how good or bad a thing that might turn out to be for her. She liked living in Progress, having a relatively quiet life, if this case looked like it merited the Anti-corruption Team's presence, that could all change.

Back in her own office, she got to work securing the conference room for the team's use, which wasn't difficult given their precedence over everything and everyone else. How to win friends, she thought. Then there was the list of identified Green activists who'd come and gone in the last six months.

It had about twenty names, the average stay was a fortnight and the first clue of the day; they'd all stayed in the Hotel Juniper. It was as good a place as any to start. Since there'd never been trouble, nobody had ever noticed, let alone looked into why they all seemed to have stayed in the same place. She began to understand some of Enya Zhao's questions.

Chapter Three - Distraction

The Hotel Lambda overlooked the Navy Quay and took its name from the lane that ran up its western side. Hardly imaginative, thought Enya. Like a lot of the town, she realised. The taxi dropped them in the vehicle airlock, unusual for anywhere outside of Vostok but essential on the exposed and equally unimaginative Harbour Road. She'd briefly seen one of the big navy ships in port as well as the three small ships, but hadn't been able to make out whether it was the Mercer or the new one, Clarke. If it was the Mercer there was a chance of bumping into Valla. Enya wasn't sure whether that would complicate their visit or not.

They picked up their keys from reception. Anatoli would already be in her room. Without a time frame she didn't know what to tell him. Should he go if this was only going to need a few days? And how much of wanting to have him stay was simply down to her personal desire?

She opened the door to the room, and heard a female squeal. Not what she was expecting. To check the room number, she stepped back into the corridor, but suddenly the door was pulled from her hand by a woman in a towel who ran past her and towards the stairs. Dark hair, lithe and, from the marks left on the carpet, wet.

"Tolli?"

She ventured into the room, still not sure about having been given a key to the right room. Anatoli appeared, from the en suite, also wet, also in a towel. Looking absolutely mortified.

"I don't know who she was, or how she got in. One minute I'm showering, next minute it's a lot more crowded, and then she runs out squealing when the room door opens. Enya, what have you got us into this time?"

She burst out laughing, then stopped. It was possible someone was listening. She gestured to Tolli about bugs in the room. He was shaking his head.

"No. I checked," he said, "used the scanner and everything. It's clean."

"I think someone's trying to distract me from the case. In an unsubtle fashion. Maybe you should go home tomorrow, in case it gets more unsubtle."

The memory of finding Tolli tied to a chair in a Vostok warehouse belonging to the gangster Frederika Tran, two years ago was still fresh. As was the memory of them armed and searching for Freddie at the Antarctic Combined Research facility in Melchior: all of which had led to Tolli's marriage proposal.

He seemed to have got used to some of the danger her job entailed, but she was increasingly sure she wanted him not to get involved with it. She wanted him safe. He seemed more serious than the flyboy she'd first met in the cockpit of his jet, but she also realised, she was no longer the stickler, beat detective she'd been back then. Change was inevitable. But still.

"I am your's to command," he said, squashing her in a wet embrace.

"Thanks," she said, whipping the towel off him to dry her face, then dropping it on the floor.

"That's not fair," he said and tried to start on her clothing.

"Tolli, later. I have to get back, I'm here to freshen up."

He was picking up the towel. "Technically, I'm not finished," he said.

She saw him reach the door of the en suite ahead of her. She checked her watch, there was time.

She arrived last into the conference room, but reckoned she looked nonchalant. Then she saw Chris smile at her, and wondered how the hotel rooms had been allocated.

On the screen was a list of twenty names with dates against them and the name Hotel Juniper. Eric had his laptop open and was typing the names in.

"Nobody had noticed because they turned up, spouted a bit about pollution, planet this, and eco that, then left," said Ray, "We all thought it was because they never got any traction. As if Progress was where they sent the noobies to see how serious about the cause they were. Survive Progress with your ideals intact and you're in the organisation, sort of thing…"

"But they all stayed at this Hotel Juniper. Where's that?"

Enya went over to the town map now stuck up on the whiteboard too.

Ray was pointing to a block out by the airport and greenhouses. "On the Back Road," she said.

"Should we head out there?" asked Chris.

"Let's see what Eric digs up first, have a better idea whether Ray's notion is right or whether something more serious was or is going on there," she said, continuing, "Anything else new? Vostok taxi, drugs, the mysterious Pat Gallway?"

She saw Ray ruffle through a pile of papers and hand her the drawing of Pat from the sketch artist.

"This been run through the database? What about ID for our twenty names?"

"On it," said Chris, taking the sketch from her hand and feeding it into the scanner slot of his modified laptop.

"I'd like to meet the sketch artist too. We had an unexpected shower guest. Somebody is definitely trying to rattle my cage."

She saw Ray reach for her phone and a few minutes later the sketch artist turned up. She took him to the far end of the table and tried to describe the woman who'd fled her room and realised during her description that the towel the woman had been wearing hadn't matched the hotel's, it had been a pale cream and the hotel had bleached white.

Enya had a good memory for faces, it had certainly been honed during her time with the Weddell City Police, so within about fifteen minutes she felt they were nearly there. Another five minutes and she was happy with the sketch artist's likeness. She thanked him as he handed it to her.

"Have we got any photo ID of our names yet?" she said coming back to sit at the business end of the table, sliding the sketch across to Chris to feed into his laptop.

"One or two. Here, let me throw them up," said Eric, as three names and accompanying ID popped up on the screen.

"When did they visit?"

Dates appeared next to the faces.

"That one was three weeks ago. Karl Leyden. Are any of the names pinging on our lists, Eric?"

"Not him yet. I've had two hits, no ID yet. And the names were much earlier. Maybe they sent big hitters then realised it was a lost cause?"

"Have we got the navy names yet?"

"Still waiting on the okay from some Defence administrator," said Chris.

"Let me see if I can shift that along a bit," said Enya, pulling out her mobile and calling Valla.

It rang for a while. She hung up and called again. This time Valla answered, slightly out of breath.

"Enya, what's up?"

“Valla, sorry to disturb you, we have a request in for the names of the crew who’re in port in Progress just now. Seems to be a bit of delay, not sure why. We’re following a lead and just want to eliminate them from our enquiries.”

“I’m sorry to hear that, I shall remedy the situation personally.”

“Thanks, out of curiosity are you still hand picking them?”

“Yes. Well. Not the last batch. We took on five, I let Veronica do the actual interviews. Why?”

“We’re looking into some Green activists, any chance you could get me those five names sooner?”

“Yes. We do a background search but it’s through Intelligence. If it’s not on their files, we don’t know about it. Let me know what you find, please.”

“I’ll keep you in the loop.”

She hung up.

More ID had turned up on the screen.

Then Chris let out a whistle, and a fresh view appeared on the screen, the sketch of the woman from the Lambda Hotel, a photo ID and a name, Isadora Ley. Enya studied the face.

“That’s her.”

“I’m not even sure she’s really an AFS citizen. Which means she’s had inside help to get the ID. She’s been here in Progress on that ID for three days, but we have a string of other names, citizenships and IDs for her.”

“Where’s she staying?”

“You’re not going to believe this Boss, but the Juniper Hotel.”

Enya looked across at Ray.

“You have no idea what goes on at this hotel? Is there a reason?”

“There’s never any bother. I’m Police, not Intelligence Agency or Anti-corruption.”

And Enya remembered what that felt like, to draw a line beyond which it was someone else’s problem. Such a long time ago, nearly eight years before, in the Environment Department building with Glenn Murcheson, looking for the reason it had shut down the local energy grid, and finding herself on the path that had led to this moment.

“Let’s go visit now. I’m kind of touchy about who shares a shower with Anatoli.”

Enya sat up front while Ray drove the unmarked police car. The twilight had gone, it was just dark, but it wasn’t really apparent till they had driven off Omega Road and away from the shopping and leisure complex. Even now, the light from it burst through on side roads between

Omega and the Back Road. To the other side of them was total blackness.

Like McMurdo and many other places in the AFS, either the land or the ice loomed over them. Long distance travel was by air or sea. The Hotel Juniper was conveniently close to the airport for a fast getaway, so she'd brought Chris and Eric. It was highly likely that Isadora would run.

The Green Movement had infiltrated AFS society at every level just as the Resistance once had and there was no doubt someone in the airport would help Isadora if she could make it there. It troubled Enya that the Greens hadn't been seriously watched so far, much less proscribed. She wondered if Gordon Murcheson had engineered the events at the Innonnox mine with Freddie Tran to get the Resistance banned, but now Gordon was himself under indefinite house arrest, and President Mariko Neish was not like Gordon. Well, she thought, not that we've been able to discover.

The entrance to the hotel was on the Airport Road. The weather meant they'd have to drive round to the vehicle airlock giving advance warning over arriving on foot, which Enya would have preferred. The snow had started while they'd been in the police station offices, and they'd been greeted with fat, wet flakes thrown horizontally when they'd stepped out to head for the car. Enya wondered what Ray had against the underground car park.

They entered the hotel through the front door airlock, with a clean and crisp suck from the door seals. Bare was the word Enya thought of. Other people might call it minimalist, but the space felt soulless. They approached the desk, and she let Ray produce her ID.

“Local Police, I’m Detective McCarthy, we’re hoping to speak to an Isadora Ley. She’s registered as staying here.”

Enya saw the receptionist look at the ID. She was aware that Chris and Eric had fanned out to examine the rest of the reception area.

“Who’re your friends?”

“Friends,” said Ray. “Is Isadora here or not?”

Enya had previously tagged Ray’s tone as sarcasm but realised it might well be a permanent level of background irritation.

The receptionist pulled a book closer on the desk to look through it. Enya knew stalling when she saw it. She turned and signalled to Chris and Eric to find the stairs and back exits.

“Keep your hands where I can see them,” said Ray, causing Enya to spin back around.

Maybe a silent alarm, surely not a weapon, she thought. The receptionist had his hands in the air, and Enya saw that Ray had pulled her gun. She went behind the desk to look for alarm buttons, motioning the receptionist to go round the front of the desk and swept her hand under the counter. She found what she was looking for.

“She’s a runner, probably on foot for the airport,” she called to Chris and Eric.

Chris had reappeared from the stair door and she watched him head out with Eric, turning back to see Ray handcuffing the receptionist.

"I'll call it in" said Ray, "and request back up. Get them to lock down the airport. If that's where she's gone, she'll not get far."

"I hope not," said Enya, aware that she herself had once escaped from Vostok by air, on a very unofficial basis.

Chapter Four - Hidden Greens

Isadora Ley, her name for the time being, heard the buzzer and knew she'd have to leave. It'd been a calculated gamble to try and seduce the pilot, which seemed to have backfired spectacularly on her. It seemed the intel they had on the Anti-corruption Team was lacking some key points. She stuffed her papers inside her survival suit and headed for the stairwell. Always empty in the AFS, often to her benefit, she had only got one floor down when she heard a door open onto the stairs. They were good. She changed tack and headed for the service lift, taking it down one more floor. Now on the floor above the ground floor, she'd lost track of which states called it first and which called it second. Whatever, it was enough to drop out of a window and land in one piece. She tried a few doors then remembered she'd been given a service key; it was unusual to be working alongside such helpful collaborators. The door opened and thankfully the room was empty. She headed for the window.

She had to hand it to the AFS, they believed in their own shit. The window opened smoothly: a well maintained, hermetically sealed window just doing its job. The snow stuck on her cheeks as she poked her head out to check the drop. It would be a standard storey height, nothing she'd not dropped from before, but she had absolutely no idea what was below her. The snow was thick, the light non existent and, she now realised, the visor was back in her room. Fuck this place, should have left it to the penguins, she thought.

Dropping from the window had knocked the breath out of her, but apart from badly jarring her left leg, nothing else was hurt. She tried not to put weight on her leg till she knew exactly what had happened to it. Technically the airport terminal should be just across the road, if she could figure out where the road was, or see the terminal building. Or, having taken a few limping steps, even see the hotel. She thought she had a good enough sense of direction so carried on in a straight line, reasoning, eventually she'd come to the edge of the road, or maybe the chain link fence round the airport. The snow was now above her ankles. Would she still feel the edge of the road through it?

Eric was first out the door. The snow was dense, the big, wet flakes were still at a near horizontal level. He pulled his visor down and set it for thermal, sweeping the area; nothing. If she was heading for the airport she either had a remarkable turn of speed in the conditions, or had completely lost direction. He saw the heat signature of car engines, two pale yellow blobs heading into the vehicle airlock.

Chris joined him.

"If she's not still inside, then my money's on stumbling around in the snow," said Eric over his visor comms.

"What makes you say that?"

"She's not native, not migrant, probably doesn't even spend a lot of time here. What's the first thing you notice about visitors?"

"Haha, yes. They're always misplacing their visors. Well, what's your plan?"

Eric thought for a moment. It wasn't usually his call.

"If she got disorientated inside, she could be heading in a different direction and still think it was towards the airport."

"Yes."

"So, we check those directions, because I don't see her in the airport direction."

"Well, the police are supposed to be locking it down anyway. I'll take the Back Road side, you take Omega Road."

"Okay."

Isadora stood very still. She could hear the fresh snow crunch. Someone was nearby, but, since everyone here seemed able to remember their visors, presumably she was directly behind them. She slipped her knife into her hand, and continued to listen for the crunching. It would only take them turning round and she would be at a major disadvantage. She trusted to luck and thought she could feel a slight temperature difference on her exposed lips.

She risked a bear hug into the darkness, drawing her knife across the resistance it had been a shock to find in her arms. She'd no idea what or who she'd struck, but she had to make the most of the advantage immediately. Running in the opposite direction, her lungs filled with freezing air, stinging deep inside her chest. Her head got control of her panic and she slowed, breathing through her cupped hands, and using yoga techniques. The pain in her lungs lessened. Who... she thought, who would choose to fucking live in this place? It was so clearly not what humans were designed for.

Eric headed off round the corner of the building. The thin strip of flesh between his visor and the survival suit stung in the constant assault of the snow. It must be numbing on the whole of your face, he thought. Scanning ahead of him, there were no thermal traces; no cars, the buildings were all well sealed, it was an unrelenting blue. He turned back to see if Chris had been more successful. As he passed the front of the hotel and got to the corner he picked up Chris's voice on the visor.

"Eric? She's got a knife. Watch out."

He stretched out behind him to find the wall of the building and got his back to it.

"You okay?"

"Bloody great tear in my suit, but yeah. She's gone off down the Back Road."

"Does the Boss know?"

"Yeah, I called it in when she ran off."

He spotted Chris, a pale yellow with a disturbing red line.

"I'm coming to get you inside."

They were back inside the reception area where a uniformed officer was watching over the handcuffed receptionist. Eric had a good look at Chris's suit.

"It's fucked."

"I know. I'll have to get one here and sort it out later. You know," said Chris, "maybe she's doubled back. The lure of the visor left behind."

"Let's go see," he said.

Together they went up to the fourth floor, finding the room door still ajar. They readied their guns and entered one after the other in the classic search manoeuvre. The visor was still there, lying on the armchair. Eric saw Chris pick it up and clip it onto his suit.

They finished checking the room out. Eric rifled through the contents of the half empty suitcase on the luggage stand, while Chris was checking the bed.

"Well, well, well," murmured Chris.

"What?"

"Another Vostok taxi receipt. You think our Mr. Gallway was in on the whole thing?"

“What’s the number after the code? You think she and him were together at some point?”

“Seven, same number. It’s possible. Are Greens bumping each other off?”

“Power struggle?” he asked.

“Same old, same old," said Chris, "We should let the Boss know.”

Chris was waiting with Eric in the now empty reception area, uniform having taken the receptionist back to the police station. He saw Enya and Ray re-enter through the door airlock.

“Lost her," said Ray, "but she can’t leave. We have all the routes being watched.”

“We should head back to the police station. Then you,” Enya was nodding at him, “need to get a new suit from the complex.”

“I don’t think there’s any doubt she’s not a citizen, carving into someone’s survival suit like this,” said Chris.

An hour later, Chris was standing just inside the Leisure Complex interior, trying to adjust to its brightness. They’d tried to ramp the levels up slowly in the airlock corridor but it hadn’t been successful. Finally, he was able to see the shops were all to the left of the entrance and the less sedate pursuits to the right where bodies were moving about doing vaguely sport-like movements in the distance.

He headed towards the retail sector, assailed by the scents promoting the products. The unmistakable smell of Progress, now an unfortunate double entendre, oozed from a technology shop front. He carried on, drawing a few head turns as the gash in his suit flapped slightly with each step.

He reached a survival suit shop. There was a selection of red, orange, neon yellow and even a neon pink on display. The assistant came over.

“You look like you lost,” said the assistant, with a smile.

Chris knew the guy would think the tear was caused by an inanimate object, like a piece of machinery. Nobody who followed the Code would slash someone’s survival suit. Chris felt there was no point in changing the assumption.

“I’m still walking, but yeah, I need a fresh suit.”

The assistant cast an appraising eye over his current suit, though Chris felt it was more than the suit that was being appraised.

“Very nice. Tailored to fit. I’m afraid we don’t stretch to that service, but I can get you something close. Got a colour preference?”

“Red,” said Chris, wondering whether Isadora had visited this shop when she first arrived.

He fished out his mobile and got up her picture.

"You seen this woman in the last few days?"

Chris thought there was a flicker of disappointment that crossed the assistant's face. The assistant came over with a red survival suit draped over his arm, and Chris felt the guy was leaning in more than was strictly necessary to see the phone screen. However, it gave him an excellent view of the assistant's face when he looked. Chris could see he'd recognised Isadora.

"No. Sorry, not seen her."

The assistant was proffering the survival suit and pointing at the changing room.

Chris carried the suit over and tried it on. The guy might be a duplicitous letch, but he had a great eye for fit. He emptied his pocket contents into the new suit and left the slashed one in the cubicle.

"I'll wear it to go, thanks."

They concluded the transaction in the least amount of words possible. Chris wondered how soon the, clearly local, Green network in Progress would find out from the assistant that people were looking for Isadora. He decided it was worth stirring the pot a bit.

"We think she murdered the guy they found at the Ethylene Plant."

He strolled out of the complex and across the road to the police station.

“You think George, the owner of our survival suit shop, the guy I went to school with, recognised Isadora?” said Ray.

Chris could tell she wasn’t convinced.

He was back with the others in the conference room. The second taxi receipt was now up on the board. He looked over at Enya.

“Tell me," Enya said to Ray, “did you have much of a problem with the Resistance?”

He saw Ray look into the distance.

“Not really. You got to know where people’s sympathies lay, but we never had anything like sabotage or murder.”

“I can see the town has a policy,” said Enya, “which I agree may have its merits. However once you get to the sabotage and murder phase of a movement’s progress, you'll find your policy is already impeding the investigation of those very things.”

Chris saw that Ray was looking crestfallen.

“You’re suggesting Progress is riddled with hidden Greens?” she said

“Yes. And there's factions within them. Maybe they’re now engaging in what they consider justified cleansing of the movement, or are themselves being cleansed. Ordinary people get caught in the crossfire and these nutters consider it collateral damage. Have you seen a Green manifesto on population control?"

"Ideas don't kill people," Ray said.

Chris could hear her defensive tone, and felt Enya needed to cool off a bit if they were going to stay on track.

"Well," he said, "let's see what happens now I've suggested Isadora bumped off Steve Jung to our friend George. I suspect Progress' homegrown Greens won't be keen on that. They will want the plants shut down but they'll be wondering how this benefits that."

"True," said Enya, "What did your contact in Vostok say about the taxi number?"

"He's off shift now, but I should get a message later. Speaking of which..."

Chris saw Ray look at her watch, it was now seven in the evening.

"Yes," said Enya, "But first can you get us a pool car? Don't want to be using taxpayer money on taxis or having you chauffeur us around more than necessary, thanks."

Chris reckoned that was as much conciliation as Enya was able to manage at the moment. He hoped Ray appreciated it. He'd had Enya Zhao as a boss since making sergeant eight years ago, he knew she didn't suffer fools gladly, but he didn't think Enya thought Ray was a fool either.

The atmosphere back at the Lambda Hotel was quite different to the one earlier in the day when they'd picked up their keys to freshen up. Chris felt everyone they came across was wary of them. Word had spread about who was in town. Whatever element of surprise they'd had was gone and they were back to their usual toolbox of cajoling, coercing and plain intimidation. He hoped the local Police were up to the job of stopping Isadora leaving town.

Anatoli was waiting in the reception area. Chris liked Enya's man; Anatoli was chill, a good laugh and easy on the eye to boot. He smiled as he thought back to his earlier encounter in the shop. Was he turning into a letch too?

"Dinner," said Anatoli, sounding less than relaxed, "Now."

The menu was typical winter fare; stews, cured meats or mushroom based dishes. Almost all the greenhouse produce would be shipped to other parts of the AFS, mostly Vostok, for a shocking mark up in price to rich tourists, or Weddell City and Saylon, the big population centres. Everyone had ordered except him and he had to read down the list again. Something was on his mind, but he couldn't tease it further into the light of his conscious thoughts. Too hungry or too tired, he thought, maybe in the morning.

Chapter Five - Fleur d'Sel

Ray was woken by the buzzing of her phone. She leant out to find it and it clattered to the floor. Shit, she thought, and turned on the light, a pool of yellow covered the bedside table and the floor. She picked up the phone, saw the time was five thirty and a missed call from the station. She cursed out loud this time. It could only be another body.

She called the station, and got the details. The early morning shift at the Salt Plant had discovered a body in the evaporation bed. It was a costly discovery and the boss wanted something done about it as soon as possible so he could deep clean and restart the process.

Throwing on her suit, she wondered if this was going to be a body the Anti-corruption Team would be interested in and decided to find out first. She preferred to work alone, and having Enya Zhao breathing down her neck didn't help her cognitive functioning.

She arrived inside the plant and was directed to the room with the evaporation bed in it. Forensics were still there, taking photographs. Drunken workmen falling from distillation towers did not merit a Forensic Team call out and so with Steve Jung, she'd had to do that all herself, but a dead body in an evaporation bed was only going to be murder. There was no accidentally falling into the chest high, stainless steel bed.

She stood on tiptoe to get a good look inside the bed. The body was naked. She was glad of the covering of salt crystals, he was no model specimen; grey under the crystal sheen, with a sizeable beer belly.

"Any clothes around? ID?" she asked the Forensic officer, as he packed away his camera.

"Nothing, the pathologist is on her way, but there's a lot of salt crystals around and inside his mouth."

Ray moved up the side of the bed and tipped onto her toes again, to get a better look at the face. Something looked very familiar even through the crystals. That was when she realised she would have to call Enya Zhao. Because this was Pat Gallway.

The pathologist arrived just ahead of Enya, which was surprising, since Enya would only have had fifteen minutes notice compared to Sheena's thirty. Enya was without her two 'huskies'.

"Ray," said Enya, "thanks for letting me know. Been a while since I've seen a body in situ."

Ray did the introductions between Enya and Sheena Ricci, the pathologist. Sheena was busy asking for stepladders, and Ray saw Enya go over to the bed to look at the body.

"He does look like he drinks. But there was no sign of excess at his room?" asked Enya.

"Functioning alcoholic. They do exist," replied Ray.

"Did you ever get the finance and phone records you asked for?"

Ray checked her phone.

"Came in late yesterday evening, not had a chance to look them over."

Ray saw Sheena directing the salt plant worker on where to place the step ladders. She and Enya stepped back from the bed. She saw Enya continue to watch the worker as he moved away.

"Where are the stepladders kept?" Enya asked.

Ray saw the worker point to a cupboard by the door as he made his way through it into the rest of the plant and the door continue to swing back and forth, as the plant manager came through from the other direction.

"When can I have the bed back? Every second costs money. This is the purest grade of Fleur d'Sel in the world, guaranteed free from micro-plastics."

Ray looked at his tall, narrow figure, dressed in decontamination coveralls, his face long, his eyes as grey as the salt covered body. She moved towards him.

"Can I take your name? I'd like to ask some general questions about access to the plant."

He was looking down at her, as if he was seeing her for the first time.

"Yes, Certainly, I'm Lief Durant, I'm the manager of the plant. I'm also marketing and public relations. None of this should get out. If people thought our Fleur d'Sel was contaminated in any way it would be devastating for our brand."

"I can't promise anything, Mr Durant. Who has access overnight to the plant? And when do the shifts change? We'll need to speak to everyone who was on tonight."

"All access is by ID card, so anyone with a registered ID would gain access anytime of the day. Shifts change at four and eight, we have rolling production. I can get you the names and details."

Ray saw him look over to the evaporation bed as Sheena was stepping down from the stepladders.

"Is that it?" he asked.

"Ray?" asked Sheena, "We can shift the body?"

"Good with me," she said and saw Sheena nod to her team to get to work.

"Probable cause?" asked Enya.

"Looks like Hypernatremia," said Sheena and elaborated, "from a presumably forced, ingestion of concentrated salt solution."

"Thanks," said Enya, "Another message perhaps?"

Ray looked at Enya for more information, this was the first she'd heard that some sort of message was part of the murders.

"Killed in the act of sabotage, at the site of sabotage, suggests to me someone has a message to make either about the act of sabotage or the person doing the sabotage. This, death by salt, in the salt plant, might be convenience, but it feels like another message to me."

"What?"

"I can't figure that out yet. It'll be good to know if the salt he's ingested is the salt from the plant."

Ray turned to find the plant manager. He'd moved over to the evaporation bed as soon as they'd lifted the body out of it.

"You got a chemical breakdown of your product?"

"Certainly, for quality control. We have processes further on..."

"Great," interrupted Ray, "send it over to me, here."

She handed him a business card, watched him pocket it to an inside pocket as he headed back to the evaporation bed.

"How did you arrive?" she asked Enya.

"Anatoli dropped me off, but I told him to go back to bed. So I wouldn't mind a lift."

In the car she quizzed Enya on the information she had on the Green Movement. This case was certainly opening her eyes to the world of clandestine operations. She'd never have believed there were natives of Progress who supported the Green cause.

She remembered George from school, five years above her. What was it that had made him want to change

Progress so drastically he'd consort with the likes of Isadora Ley and Steve Jung?

She let Enya out at the Lambda Hotel and carried on round to the police station, properly fired up now. There used to be the Code, the protection of life against the elements regardless of whatever else was between one person and another. The size of the AFS population, the environment, it had always seemed to make sense to Ray. But this was different. It wasn't Antarctic to cold-bloodedly murder people for a political ideology. That sort of shit belonged back in the UN.

Enya got back to the hotel and the room. It was just after seven. Tolli had gone back to sleep and she didn't want to wake him. She sat at the table and opened her laptop. Some emails had come in. The list of five new navy recruits from Valla. The full crew lists of the ships in port from the Defence Office, and as of a minute ago a forwarded email from Ray with Pat Gallway's finance and phone records. She'd get Eric to go through the navy lists for cross referencing, so opened Ray's forwarded mail. The first file was the phone records for the last six months. There was a batch of calls two days ago to one number, but, what caught her eye was a single call to a number yesterday, which had only occurred one more time. His last received call.

Two months earlier he was making calls to Vostok numbers. Presumably while in Vostok. If the last number had been Isadora, the phone was probably dead now, but she sent on the number to be checked, maybe it would match her current name or one of her other identities. It might even be a new identity which would be more helpful again.

Her phone went off with a solar flare alarm. It was another irritation. Comms would be down for the next few hours at least, the day at worst. She looked over at Tolli sprawled across the bed, his tousled dark hair, the muscles on his out-flung arm. It was unlikely he'd be leaving today. She didn't like the fact that Isadora knew which room they had. She decided she'd ask for a new room, in case the alarm stayed up. Distracted, she pulled herself away from admiring Tolli and got back to looking at the downloaded files.

For a drunk, or functioning alcoholic, apparently unable to put down a deposit on an apartment, Pat Gallway had a very healthy bank balance. With a recent payment of two thousand dollars, he had more than enough to buy a decent flat. Was it a bribe to him? For bribing others? For materials in some nefarious task? His outgoings were minimal so it didn't look like he was bribing anyone or buying kit. Maybe, he had been blackmailing someone.

She heard Tolli stir.

"Good morning sweetheart. I didn't expect you to be here," he said.

She saw he had a wicked look in his eye.

"Better company here," she said giving up on the files completely for the moment.

She saw him pick up his phone and see the alert.

"Ah," he said, "doesn't look like I'll be going anywhere today."

"That's where you're wrong. I need you to get them to shift us to a different room. I'm not keen on Isadora Ley's next potential visit."

He looked like he was going to make a joke but then thought better of it. She missed his spontaneous jokes and utterances. He had definitely got more serious.

"I can do that. I'll maybe swing over to the airport after, in case the alarm gets cancelled."

"Come by the station. We have tonnes of paperwork to look through even if the comms stay down."

"You say the sexiest things," he said. "Let's skip breakfast."

Chris was already awake, but now the noises from the room next door gave him a reason to get up and go get breakfast. He saw Eric was already at a table.

"Morning. I thought I'd be on my own." Eric said.

"Just me. I think," he answered.

"Oh."

"I wish I could say get a room, but the problem is actually where that room is."

"He won't be leaving today either."

"It's not that I mind Anatoli, and there's no impact on work. He's been handy in a tight spot or two. I just wish hotels didn't allocate all the rooms together."

"How long do you think the alert will be on for?"

"Maybe twenty four hours. The cycle's ramping up. This is a resilience test for the whole world." Chris paused, he'd noticed the change of subject from Eric, "I don't think there'll be a Carrington level event, but everyone said that the last time too."

"Did you hear Enya go out early this morning?"

"Yeah, I guess we'll find out why later."

Chris wondered about Eric. He was young, only two years qualified, but he could see why Enya had chosen him to join the team. He had the analytical skills and the straight-down-the-line sense of what was wrong that Enya had. But maybe that was the problem. He felt Eric didn't like Anatoli, or didn't think he should be chartered to fly for them, or maybe it was simply that he didn't think he should be along on a job with Enya. Chris couldn't quite figure it out.

Chris and Eric took the pool car over to the station since Enya hadn't turned up after breakfast. Chris could see Ray was talking to another woman when they entered the conference room.

"Chris, Eric, this is Sheena Ricci, one of our pathologists. Last night we had another body. Pat Gallway was found in the evaporation bed of the Salt Plant at half five this morning. Has Enya said anything?"

Clearly Ray had sussed a few things out already about their team dynamic to have even asked. The conversation over breakfast came back to him like acid reflux. Maybe Anatoli was interfering with things after all?

"No, she didn't come down for breakfast. I'm sure she'll be here shortly. But, Pat Gallway is another body?"

"Yes. Sheena's been telling me someone must have forced him to drink a large quantity of highly saline solution, about five hours before we found him. We're waiting on the plant's manager to give us the chemical breakdown of their salt product."

"Drinking salty water, won't he have gagged, or been sick?"

"There's way's of bypassing the tastebuds, " said Sheena.

He saw Eric had sat down at the table and was busy logging on.

"You were after his records weren't you," Eric said to Ray, "what did you find?"

"He's probably been blackmailing someone," Enya said.

Chris hadn't even heard the glass door's twang. He turned around to see Enya with Anatoli in tow. He checked Eric's face immediately, especially after his recent thoughts. But the idea of blackmail seemed to have totally overridden any other concerns on Eric's face, there was only curiosity.

Chapter Six - Closet Greens

"I was going over the files you sent. I managed to get a request away on a phone number, but who knows when we'll get an answer to that now. In the meantime we have the navy names, and Pat Gallway to concentrate on," said Enya.

Anatoli loved listening to Enya when she was like this, her surety and command. But it also made him feel superfluous, especially with Chris and Eric around. He wasn't trained in Police work, and they knew it. He was good enough in a fight because he always met his militia training targets, but this kind of paperwork analysis, he didn't have the patience for it. Even in his new business partnership, he was leaving a lot of the paperwork up to Gary, and concentrating on the engineering side of the airship designs.

He checked his phone again for an all clear, knowing it would be obvious from a chorus of all clear messages on everyone's mobiles if it *had* come through. Enya had made him bring his laptop, even though he didn't have the security clearances the rest did, and there was nothing downloaded on it. What did she have in mind, dragging him over here?

He watched Eric and Chris get down to work on the names.

"Anatoli, can you set up here?" said Enya, "I'd like you to trawl the..."

"Pubs, I should trawl the pubs," he interrupted, "see who knew Pat Gallway, what he was like."

He saw her pause. It was a good idea, but he knew why she didn't want him to be doing it. She'd dragged him over here despite him not being in the team, so if he was going to help then he was going to do things he was good at.

"Okay, but take Ray with you. And look out for Isadora."

This Isadora woman had needled Enya somehow, it sounded personal now. Was the only reason he'd been brought to the office so Enya could keep him safe? Sometimes, she really was overprotective.

He sat up front in Ray's car. Having only sat in the back before, he hadn't realised how untidy it was up front. Poor Enya must have had a hard time ignoring the mess. Ray was telling him about Progress' pubs, both licensed and unofficial. Despite his short time in Progress, he wasn't surprised to find the nearest unofficial pub was round the corner from the police station, or that it was patronised by quite a few of them either.

"It's a total dive, but it's a safe place to let off a bit steam, even have a rant about your boss. Nothing leaves the Confessional. That's how it got its name in the first place."

"And Pat Gallway might have drank here?"

They'd pushed at an inconspicuous door in a single storey building and entered a dark room, pools of light hit onto tables from suspended lighting, there were a few booths to one of the walls, and a long bar opposite them.

"Nah I doubt it, we're just being thorough. Your Enya would want to know why we didn't check it out."

"True," he admitted.

"We can have a drink here, so we smell right for the other places, that sound okay to you?"

"I'm a professional pilot, we drink anytime, except ten hours before a flight, and I'm not flying anywhere today."

"Ah the rumours are true then?"

"All of them," said Anatoli, beginning to warm to Detective McCarthy.

The bartender slid them the two beers Anatoli had seen Ray order with a hand signal on approach.

"How did you meet Enya?"

He hadn't had a drink for over a week, he'd had three charter flights, then Enya's call. When they'd left he'd expected to be turning around either immediately or within twenty four hours. Now he didn't know when he'd be leaving. He wondered if he should have gone yesterday evening, but he thought Enya and he had both avoided talking about it, and...

"I'm sorry, my mind went for a wander, what did you say?"

"How did you meet, you and Enya?"

“Oh, she brought my dinner to the cockpit while I was flying her and some friends to McMurdo from Vostok. We got talking. Usual sort of thing.”

Although it hadn’t been the usual sort of circumstances. Meeting up with Valla Torres, back when she was a General in the Resistance and it was a proscribed organisation. When Enya should have been arresting her, but ended up fighting alongside her against UN forces. He didn’t generally admit to his part in all of that. People started asking him questions he either didn't want to answer or didn’t know the answers to.

He saw Ray take a big swig of the bottle.

“You related to Senator Dale?”

Ah, he thought, this run of questioning now.

“Dad. You Glencor then?”

“Nah, Larsen. Thought about moving, couldn’t be arsed in the end.”

“Who would you go to?”

“Maybe Torres. I like that Valentina Torres. Thought she should have stayed on as President. And she keeps good order on her navy boats.”

Anatoli always found it difficult to have conversations with people who discussed his friends like they were entities or celebrities and not just other people. He wondered if Ray really did think like that or if this was some sort of test? He’d been hanging around with the

Anti-corruption Team long enough for some paranoia to rub off.

"So why the police?"

He decided to counter back, and saw her smile. He took a big swig of the bottle feeling more secure about the direction of the conversation again.

"Would you believe a boy? Who then dropped out of the training. But by that time I was hooked. He'd lasted till just after the detection module. I could have been doing something completely different otherwise."

He saw she was half way through the small bottle, and he took another swig to catch up.

"What happened to him?"

"I arrested him. I think, after that, he left for Vostok. So what's the deal then? You a proper part of the team or just chartered?"

"Beats me," he admitted. "Honestly sometimes I feel like… well like now. I'm not Police, I haven't got security clearance, so what can I do if I am in the team? But other times, yes, we work together, and it works well."

"The other two, they're like her huskies. You're not in the pack."

It struck Anatoli as an odd way to put it, but the more he thought about it, the more right it sounded.

She finished her bottle.

"Drink up," she said.

"Aren't you going to ask about Pat Gallway?"

"Oh yeah. Hey, Colin, you seen this guy in here anytime?"

All of a sudden the bartender was in front of them, Anatoli hadn't even seen where he'd been before that. Ray had unfolded a copy of the sketch artist likeness.

The bartender shook his head, and Anatoli thought Ray looked satisfied. He swigged the rest of the bottle and stood up.

When they got outside he could tell Ray was not satisfied.

"Well, I'll be strung up like a kipper. Colin. You can just never tell. Though, I wonder how much overlap there is between ex-Resistance and the Greens?"

"What? He did know Pat? How could you tell?"

"There's facial tells, eye movement, delays. It's all in the training. He was in the Resistance, but I always thought mostly to get the girls. Maybe it's the same with the Greens."

"We're still checking out the other pubs?"

"Absolutely. I'm extra keen to find out who else in town is a closet Green."

After two hours they had covered all the pubs that Ray knew. She'd said she doubted there were more than one or two other unofficial ones that might have sprung up, especially after she'd found three had disappeared. They were driving back to the station, when the all clear came through on their phones.

"Damn," he said.

"Would it be so bad to fly now?" asked Ray.

"You don't know the half of what I've done, unofficially shall we say, and got away with. I can't afford to get caught out in a breathalyser test."

"Maybe it stays off."

He didn't feel hopeful.

Ray had enjoyed herself. There was no denying Anatoli Dale was highly personable. To begin with she couldn't see why he'd not followed his father into politics. Over the course of their pub crawl she'd found out why.

Like most people, she hadn't been surprised when Gordon Murcheson, senior Glencor senator, had been put on trial. But at the time it had been a surprise he'd resigned as President. It had been even more surprising that they'd managed to find him guilty of anything, so the stories that Anatoli told her, about inner Glencor politics weren't a complete shock. But she also had a better appreciation of the reasons Valentina Torres set up the

Anti-corruption Team and why the easy-going Anatoli Dale had gone for his wings instead of a seat in the Senate. Many of her fellow officers had seen Gordon's trial as evidence the system was fine and there was no reason for more controls, rather than it being the prime motivator in setting the Team up.

But what had really opened her eyes this afternoon, was the number of bartenders who appeared to recognise Pat Gallway while denying the same. A few down near to the Chemical Plants did acknowledge him, and confirmed his reputation as a bit of a drunk but Ray knew it was possible to act drunk, or drunker than you were.

As soon as they had arrived back in the conference room the team had stopped working and she saw Enya waiting to hear what she had to say. She watched Anatoli pick up his laptop and move to the far end of the conference table, and watched Enya's reaction.

He'd confessed to Ray he thought Enya was worried about what Isadora might do to him, and had told her about being tied up at Freddie's warehouse. She could see something like worry in Enya's face, and realised she was being drawn into analysing the Team's dynamics. She tried to put it to the side and began her report.

"We found five bars where they said they didn't know Pat, when I know for certain they did. Three bars down near the Chemical Plants acknowledged him as a regular, and a heavy drinking one at that. What's a bit disconcerting is one of the bars denying any knowledge is the Confessional, where the police often drink. If that has Green sympathies then it would be easy for them to stay ahead of anything we might try. I'm concerned Isadora has a way out of Progress now the solar alarm has lifted."

"Do you have officers you trust we could put on the airport? I still think she'll head for there. Also do we have any idea where she might be just now?"

Ray heard the personal concern in Enya's voice, and noticed that her huskies had heard it too. She saw Eric looking over at Anatoli, who was buried in his laptop. How could Enya not be noticing this?

"I have a couple I trust," she said, "I'll see what they're up to. I don't think we know enough to even speculate where she could be. What have you found out while we were out?"

"We have bad news for Valentina Torres, one of her newest recruits has been to Progress before, stayed at the Juniper Hotel and we suspect has ulterior motives for joining the navy. He's on the MS Mercer which is also in port just now," said Chris.

"It's not a crime to support Green policies," she said, "we need to tread carefully here."

She saw Enya nod her head.

"You couldn't smuggle a person onboard a navy ship, but I alerted Valentina just the same. I imagine they're doing a full vessel search as we speak," said Enya.

"But you have more, I can practically feel the suspense," Ray said, and it was no joke, there seemed to have been a breakthrough of some kind.

"Yes," said Eric, "we searched back through Pat's finances using our own channels. He got the recent money from Rafael Dupont, via several front organisations. Rafael is a member of the Planetary Cooperation Group, an association of right-wing politicians across the world who want to subvert the Green Agenda and Eco-movements in general. They see money to be made in disasters. Global's heavily invested in them. It's the least Green thing you could imagine really."

"Senator Rafael Dupont? And you still think it was blackmail?"

"Yes and yes," said Enya, "Pat was in Vostok at the same time as Isadora as far as we can see. Your contact came good and both receipts belong to the same taxi firm. Maybe he got cold feet when he realised Isadora was an assassin, wanted out?"

"Do we know where she's come from, maybe have an idea where she's heading for?"

"No. We need to lean on some Greens here in Progress, get a decent picture of all the factions," said Enya, "I don't think it's Rafael who's paying Isadora."

"Well," she said, "we still have the Juniper's receptionist in the cells. Going to have to release him in ten hours time, but nobody's spoken to him yet. One of you? Or would you rather I did it?"

She saw Enya thinking, and clearly having trouble making a decision too. The huskies were looking expectantly at Enya. Ray could imagine Chris being sufficiently scary, but reckoned Eric couldn't make a convincing threat.

"You start. Let Chris sit in, we can play it by ear," said Enya.

"Good," she said, "After lunch then?"

"Yes. But delay his lunch due to some unforeseen mishap," agreed Enya.

There was the shutting of laptops which she saw, was enough to get Anatoli to look up.

"Is this lunch?" asked Anatoli.

"Yes, come on. I saw today's specials, they have your favourite," said Enya.

Ray watched them leave, Enya and Anatoli, then Chris with Eric bringing up the rear. Group dynamics was a fascinating thing to watch unless it directly impinged on your own well being. She hoped Enya wasn't as blind to the tensions as she appeared to be.

Chapter Seven - Steel

Isadora had never considered herself lucky, it was simply good planning. But she'd had to admit she'd been lucky to escape from the officers who were searching for her. The planning had been: always carry a knife. The luck had been to run in the direction that had led her to finding a building. Perhaps it was also lucky she hadn't killed the officer and brought the whole force out looking for her. She'd got into the shelter of the building's bulk and called her only contact in the town. Some guy called Colin apparently. He'd told her to stay where she was and he'd come find her.

By the time he'd arrived she was shivering, taking one look at her suit and shaking his head, the next thing she knew, he was parking up in the brightly lit shopping complex she'd normally have avoided. The guy in the shop had been very disparaging of her suit, which she'd spent a lot of money on back in Europe. The shop there had said it was the highest spec they had, but the guy here had made it sound like some sort of designer knock-off of the real thing.

She had to admit the suit she had on now was much better. She hadn't asked what the differences were and why they couldn't be bought in the UN states: she'd heard the rumours about animal fur and other materials. Her ethics were a complex web of contradictions and involved not asking direct questions in order not to hear certain answers.

Colin had supplied a fresh visor, and when she'd told him she had to get in touch with someone she'd arrived with, he'd supplied a burner phone immediately. It was pretty obvious no one local actually knew what was really going on. They were all fired up idealists as far as she'd come across, which was sweet, but also dangerous, and not just for them.

She'd met Pat at the place they'd agreed to hide out at, an unused room in the same apartment block as his original room.

He'd been undercover here for just over a year, waiting. When she'd got in touch four days ago he'd seem relieved to be doing something. They'd first met two months ago in Vostok at a meeting hosted by a representative of the Green Movement. Or at least that's what they'd claimed. She was even less sure now. It felt like she was going to be somebody's scapegoat over this whole episode and she wasn't going to allow that to happen.

Pat had seemed nervous when she'd arrived at the hide out room. He'd babbled about not knowing who the guy he'd given his work-suit to was, and that now he was dead, they were looking for him. Pat had sounded like he was going to be a liability. It was midnight. She suggested he had a drink to calm his nerves. Pouring a glass of whisky for him, she had made sure the paralysing agent was mixed through it. Once he was still, she got to work with the salt she'd bought from a few different places. There was no way she was making it easy to trace.

She remembered seeing the fear in Pat's eyes as she began to pour the saline mixture down his throat. She'd restrained his arms so he couldn't make himself gag as the effects of the paralysing drug wore off. When she'd finished he appeared drunk. Dragging him up, they'd staggered out the room and across the road towards the Salt Plant.

She'd placed her phone in front of the ID checker and let the app do its work. There'd been about thirty seconds of rapid flickering till it had mimicked an ID code and let her in. She'd persuaded Pat up into the evaporation bed, helping him undress. The salt had affected his cognition, he was confused and malleable. She told him to lie down and have a rest, knowing he would never wake up again.

Now, she was here in the hide out room, hiding out. The solar flare alert had woken her up and the smell of salt filled her nostrils. It couldn't be helped. Using an old cloth she'd tried to get rid of as much possible in the shower, but it was too great a risk to run the water in a room that was supposed to be empty.

There was nothing to do now but wait for the all clear: here, at the opposite end of town to the airport, however, Progress seemed to have had insufficient murders for the Police to have become proficient at solving them, they'd be over stretched, hopefully to her advantage.

It was hardly ideal, but she did consider it lucky. Once she got to the airport she'd ditch the Isadora persona and get back to the relative safety of Europe via Vostok. Any destination would suit her. In the meantime she'd attempt to work out who was trying to play her, because there would be a reckoning for that.

The interview room was small, the light was painfully bright but steady and Chris felt they were missing a trick or two. The interview suites back in Weddell City had a selection of issues that were guaranteed to put your interviewee at a disadvantage immediately. The receptionist had been deposited ahead of their arrival and had his handcuffs chained to the desk. The room was very small, the table was a standard width but he still felt that interviewer and interviewee would feel closer because of the room. He let Ray go in first, and then sat nearest the door, so his larger frame covered part of the doorway.

"Mr. Choudrey," began Ray, "Why did you alert Ms. Ley to our presence, using a hidden alarm button?"

"I have no comment to make," said the receptionist.

"You are aware that currently you're an accessory to murder, twice?"

Chris could see that the receptionist hadn't expected that. He saw concern flit across his face.

"You have no proof, you'll have to let me go in nine hours time. I know my rights."

"I have enough to charge you with accessory. But, I can see, you didn't think you were alerting an assassin that the police were hot on their tail, but rather a comrade with merely some shade in her past. I've lived all my life in Progress," said Ray, "I can tell you it's come as a surprise to find so many of its inhabitants willing to see an increase in pollutants and, in murder, for a political ideology. I had't realised the Code was so dead here, and the UN attitude so prevalent."

Chris could tell that had also hit home. Ray went up a notch in his estimation. He saw her sit back in her chair and simply look at Adil Choudrey. Chris saw Adil look down at his hands. He waited. Ray clearly thought she'd done enough so he continued to wait. Maybe a minute later, he saw Adil look up.

"Okay," he said, "Isadora arrived at the hotel with Pat Gallway, three days ago. Pat's been working here for a year, he vouched for her, that was good enough for me."

"We need to know about factional in-fighting, we think Isadora was being paid to murder Steve Jung because he was in the wrong set of Green activists. We know Steve was staying at the hotel but Isadora murdered him at the Ethylene Plant as a message," said Ray, "Are you sure you're in the right faction?"

Chris thought it was the perfect tone.

"Steve Jung was a nutter," said Adil with vehemence.

It took Chris a little by surprise, but not, he thought, Ray.

"Ah, so Steve was in a different faction to yours. Do you know who his associates were?"

"Some nutters just work alone, but yes, I think Steve had back up. He mentioned he'd been specifically asked to come to Progress. Said something about people needing woken up to the dangers of the Chemical Plants. I mean, I don't like them, but I heard he was sabotaging the process to increase flaring. That's not Green."

"And you didn't think to tell us at any point?"

Chris saw Adil give Ray a sarcastic look as an answer.

"Did you know Steve was wearing Pat's work-suit when he was murdered?" asked Chris.

Again Chris saw Adil's anxiety, a deepening furrow on his forehead. It seemed Adil couldn't smooth it out.

"Pat wouldn't have worked with the likes of Steve Jung knowingly. Someone must have got one of his suits, maybe to shift the blame."

Chris heard Ray sigh.

"Who do you think would have done that? You must have some idea."

Chris saw something dawn on Adil's face. He wondered if they'd scared him enough that whatever revelation he'd had, he would share with them?

"I suppose Isadora might. Nobody I know from Progress would have helped Steve Jung sabotage the Ethylene Plant. If you didn't know what you were doing you could have half the town away with an explosion."

"There's nobody else from outside visiting?"

"Winter's our quiet time. We get more guests in the summer; ecologists, biologists, as well as activists."

"So," said Ray, "winter is just for assassinations?"

Chris saw Adil swallow hard.

"We're going to let you go for the time being," said Chris, with an edge of threat, "and we're going to expect you to tell your friends that any misplaced loyalty that saw them help Isadora will only be treated favourably if they come forward with any information immediately. We will be reserving the options of aiding, abetting or accessory to murder, should we feel it is merited."

He could see a still uncertain relief un-crease Adil's forehead.

"I can go?"

"For now, as long as you spread the word. Isadora is who we're after and she's not your ally," said Ray.

Chris saw Ray unlock the handcuffs, and Adil rub his wrists. Chris got up to open the door and stood out in the corridor while Adil came out. He saw Ray guide Adil down the corridor towards the front desk to be signed out. Chris headed back to the conference room. He wasn't sure they'd gained more information but they'd had plenty of what they already suspected solidly confirmed.

He hadn't been taking notice as he walked towards the conference room of what he should have seen through the glass. But when he opened the door it was unavoidable. Anatoli and Eric were face to face. Close. There was no sign of Enya. Neither of them turned at the sound of the door opening.

He hadn't caught the tail end of what Eric was saying but he saw him tap Anatoli on the top of his arm with some force. He felt that was a mistake. He'd been with Anatoli out at Melchior. While he was easy going, Anatoli also had a core of steel it wasn't wise to mess with.

"I think," said Anatoli, without any emotion, "that if you have concerns about your Team Leader it is best not to take them up with the charter pilot, but the Team Leader. I'm chartered by the team and currently my charter hire has not been terminated."

Then Chris heard the steel.

"And if you touch me again, you *will* regret it."

He saw Anatoli then turn, make brief eye contact with him and pass him in the still open doorway.

Chris properly entered the room. Eric's face was red. And Chris was sure the enormity of whatever had been said was slowly dawning on him. Chris didn't know if it was a lapse of judgment that Enya would forgive.

The door opened and he turned, but it was Ray not Enya.

"Where's Enya?" she asked.

"Forensics, they have the salt analysis," said Eric, unable to keep the terseness out of his voice.

Chris saw Ray look at him and he shrugged his shoulders. In these situations it was best to stay well out of it, but it didn't look like Ray subscribed to that idea.

"What did I miss?"

Chris shook his head in warning at her, but she wasn't letting go.

"Wait. Where's Anatoli? He's been a near constant fixture since you arrived."

Still it looked like Eric hadn't learnt.

"Hopefully he's gone to the airport," said Eric.

Unfortunately at that moment Enya had returned to the room and Chris saw she'd only heard the word airport.

"Have they got her?" asked Enya.

The shit was now squarely aimed at the fan and he had no excuse to leave the room. Normally he'd be the one to try and smooth things over between everyone, but this was entirely Eric's mess and there was a lesson here he had to learn. He saw Ray was waiting too.

"No," said Eric, "I think Anatoli has gone to the airport."

"Fuck," said Enya and left the room heading for the exit.

"You're in the shit," he said to Eric.

"It needed to be said," said Eric.

"Yes, but as Anatoli pointed out, not to him."

"You're taking his side."

He saw Ray's face and wished Eric would just shut up.

“It’s not sides. It’s what’s right. You should know that. Don’t be daft, it’s still salvageable if you apologise.”

It was clear there was a bit of hero worship going on with Eric as far as Enya was concerned, but Chris realised now, in a choice between them, Eric had been right, Chris would choose Anatoli.

Chapter Eight - Peanuts

Isadora was gambling on the solar alert meaning the security would have relaxed a bit at the airport even if the all clear had just come through. Colin had dropped her with bolt cutters near the perimeter fence, behind the hangars, and cutting the fence with practiced ease she ran for the nearest. Her plan was to hide out, till it looked like someone was preparing to leave on one of the small private jets and then hijack it. She rather hoped it would be the Anti-corruption's charter. He was cute, and it'd certainly mess with their boss.

She squeezed inside and saw two small jets both closed up. One had Torres Mining painted along the fuselage and its identifier WD222, the other was unmarked except for its identifier, VO570. A choice was even better. She looked for a place to hide and found it at the back amongst de-icer machinery. It was cool inside the hangar but not freezing, there was a slight warmth coming up through the floor; she got comfortable. From past experience she could sit for nearly ten hours like this. She hoped it wouldn't take that long though.

She heard voices and at once was fully alert, it had been nearly three hours. A man and a woman, the man had a slight Australian twang to his accent, but the woman was native, she'd heard it often enough to spot its broad strokes. She moved carefully to get a view. The couple were heading towards the Torres Mining jet. She heard the hydraulics of the jet door kick in, and decided it was worth getting closer. This could be her only chance. The other jet gave her some cover, as she crouched behind its wheels.

They went up the steps and inside. She ran for the door, her knife in her hand, making no sound as she went up the steps and turned into the cabin. The man had his back to her, but there was no sign of the woman. He was slightly taller than her but she had surprise on her side. Getting behind him, she brought the knife round quickly against his throat. He made to move as if by instinct but stopped himself as she brought the blade into contact with his skin.

“If you have any weapons drop them now,” she whispered at his ear.

She saw him put his hands wide. She didn’t want to frisk him one handed.

“Come on, all you guys carry. It’s militia rules. Get your gun out and drop it to the floor.”

She pressed in deeper with the blade, it was sharp enough to cut survival suit material, as she had discovered, so it didn’t take much extra pressure to break the skin. She smelt the blood.

“Okay, calm down. I’m just going to take it out now.”

There was something about his tone, she recognised military training. She couldn’t risk him being conscious a second longer. She hit him hard on the side of his neck with the edge of her free hand. She’d not spent her life on picket lines and demonstrations without picking up a trick or two. He wobbled then crumpled to the floor. She jumped over his body to put it between herself and the cockpit, where she presumed the woman would come out from.

A tall, striking blonde came through the cabin door and she saw the woman take in the scene with a glance. She could see calculations already churning in the woman's face. Keeping the blade against the man's neck, she made sure the woman could see the blood already drawn.

"Gun. Now. On the floor, slide it towards me, and nothing happens to either of you."

She saw the blonde go inside her survival suit one handed and pull out a hand gun, crouch down and slide it along the floor. It stopped just ahead of the man's body.

"Right. You're taking me to Vostok now. Get back in there and get it sorted. No funny business."

She saw the blonde turn and leave. It made no difference whether she alerted anybody as far as Isadora was concerned. She had all the aces. She searched the man for his gun, found it and stowed it, then leant over to gain the gun from the floor, sheathing the knife. A gun was a more dangerous object on a plane. She checked the pulse of the guy, it was steady. She pulled him up into a chair and strapped him in. He'd need restraints but the gun would do for now.

She turned as she heard the hydraulics kick in and saw the steps raise and fold, then the door shut into the fuselage. It looked like she was going to make it.

Anatoli heard Valla on the radio calling the tower. He'd never heard her like that before. Something was dreadfully wrong. He'd seen her jet leaving the hangar as he'd approached it to get to his own, and never thought a thing about it. But now, sitting in his cockpit and hearing the tension, the faintest wavering, he felt something turn in the pit of his stomach.

Valla was posting a flight plan for Vostok, which was suicidal given the winter storm due to hit there in two hours time and anyway she'd have insufficient fuel for the journey. If, as he suspected, she'd come to pick up Martin, then she'd have posted a plan for Weddell City. This, sounded like she'd gained an unwelcome visitor, one he'd also met. He called Enya.

"Where are you? Are you all right? What's happened?"

As soon as they'd connected she'd started with a volley of questions.

"Enya, I'm fine. Listen. Valla has just left for Vostok and I don't think it was willingly."

"Valla?"

"Yes, she was taxiing out of the hangar as I came in, I never thought anything of it, didn't even look up. But I've just heard her call the tower. She didn't sound right, and she wouldn't be going to Vostok."

"I'm going back for the others. Get fuelled up."

"But Enya, she's not going to get to Vostok, it's too far for a single hop. There's a winter storm due to hit it in two hours time anyway. The forecast is for a full thirty six hours of high velocity winds."

"Fuel up, that's an order. And think about where they'll have to divert to when that assassin woman realises she can't get to Vostok."

"Ma'am," he said, hoping it would make her smile even just a bit.

She'd hung up. He wondered what had been said about the conversation he and Eric had had in the conference room. It had taken him by surprise, he'd no idea Eric didn't like him. Most people liked him. He hadn't had to deal with hostility like that since high school. And that's what it felt like, something schoolboy-ish. He reckoned Eric was early twenties. Had he acquired a rival for Enya, without her realising?

He put the concern aside and dug out some charts from the cupboard behind his seat, taking them through to spread out on a pull down table. There were really only two places to divert to since the storm had already reached Saylon; Kunlun, or Mellor Station, but Mellor only had a skeleton crew of three researchers till spring.

He checked on the latest weather forecasts. The storm's track bypassed Kunlun somewhat but he still wouldn't want to be landing in what weather they'd get there, with no fuel to spare. It would be sheer winds, downdrafts from the mountains, whirlwinds, visibility would be nil. This storm had travelled over the Southern Indian Ocean picking up moisture to dump right across Antarctica from Saylon to McMurdo in a more or less straight line. The snow would be relentless.

He'd flown twice to Kunlun, the runway had about ten metres either side of it to a straight edge down. It would take total concentration to land there with side winds pushing back and forth towards the edges.

He heard voices in the hangar and went to push his jet door open and put the steps down.

The fuel tug had turned up a while back and was connected. The guy was shaking his head as Enya, Ray and Chris came towards the jet. There was no sign of Eric. Ray was pulling a trolley behind her loaded up with boxes of various sizes. His curiosity was piqued.

"What's in the boxes?"

"Snow search kit, mountaineering bits and bobs, spare and specialist visors, a heat suit. A bundle of just in case stuff really."

Anatoli watched the three of them load Ray's stuff into the cabin stowing it under seats and strapping some of it into the spare chairs. Nobody had yet mentioned the lack of Eric, and he certainly wasn't going to. He showed them the charts.

"It's got to be Kunlun or maybe Mellor Station," he said.

"And we have enough to get us there?"

"Kunlun just, but there's no wriggle room, unless we tried to land at Mellor Station to refuel on their spare supplies."

"And Valla would know this too?"

"Yes. Why?"

"Well, maybe she's going to land at Mellor Station and do something heroic. Can you get a message through to them?"

"It'd have to be on the Sat phone," he said pointing to the back of his cabin.

He watched Enya head to the Sat phone and saw Chris catch his eye. Chris gave him a conspiratorial smile. He wished sometimes they'd realise he didn't overthink everything, and conspiratorial stuff mostly went over his head. He went to speak to Chris, while Ray was busy with one of her boxes.

"So, where's the boy?"

"To paraphrase Ms McCarthy, Eric is in the doghouse."

"Well, we could have probably done with an extra gun, but it's her team."

"He'll come to his senses. We've left him with lists of names to be getting on with."

Anatoli didn't continue the conversation since Enya was coming back from the Sat phone.

"I gave them a heads up," she said, "Their fuel tanks are full and operational but they said they 'might develop a heating issue' before Valla lands. There's only three of them there at the moment, all ice sheet scientists, but they assured me they all had their militia training up to date."

The fuel tug operator rapped on the fuselage and Anatoli stuck his head out the door.

“You’re as mad as the blonde,” said the tug operator.

“Yep,” he agreed and watched the fuel tug depart through the wide open hangar doors.

He came back inside bringing the steps up with him and shutting the door for take-off.

“Well, let’s go if we’re going,” he said and headed into the cockpit to start the pre-flight checks.

Valla had seen Anatoli walking into the hangar, but he hadn’t seen her. She made a point of dragging out the comms with the tower in the hope he’d catch some of what was going on. The wound on Martin’s neck didn’t look deep, but Enya had divulged enough about this assassin woman for Valla to be sure it was the same person, and she would kill Martin if she thought it necessary. Valla was determined not to give her any reason to.

They didn’t have the fuel to get to Vostok, and at some point she was going to have to tell the woman. But she felt it would be better once they were in the air. The only places she could think to refuel were Saylon or Mellor Station and the storm had already hit Saylon. If she planned on doing something about the assassin then a few more bodies to even up the odds would be better, and hopefully Martin would have come round by then.

She heard the cockpit door open.

“We don’t have the fuel to get to Vostok. We’ll need to refuel at Mellor Station.”

“I don’t believe you.”

“This is a small jet, WD222, look it up in the AFS aviation app, you’ll see my range.”

“How long till we get there?”

“Two hours.”

“What’ve you got to eat?”

“Peanuts, in the bar at the back.”

She heard the door shut. It was a standing joke amongst Torres that there was only ever peanuts to eat on the jet. She wondered what the eco-assassin was making of the leather and wood. It’d been something Alison had commented on once or twice. Then she turned her mind to how she would disarm this assassin given she had both their guns and a very sharp knife which she clearly knew how to handle. If push came to shove, Valla thought, Enya would just have to come to terms with a dead assassin.

Chapter Nine - Doghouse

Valla fought her jet down onto the blue ice runway at Mellor Station. The wind was building and her jet had tilted and slewed in the final approach despite having the runway oriented for her to land directly into the wind. The storm was moving so fast the wind direction was constantly changing. Her jet touched down, travelling along with small slips side to side that she was able to reduce till she was straight and could begin to apply brakes, heading towards what was called the 'catcher net'.

Taking about half an hour to make, the net was a creation of wide, frozen 'tramlines' of ice ridges with a ribbed area between them. She brought the brakes on to full and began to increase the reverse thrust as she felt the jet run over the frozen ribbing and a tramline ridge catch a wheel into a more secure path. In the mush of fresh snow and ice fragments from the net, her jet came to a shuddering halt.

She taxied away and secured the plane as much as possible in these wind conditions. She unstrapped, took a deep breath and entered the cabin. It was hot, she'd kept the heating ramped up, trying to make the woman drowsy, but it didn't seem to have had much effect. Martin looked like he was still out, which was either worrying or a subterfuge, either way, she still didn't have a workable plan to overpowering the woman.

"I'll have to go speak to them and arrange the fuel, they said something on the radio about the fuel tank heating being off, it might take some time."

"I have all the time in the world," said the woman, "your man here not so much."

It was all Valla could do to keep her emotions from her face. She zipped up past her chin, and brought down her visor, with a quick look back at Martin. She could see a pale yellow against the oranges at the side of his neck, presumably where the woman had hit him. That wasn't good. She hoped someone at Mellor also doubled as a medic.

She stumbled towards the blinking target showing the start of the line and clipped on feeling her way to the station buildings. She entered the airlock, heard the hiss of the seal and opened the door. Three armed guys stood there, all aiming at her. She put her hands up. Somebody had obviously told them something.

"I'm Senator Valentina Torres, I have an armed individual onboard my jet and a concussed passenger. What do you already know?"

She was pleased to see them lower the weapons and stow them.

"I'm Roy, nominally in charge here, we got a sat call from Progress about your situation. A woman called Enya Zhao, said she was the Anti-corruption Team. We said we'd fix it so you couldn't leave. But what do you want us to do? Could we rush her?"

"No. She has the concussed passenger as a hostage. We've got to subdue her some other way. I tried turning the heating in the cabin up, but she's still awake."

She saw Roy look to one of the other guys.

"I'm Philippe, I'm the medic, chemist and cook. You need an anaesthetic into the air intake. But I don't have… wait. Poul, do we have acetylene?"

The final guy spoke up.

"Hi, Poul, mechanic amongst other skills. Yes I have two full tanks, why?"

"It has anaesthetic properties," said Philippe.

"I did not know that," said Poul.

"Do we have a plan?" asked Valla.

"I think so," said Roy.

She watched them, pale blue figures, dragging the acetylene tanks as long pale blue streaks, from the work shop onto a sled. She could see Roy over by the fuel station, pulling on a hose, as though they would begin to fuel the jet. The tanks moved towards the jet's engine. Between the two acetylene tanks, Valla knew, was a third much smaller bottle which Philippe had said was the station's only tank of medical anaesthetic. She had Roy's handgun stowed inside her suit.

She re-entered the jet, closing the door behind her. It was very warm inside, the woman hadn't shrugged off her survival suit and Valla could see she was less alert than earlier.

"I have to unlock the fuel cap. They've brought the fuel line over but there might be some fumes. They said about forty five minutes."

She saw the woman check Martin's pulse.

"He's still alive, but I'm wondering if I hit him a bit hard. You better hope there's good medical attention at Vostok."

Valla nodded, and headed into the cockpit, to turn on the air conditioning to full air intake. She fished the chemical filter mask out of her survival suit and put it on. There was a need to be very careful not to create sparks as they filled the jet up with acetylene. She'd have to be damn sure the woman was out cold before she went into the cabin, and Philippe had been a bit vague on timings. They'd agreed to give it twenty minutes.

It was the longest twenty minutes Valla thought she'd ever sat through, and that included certain senate sub-committees. She shut off the engines and closed the air intakes, stood up and opened the cockpit door carefully.

The woman was sprawled across the table, the gun in her left hand hanging down off the edge. Valla walked slowly towards her. She took the weight of the gun in her hand, prised the woman's fingers off it and stowed it in her suit. She pulled the woman back into a sitting position and searched her for the other gun and knife, finding a bundle of papers as well. She let out a sigh in relief.

She checked Martin's pulse for herself and then went to open the cabin door manually, desperately careful not to let anything grind. The freezing air rushed in carrying snowflakes with it, as the heated interior air/acetylene mix escaped. Roy was at the end of the walk-line, a pale blue body with a yellow streaked face in her visor. She saw him begin to come along the line.

Roy arrived, masked up, handed her some cable ties and she watched him lift Martin over his shoulder and turn for the door. She tightened the cable ties on the woman wrists and followed him, leaving her jet open to the elements, clipped onto the line and let the relief wash over her.

They'd agreed Roy would collect the woman once they'd figured out where to keep her and they'd close up the jet at that point. She didn't care about the state the interior would get into. What mattered, Martin, was now safe in the medical room, where she was now with Philippe.

“Is he going to be okay?”

“She must have hit him hard to cause a temporary blood flow issue. That's what knocked him out. It looks like he's not sustained external head injuries, so the heat's probably kept him out, it's not ideal for brain injuries.”

Valla nearly broke when he said that.

“We'll get him hooked up and stabilised, see what happens. I can't say anything for certain right now.”

She continued to stand in the room, watching Martin lying on the bed, wishing everything was different.

"Go. Go and get something to eat. Sort out with Roy where we're keeping the hijacker. Go do things, Senator."

She turned and said thanks, and left the room in a trance. She found Roy in the communal living quarter, and they discussed where was secure enough and warm enough to keep the woman. There were lockable cages, but they were in outbuildings and not particularly warm. It was all Valla could do not to insist she was placed there anyway.

For Valla, the Code was under strain and she realised now how important it had always been to stick to it. Enya had said the woman was an eco-assassin, and Valla recalled Arnaud Cheung, the self-styled assassin in the Resistance, who'd ended up shooting Daniel Ektov instead of Gordon Murcheson. She was better than them. There would be a trial, and justice.

"...and bring the cage inside," said Roy.

"What?" asked Valla.

"I said, we could empty the small cage with the welding gear, especially now we have no acetylene to contain, and bring it in here."

He was pointing to a corner of the room that was mostly empty.

"Okay," she agreed.

Eric expected to be left behind. He'd made a fool of himself and he was happy to put some distance between himself and the people who'd seen it. He had his list of names, so he started with the recent navy recruit and burrowed fully into the man's life as far as digital records would allow. If anything untoward popped up he'd go down and visit the Mercer. He was also running a series of investigations into the multiple profiles of Isadora Ley, searching back for the primary person she had been, and how she had developed into an eco-assassin for hire.

He mused on recycled bullets briefly as an idea, then heard a ping from one of his searches. He shuffled the various open windows on the laptop till he found the culprit. It was the navy guy, Jonathan Blackbird Renner, mostly known online as Blackie.

Renner had been at school with Thierry Vonne, in the football team with him too. In the AFS it was pretty difficult to stop people finding out about you. The population was so small and moved about across the continent, most people knew someone who knew someone. He chased down the details of the other team mates and got in touch with some general questions the state negotiator with the Special Stranger training, Alison Strang, had constructed for situations like this. He issued the emails from the National Statistics Office address they had permanent access to. He had limited faith in the idea, Special Stranger techniques sounded like psychobabble to him.

There was a knock on the glass door and he looked up, there was a uniformed officer opening the door.

"Sorry to disturb you Sir, we have a gentleman who's come in and wishes to relay some information about our inquires into Isadora Ley."

"Thanks, show him to an interview room, I'll be there shortly."

He shut down the laptop after setting the security protocols in place and headed for the interview suite.

He sat down in the narrow room and asked the man to sit. He'd been standing in the room when Eric had arrived and was still standing now Eric was sitting at the table.

"I want to stand."

"Fine. Can I ask your name?"

"I'm Colin Rosko, I own the Confessional bar. I drove Isadora to the airport fence with bolt cutters, but George is saying she killed Steve Jung."

"Okay. Please, Colin, take a seat, you're not in any trouble. We're trying to build a picture of what's going on. It's not illegal to support Green policies. But we think the Green activist movement is being subverted by outside organisations."

He saw Colin look at him, some of the agitation from when he first entered the room had gone. Colin pulled out a chair and sat down.

"I helped her. I found her in one of those stupid suits they buy before they arrive and took her to George. We helped her. I gave her a phone."

"Did you?" he interrupted, "Was it this number by any chance?"

He scribbled down the last number Pat Gallway received on his mobile.

"Yes. Why?"

"Don't worry. What happened next?"

"I dropped her off at Five and Hydrogen and then today she asked me to pick her up and take her to the airport with bolt cutters."

"Colin, how did you know her?"

"I didn't know her. But she knew who I was. My number is given out to activists all the time. I'm the Green contact for Progress."

"So, who gives out your number to activists?"

"Central Office, Maddy Clearbright, she's the Networking Coordinator."

"So, Steve Jung would've had your number too?"

"I knew Steve already, but he'd changed when I met him recently. He'd been on an activist course in Vostok, and came back with these wild ideas about direct action. I didn't agree with them, but he didn't deserve to die."

"When did he go on this course, did he say?"

"About two months ago"

"Thanks Colin, you've been very helpful. You don't need to worry. We'll get Isadora and she'll be tried for her crimes. In the meantime please let us know if anything suspicious or odd crops up, a new activist or maybe a message from Maddy about Isadora."

"I will."

Eric got up and held open the door for Colin, watching him wander down the corridor towards the uniformed officer who would show him out. It looked like Colin was still doing a lot of processing, it was possible he'd see him again.

He read over his notes, and saw the streets Five and Hydrogen mentioned. Where Pat Gallway had had a room. He headed towards the Chief's office to ask for a search of the whole building.

He'd spent another two hours on his names when his phone rang. It was the uniformed officers who were going door to door in the company accommodation on Five and Hydrogen. They'd found an empty room with traces of salt in the shower tray and on the bed. Now they knew where Isadora had been hiding, he told them to get Forensics in and asked for the CCTV files to be downloaded.

The Forensic report on the salt, which had mostly got forgotten in the recent event he was now wishing to forget, had said it was a mixture, salt from the plant and rock salt from a local shop. He was sure he'd read the proportions, if they matched what was in the room and the CCTV showed her coming and going then they had her tied to the murder of Pat Gallway.

But they still had to catch her. He hoped the team were okay in the weather. The wind had picked up in Progress, the view towards the complex was now just a barely lit curtain of dense snow. The one thing he'd give Anatoli was his piloting skills, if anyone could fly in this weather it was him.

Anatoli felt welded to the jet's controls, he'd become a part of the jet. He felt the winds and the updrafts and adjusted, careful not to over compensate. Even still, the jet was being heavily buffeted and occasionally it would plunge in a downdraft. He checked the weather stats again. The wind speeds were increasing as he approached Mellor Station, the numbers danced wildly, confirming what he could already feel were strong gusts coming in around 40 knots.

Valla had about an hour on him, she'd have landed in less severe winds, but crucially she'd also have landed into the wind. Anatoli had to assume they hadn't cleared a fresh runway for him or reformed the net. He would experience these gusting cross-winds on a less than optimal runway. All his concern was for his jet and passengers, he'd never landed in such conditions, anywhere, much less on a blue ice runway and had been slowly descending almost as soon as he'd reached cruising altitude.

It was the breakdown of the Polar Vortex that allowed these fast moving storms to sweep across with massive amounts of precipitation, changing every aspect of Antarctic weather. This one was a relatively long lived storm, and that was due to its size, the eye was tracking directly to Vostok. Mellor Station was about two thousand kilometres away and still affected.

Normally, slots were allocated to aircraft to give the airports time to react to changes in the wind directions where possible, and it wasn't unheard of for flights to be cancelled because of unpredictable winds at locations without the space for a full choice of runway direction. While Mellor Station did have the full three sixty degrees, they were only three guys and, who knew what was happening with Isadora.

As he got closer the snow intensified, there would be little to no visuals and he switched to the projected simulation which used his jet's instrument data and the signals from Mellor Station's runways area.

He was fighting the controls to keep the jet on course, aware of the aching in his arms and legs on the periphery of his concentration. The luxury of position recovery he'd had earlier, was gone due to the proximity of the ground.

The whole jet felt like it was being tossed from one giant, unseen hand to another. The ground rushed up in the projection cast onto his window, as he prepared to land the jet, ready to turn against the cross wind just ahead of the hard contact.

There was an uneven bounce, the jet was pushed by the cross winds and he fought it back and down, feeling the wheels slip on the fresh snow layer. The jet continued its slip to one side as a strong gust caught it. As he tried to correct, the jet now slid further in the opposite direction. With another correction he realised the jet was increasing its fishtailing. He neutralised the rudder, and let the jet slide, he had space either side to play with, but his speed was still a concern, especially since the net at the end of the runway would be chewed up from Valla's landing.

Slowly, in small increments he crabbed towards the runway proper, his legs really began to complain. The recent snow was a lubricating layer over the ice and he could feel the jet still slipping sometimes, he was finding it hard to control his legs for the small adjustments needed. If he could just get to a decent bit of net, he'd be in with a chance. He felt the rumble of the wheels over the ribbing but no sense of a tramline.

The whole aircraft was now shaking with the strain of braking; the ribbing added to the shuddering of the flaps, sending vibrations along the fuselage. Finally, he felt the jet line up as the edge of a tramline, a mere ten centimetres of frozen ice ridge, forced the wheel which had met it to straighten, and he engaged the reverse thrust. The noise was intense. A glance at the visual display showed the jet was running out of net area, but only seconds before that happened, he managed to stop.

He could hardly move, his legs in particular quivered from his efforts in landing. He tried to stand and had to hold on to the back of the chair. Enya came in and saw him.

"I need to taxi nearer to the station buildings," he said, "Everyone okay?"

"Yes. Are you?"

"It's not something I'd like to repeat."

Chapter Ten - Unshakeable

Anatoli could see someone coming towards them, but only because he had short range radar on. There was no visibility, and the station may as well have had its lights off for all the good they were doing. There was a knock on the door, and, already zipped up, he put down the steps. They all got out clipping onto the line that the person had brought to the jet for them. Anatoli left last, his legs still shaking inside, and every part of him ached. He shut the door up, and hoped the winds would begin to ease soon. Through his visor, his rapidly cooling jet was shaking violently in the onslaught of the winds.

They got inside, stomping the snow off their boots. Anatoli saw Valla straight away, she looked smaller somehow. He went over to her. She turned to face him and he could see she was on the point of tears.

"Valla?"

She hugged him. Anatoli had always thought of Valla as an unshakeable rock, he'd been too young to be considered a contemporary of Valla in her youth but he'd hung around with people who had. Whatever had happened to her seemed like it had been an earthquake to her rock.

"I turned up the heating, what if I made it worse?"

"Valla, tell us what happened?" he asked, confused.

And so they all heard. It was near the end of her story when he finally noticed the cage in the corner, as Valla described hauling Isadora out of the jet. By the looks of things, Isadora was still out from the anaesthetic.

"We'll have to stay here for at least another twenty four hours, till the storm has lessened," said Enya.

He saw Enya turn to look at Roy.

"We can order an emergency drop of any extra supplies we take from your store," Enya said.

"Sure," Roy said, "we usually carry spare, you're not the first to have to make an emergency stop-over in winter, just the first to have...what did you say she was?"

"An eco-assassin," said Enya.

"That's a thing is it?"

"Apparently so."

"Well if you're here for a while we'll shuffle a few sleeping arrangements around. We should have a guard in here at all times though."

"Agreed," said Enya.

"I want to sleep in the medical room, please," said Valla.

Anatoli was the last to go on guard duty, at seven in the morning, still stiff from the landing, his walking stilted, ever conscious of his back. As he entered the room, it looked like the anaesthetic had worn off sometime while he was asleep. Isadora was awake and watching him. Relieving Poul, he didn't say much, just a few hand signals, and wondered what Enya had in store for Isadora when they got back to Progress, presuming that was where they'd go. Though, now he thought about it they could make another hop to Slessor Station and then on to Weddell City.

His was not to question why, his was just to plot and fly, he thought, amused with his witticism. Then he realised his reluctance to return to Progress might have something to do with Eric still being there and he felt less happy.

“Hey. You're the pilot, aren't you?”

Isadora was trying to get his attention, maybe she'd tried with Poul too, but he suspected not. She seemed to think he was the weak link. Anatoli wondered if he was, then discounted the idea. It was Eric's jealousy that had set the argument in motion. Continuing to ignore Isadora, he decided to make some coffee.

Valla stumbled in from the medical room. He turned and waved a mug at her.

“Yes, coffee. Martin's awake, but Philippe said no stimulants, so a glass of water too.”

He saw Valla was studiously avoiding looking at the cage. It must be hard. He couldn't imagine how he'd feel if something had happened to Enya: the worry about what might, was enough. Pouring the boiling water onto the coffee granules, the aroma made everything seem briefly mundane. He ran the tap and filled a glass with water, then watched Valla go back through the door.

Valla came back into the medical room. It was cooler than the living space, water condensed in the air above her coffee cup creating a tiny cloud, as she put it down on a nearby table. She went over to the bed where Martin was lying. She sat in the seat she'd pulled up to watch over him.

"Hello, I've brought you some water. I think you might need to lift your head a bit to drink it."

"Who are you again?"

It was like a knife thrust into her.

"I'm Valla, remember. I was here when you woke up."

"I like you. I think I know that already. Yes, I can move."

She watched him lift his head from the bed slowly, like he was experimenting with his own body. He was leaning on an elbow. Giving him the glass of water into his other hand, she watched him take it, bring it to his mouth and drink it in one go.

"It was cold, thanks. Valla."

She saw him smile. She lost the last shred of restraint, the stinging heat that had sat behind her eyes gave way and she started to cry.

"Oh, now. Why are you crying? Come here."

He was trying to put the arm which still held the glass around her. She took the glass from him and leant in, sniffing back her tears.

"So," he said, "why are we here? Where is here? Who am I? And why were you crying?"

She let him wipe the wetness off her cheeks.

"We're here because of the storm. At Mellor Station, in the Antarctic Free State. You're Martin Kostov, the executive officer of the MS Mercer, an AFS navy ship, and I was crying because you smiled."

"I am? I did? I'm sorry, I won't smile again," he said, smiling, with a familiar twinkle in his eye.

Then she saw him look thoughtful.

"Wait, I do know you. We were going to fly to Weddell City. How did we end up here?"

"Martin, you've suffered an oxygen loss to your brain, you've got to take it easy. We're here because we got hijacked. But it's all right, we've got her locked up."

"Well I guess I can see why some of that would make you cry, but why my smile?"

She pulled back to look him in the eye. He was smiling again.

"Because."

She kissed him, and then he kissed her back.

The door opened.

"Whoa. I'm not sure the doctor ordered any of that," said Philippe.

She sat round on the chair. Philippe was picking up some instrument from the table where she'd put her coffee.

"May I?"

He was gesturing to the chair she was sitting in. She got up and moved to stand somewhere she could still see what was going on, watching as he shone a light into Martin's eyes, one by one, then asking Martin to follow his finger as he moved it from side to side. Then he asked Martin to count back from ten, then fifty, then asked him what latitude Progress was at, and who was President. The questions continued. Valla was pleased to hear the answers.

"Doesn't sound like any permanent damage, which means you're a very lucky man, Mr. Kostov."

"I know," he said.

Valla saw Martin was smiling at her.

"However," said Philippe, "you're still recovering. I understand you're going to be here for a while, so plenty of time to get back up to speed."

Valla saw Philippe cast a meaningful glance in her direction.

Then she heard the door open and turned to see Anatoli come in.

"Ah, glad to see you're awake. I've got sort of bad news, the storm seems to have stalled over the interior and we'll be here for another twenty hours not twelve as we'd hoped. Probably better for you, Martin."

She saw Martin study Anatoli, then he smiled.

"You're Anatoli. Where's Enya?"

She saw Anatoli pop his head back through the door, laughing, then Enya came in with him, and Chris Saraband too.

"So, Navy, relying on the Anti-corruption Team to save you? I hope this squares us for Melchior now?" said Enya.

She saw Martin think, then smile, as he got the references. There was clearly still something going on, thought Valla, which she wanted someone in Weddell City to look at, as soon as was practicable.

The three Team members disappeared back through the door into the living area.

"Any chance of food, I'm starving," asked Martin.

Enya was sitting at the table, thinking. There was a lot to think about. She had to decide where was best to take Isadora. Progress had a few relatively harmless Green activists, but Weddell City was a complex political arena, taking Isadora there meant more danger. Some of those trying to subvert the Green Movement had plenty of money and would use it to silence their erstwhile assassin. But Glenn and Alison were due back into Weddell City in two days time, and Alison was a resource she could use to crack Isadora. They had to know who had paid Isadora. She wondered what Eric had managed to dig up on his own back in Progress? If she left him there and headed to Weddell City, how would he take that? This Team stuff was hard, she preferred it when they all played nicely.

Enya had her back to Isadora, entirely on purpose. It wasn't clear what it was about Isadora that she found so irritating, but somehow the woman had gotten under her skin. Maybe it was the way she talked to Anatoli and no one else. If it was that, then going to Weddell City would fix that too. It felt like she had made her mind up, despite the added danger of Weddell City, it held more positives than negatives.

She watched as Philippe came over to put breakfasts down on the table, and the others began to join her. They'd already shoved some bread and water through to Isadora. The Code didn't go as far as feeding someone a cooked breakfast, merely requiring them to be kept alive as far as possible.

Anatoli came and sat next to her, also with his back to the cage. She leant in to whisper in his ear.

"I should take Isadora to Weddell City, Glenn and Alison will be back soon, it's not safer, but I think it's better resourced."

She saw him nod then lean in to her ear.

"I think Valla is heading that way too, Martin has his memory back, but there's delays, she'll want to leave as soon as it's safe."

"I need to go to the toilet," said Isadora.

Enya looked round.

"There's a pail, nobody will watch."

She motioned to Roy and Philippe to turn their chairs around.

"This is inhuman. I have rights," Isadora protested.

Enya turned around again.

"I'm sorry but you're Isadora Ley, an AFS citizen, your rights extend to the application of the Code and no further at this point in time. Surely you know that as a citizen?"

She turned back to the table. Let her chew on that for a while, she thought. There was the sound of peeing and the unmistakable smell of the same, which finished breakfast for everyone regardless of what was left on their plates.

Enya stood and motioned to Anatoli, Chris and Ray to move to the opposite corner from the cage to discuss their departure and what they'd need to have in place ahead of their arrival. Behind them they heard Roy and Philippe clearing the table.

“We’re going out to take some measurements, we’ll be gone for about an hour, make yourselves at home,” said Roy.

She turned to see them zipping up and heading to the airlock. She recalled being relieved by Poul on guard duty at three in the morning, he ought to be up soon. In the meantime she laid out the plan to Chris, Ray and Anatoli, knowing Tolli wasn’t going to be happy. She was sending him back to Progress with Ray and she and Chris would hitch a ride with Valla. It was Chris who looked the most upset though. She didn’t understand them sometimes, but she was pleased neither had expressed any reservations about the plan.

The door from the sleeping accommodation opened and Poul came through. She saw him wrinkle his nose at the smell of cooling urine.

“When are you going to do something about that?”

“Soon,” she said, thinking about all the things that could go wrong while retrieving the pail of liquid. It would be a two person operation and neither of those people would be Tolli.

Roy and Philippe arrived back through the airlock and she looked up as they stomped the snow off themselves.

“Smells better than when we left,” said Roy.

She saw him glance at the cage. She knew it looked like Isadora was sleeping, which was technically correct, but they’d cheated a bit, and used something Poul had pointed out to them in the medical room. Valla had grinned a bit too much when Enya described how they were going to get the pail.

The Code was a flexible thing in Antarctica, it most certainly wasn't written down anywhere, but it was an understanding that a fellow human being would not be left at the mercy of the elements regardless of anything else going on between them and the rest of society. Even the gangs held roughly to the Code, though less and less these days. You'd never find someone left outside to die, but you might find someone outside who was already dead. You'd never find someone who'd refuse to let you inside, just sometimes, you'd wish it was better to have been at a different door.

Enya had heard rumours about the Senate trying to create a written piece of legislation to enshrine it. She knew that would be the beginning of the end for the Code, but Antarctica was hardly a frontier land anymore, it was a settled country now, and, it was only a matter of time before they decided on some kind of permanent army too. People were finding excuses to avoid militia training. If it was falling back to a core of willing then it would be better to formalise it as such. In other circumstances she'd be having an animated conversation with Valla right now about that, but Valla was in the medical room and didn't look like leaving it till they were leaving Mellor Station itself.

She went to see Valla.

She saw Martin and Valla on chairs, holding hands, chatting. They didn't look terribly comfortable.

"Hi, I wondered if you'd like to use the room they gave Anatoli and I? Everybody keeps walking through here, and I'm sure you'd prefer a bit of privacy. Roy and Philippe are back and I think they use this room for samples too."

"Oh, I didn't realise. Thanks. I couldn't sit in the same room as that woman just now," said Valla.

"I know what you mean," agreed Enya.

As Valla was standing up, Enya saw her fish inside her survival suit and pull out a rolled up bundle of individual sheets of paper.

"I found these in her survival suit when I was disarming her. I haven't even looked at them."

Enya took them from Valla and went back to the living area to unroll them.

Chapter Eleven - Even

Enya again sat with her back to the cage, even though Isadora was still out cold. She unrolled the sheets from each other. It seemed Isadora was old school in her admin habits. Which struck Enya as odd for someone who wanted to save the trees, amongst other things.

The first sheet she unrolled was a typed out list of contact numbers, a few names but mostly just numbers, something for Anatoli to take back to Eric. The next sheet was a hotel invoice from Vostok, dated two months ago. The sheet after that appeared to be blank. Enya knew there were various inks and tricks to that, she'd take it back to Weddell City and make sure it was blank. The final sheet was a list of facilities, including the Ethylene plant at Progress, and some had stars against them. Another thing for Eric to investigate.

Ray would not be coming to Weddell City; Enya wanted the detective in Progress, running down the source of tubocurarine and investigating the murders. So it was her and Chris escorting Isadora hitching a ride on Valla's jet. And it would be a long haul, via Slessor Station with potential delays for weather and solar alarms. They'd stock up on food and drink, but she wondered how much of the tranquilliser she could requisition from Mellor Station?

She did not want Isadora conscious and she wondered how ethical it was, even if currently it was still legal. Senator Castillero's senate committee were now two years into a complete overhaul of the AFS's legal code. Enya reckoned their next target would be some of the actual legislation. And then what would they do with people like Isadora?

When she'd first come back into the living area, Ray and Chris had been playing cards near to one of the heaters on a low table and had said Anatoli had gone out to check on the jets. She checked the weather on her phone, expecting Anatoli back soon, so turned when she heard the airlock outer door closing.

Anatoli was first through the door followed by Poul and they were laughing. She was pleased to see Anatoli had lightened up but with a twinge of regret that she had to send him back to Progress. There was no way round it. Something was definitely going on in Progress, confirmed by the additional facilities listed on Isadora's sheet; the greenhouses, the Natural Gas Plant and Navy Quay, however the other facilities in the list all sounded like they could be in Kunlun, though she didn't recognise them particularly.

Was there a concerted attempt to stir the least Green places in the AFS to some kind of Green action? Through sabotage, such as Steve Jung's attempts to increase flaring? And who benefited from this agitation?

Thierry Vonne was high on her list, but she was also aware that Rafael Dupont, and his Planetary Cooperation Group could make capital, both political and financial from this. The AFS was the main exporter of aviation fuel, raw minerals and plastics, any suggestion that the supply of such things could be disrupted would send prices sky-rocketing, and make Global Corp enterprises in the UN states more competitive.

Anatoli had come and sat beside her, pushing his freezing nose into her neck.

"Make the most of it," she said, grinning at him. "How's the jet?"

"Still upright, bit frozen. It will take a good hour to defrost before take-off, but I checked the weather stats and the storm has started to shift again, so fingers crossed it'll be good in seven hours or so."

"I want you to give these to Eric, he can send copies on to me."

She handed him three sheets.

"Make sure Isadora doesn't know you have them," she said.

"Poul said you were going to knock her out for the journey to Weddell City. What happens if she admits to being from somewhere other than the AFS?"

"First she'd need to be conscious to do that, and second I don't think she'll blow her cover. Not yet."

"Sweetheart, sometimes I remember a Detective Inspector from Weddell City Police who wanted to arrest senators and gangsters, and talked about staying inside the lines."

She could tell he was teasing her, but, coupled with her earlier thoughts, perhaps it would be no bad thing, if Dante Castillero did look at the legislation?

Roy and Philippe had insisted on a final cooked meal before they set off, so everyone had squeezed around the dining table. They'd ensured Isadora had been fed, watered and relieved well ahead of time, but Enya had decided to hold back on the tranquilliser until it was time to move. As a consequence the conversation around the table was light-hearted. Roy was detailing an extensive list of wants to Enya, that went beyond what they'd used up at the station.

She indulged him, as Anatoli and Poul added more exotic, and ridiculous items to the list. Valla and Martin had been given seats with their back to the cage, which meant Enya could see Isadora, sitting in the cage. Thankfully it was dim enough across the room for her not to see the woman's face. Enya had no desire to know what Isadora might be thinking.

Isadora watched them. Laughing and joking they looked like ordinary people, but she had to remind herself they were all part of the Antarctic Free State and some were part of the establishment too. She'd realised from snippets of conversation she'd heard while awake, that the jet she'd hijacked belonged to Senator Valentina Torres, the Defence Portfolio holder, arguably the second most important person after the President. She was, at the very least, partly responsible for the current Senate's refusal to operate to UN eco-standards. She was an enemy of the planet, not an ordinary person at all.

When Isadora had been asked to attend the Green Activist Conference in Vostok two months prior, the invitation had been anonymous. However, it had suggested the Planetary Cooperation Group was involved in radicalising activists to benefit Global operations back in the UN. It had asked her to attend and make a report. She'd been intrigued enough to reply, and had received identity papers and a hyperplane ticket by return email.

Whoever had invited her, had clearly expected her to be open to the job offer that followed shortly after to eliminate the radicalised activist Steve Jung. He'd been increasing the flaring events at the Ethylene Plant and the subsequent pollution output. She'd initially suspected Thierry Vonne, the only openly Green senator was behind the invitations, but the more things had started to go wrong the more she wondered if that was what she was supposed to think.

She'd heard rumours about Valentina Torres. Back in Europe, she was considered an influential female figure. But the rumours had also included her ruthless strategising, and her ability to take hard decisions. If it had been Senator Torres behind this, then she'd got her fingers burnt, which Isadora took some comfort in.

But, there was now something personal between her and the little woman in charge of the Anti-corruption Team, the lover of the cute pilot. The enmity she could feel coming from the woman they all called Enya, triggered something old in her. There had been much talk about this Code of theirs, but she felt Enya might be pushed past that quite easily in her case. And she recognised the temptation to push, something she'd thought she'd long got control over. A self-destructive urge to push people into hurting her.

She'd been caged and humiliated but it was nothing to her, even drugged, these were things she'd experienced before, long before she'd decided to fight back. There would be opportunities, she just had to be ready for them. And then she'd get revenge on them all.

Karl Leyden had climbed up onto the hangar roof at Weddell City Airport, thirty five minutes before the jet was due to land. He was wearing a native made survival suit but he knew its protection wouldn't be enough so he had the heat pad ready, giving him twenty minutes over what the suit would provide. He hoped the heat would be enough.

He wondered how he would feel seeing her again. Would he even recognise the woman now called Isadora from the fragile and angry creature Enid had been when they'd first met?

He heard the jet overhead and shuffled forward to the edge of the roof. He could see the red van and two cars but it didn't look like there would be any security sweep. He was surprised.

Rafael had received an anonymous tip-off about the jet, so surely they wouldn't simply rely on it being a secret? The sniper rifle was in its heated bag, waiting till the jet taxied up, he brought it out and set up. There was no time for a test shot, but he had some faith in his acquired abilities.

They really were hoping their secret had been kept and he smiled in anticipation of their disappointment.

Sighting on the jet doorway, he saw the steps come out and the door open.

He saw her, just as he remembered her; so helpless between the two agents. He hesitated. Memories of their time together filled his chest with odd feelings. The agents had got to the foot of the stairs. He was running out of time.

Valla's jet touched down on the runway, the different lights marked out her route and the floodlights, illuminating the private hangar area, shone ahead of her. She was glad to be finally landing in Weddell City. She had called ahead at Slessor Station while refuelling, arranging an appointment for scans for Martin, and had overheard Enya making arrangements with the Intelligence Agency to receive Isadora. Less than a handful of people knew who they were bringing in.

Valla brought the jet up to the hangar used by Torres Mining. She could see the red van and two cars waiting. Isadora was groggily coming round from the shot of tranquilliser they'd administered at Slessor Station. She'd need help getting down the steps, or she'd need a stretcher. Valla knew which method she'd have chosen, but it wasn't her call.

Valla was in the cabin when the two agents came on board lifting Isadora out of the seat and checking her restraints. She had just turned to speak to Martin when she heard the crack. It was unmistakable. Someone had fired a single shot. She saw Chris and Enya pull their guns. Chris stayed seated near Martin, as Valla edged to the side of the open door and quickly looked out. The agents had got down the steps onto the apron, and it looked like that had been when the sniper had hit Isadora. An agent was on their knees at her body as it lay on the apron, while the other was shouting into his visor and scanning round, trying to locate where the shot had come from.

Enya had joined her at the doorway. Valla watched as a car slewed up to the agent with Isadora and two more lifted her in. Other agents were now fanning out, all looking for the sniper.

"Where's Wylie when you need him?" said Enya rhetorically.

"Who knew she was onboard?" asked Valla.

"I told Kairns in Intelligence, who did you tell?"

"Nikau."

"I'm prepared to believe the Intelligence Agency is still a bit leaky, but maybe you need to check who else Nikau told."

"Yes," said Valla, in as flat a voice as she could manage, because deep down a small knot was forming. Nikau Burns was her right-hand man, or had been. He'd been her father's right-hand man before that, but lately Nikau had been working more for President Neish than for the Torres Family.

Which had been fine by Valla. The administration that Mariko Neish had set up was a very inter-Family affair.

The five Families that made up the political allegiances of the citizens of the AFS had changed from a hereditary set-up to a more loose affiliation and the senate structures had begun to reflect the increase in consensus politics that resulted.

Valla knew from previous experiences Nikau was more than capable of working in an underhand manner, and she'd always had her doubts about the apparent openness of Mariko's presidency.

Mariko Neish was a Lomonosov senior senator; had grown up politically under Daniel Ektov and his own devious brand of politicking. When Valla had been offered the chance to become interim president, she'd only taken it in order to set up the Anti-corruption Team and get Dante Castillero's legal review underway and, it was because she hadn't trusted the obvious winner of the presidential race, Mariko Neish, to do either.

She saw Regional Controller Kairns coming towards the jet's steps, climbing them slowly, puffing and panting as he did so.

She and Enya stepped back from the door as Kairns came in and headed for the nearest seat.

"She's alive. At the moment. Shot to the chest. I've posted guards to the hospital. Who knew?"

"We were just asking ourselves the same thing. Nikau Burns and you," she said, "I'll get in touch with Nikau and see who he might have told. You had plenty of agents tonight, quite sure of them all?"

She saw Kairns shrug his shoulders. There was a time when Kairns, even as a field agent, would have looked the other way to a Torres indiscretion, but she thought the Agency had matured beyond Family loyalties. Then again, she realised, this is Green politics, nobody is playing by Antarctic rules.

Chapter Twelve - Holes

Anatoli touched down at Progress and felt like he was returning to hell. The Ethylene Plant had been flaring again as he passed over on approach and the greenhouses had an unearthly glow about them as he landed and ran parallel with them, on the runway.

He'd let Ray sit up in the cockpit since it was just her and him. They'd had a pleasant enough conversation, revisiting topics from their investigative pub crawl, but he'd been happy when she'd dozed off in the end. He liked flying alone, it gave him time to think.

It was his long term plan to work with Gary, Alison Strang's son, to develop an airship design that would be powered by hydrogen fuel cells, with the ability to transport cargo as well as passengers. It would meet the stringent UN criteria for carbon footprint. They had some competition but he'd been surprised when they'd first investigated the idea how little there was. The world seemed to have fallen back to the sea for primary transport

Digging deeper, they'd found that was being driven by governments' nationalised shipyards. Global didn't seem interested in new transport either, so it was them and about ten other small entrepreneurial companies, spread around the world, all of them based inland of large landmass areas.

He should contact Gary, now he was stuck in Progress. It made sense to do some work on their designs till Eric got called back to Weddell City.

He wasn't sure how to handle Eric. Chris had seemed to suggest he'd apologise, but Anatoli wasn't expecting much sincerity with it. So it was a surprise to find Eric waiting at the private hangar barrier with a car to collect them. It was late evening and past time for dinner according to his stomach, hopefully Eric was taking them back to the hotel and not the police station.

"Can I drop you off, Ray?" asked Eric.

"Sure. I'm on Alpha Road, so on your way. What's been happening?"

"Lots of paperwork, some interesting information bubbling up in my online searches, and Colin visited. It seems the Greens here have had a rude awakening to the realities of political activism UN style."

"Colin? I'm probably not as surprised as I should be. He hears a lot of shit working at the Confessional, it would make anyone want to change things. I expect."

Anatoli had sat in the back seat, and just relaxed after the flight. The weather hadn't been terrible, but it was still a long flight, in a small jet, and required concentration. He was happy to be left out of the conversation. His back was fine after two years of physio work, but he was more careful with his posture and assiduous with the exercises. Maybe he'd been tense flying back, but he was keen to eat and then get to his own room and do the stretches.

He watched Ray wave briefly before she disappeared into the building. The street lights were already dimming in the increasing snowfall and by the time Eric was driving into the hotel's basement car park the world had shrunk to the car. It felt claustrophobic when added to the awkward silence. Anatoli was determined he wasn't going to be the one to break either. He got out and headed for the lift. Eric was trailing. The lift door opened and he stepped in, turning to press the main floor button, seeing Eric's approach deviate towards the stairs. Anatoli shrugged internally and pressed to close the door. He'd made his case for being the charter pilot and he was sticking to that role.

Eric headed for the stairs. A confined space alone with Anatoli was going to be too much. He'd not quite made up his mind what exactly to apologise for and there were things he still felt were right to have been said to Anatoli's face. Having eaten already there was no chance he'd bump into Anatoli at the restaurant, he headed for his room, to continue working on the case.

Opening his laptop he saw some mail replies from the people who'd been at school with Jonathan Blackbird Renner and Thierry Vonne. He opened the first reply.

Knowing how innocuous the questions had been, the candour on show in the answers was surprising. He'd heard about Alison Strang, and hadn't believed half of the things about Special Strangers that had been included, but he had to admit there was something to it after all. Collating the answers from the three classmates who'd replied built a picture of a strategic thinker in Thierry Vonne, and his willing enforcer in

Jonathan. This was more than a casual link and, he was willing to bet, it still existed.

What he still didn't have was anything on Isadora Ley, or an idea of who was backing her. He'd really have liked a link back to either Thierry or Rafael, because that would be enough to bring him home to Weddell City from Progress, but it was slow going, through the bureaucracy of the Department of Citizenry, to find out who had issued Isadora's ID, getting bounced around the department. He composed a more forthright email, bringing the full weight of what the Anti-corruption Team could do to anyone considered as impeding the investigation and sent it off.

Lying back on the bed, he let his mind wander, mostly to see if he'd been able to compose an apology. He'd recognised the anger was still there, while composing the email to the Department of Citizenry. Tomorrow, there might be a chance at breakfast, but he'd already decided, he wasn't going out of his way to create meetings.

The alarm to wake him went off, he showered, got dressed and heading down for breakfast. He had mixed emotions seeing Anatoli already at a table. Well, he *had* said to himself he would try. He went over and sat down. Before he could say anything though, Anatoli spoke.

"I have something for you."

That was unexpected.

"I forgot about it until I was back in the room, they're papers Valla found on Isadora. Enya wants copies sent to her," Anatoli continued.

Anatoli was pushing over three curled up sheets of A4. Eric unfurled them on the table, letting them re-curl as the waiter came over to take his order.

"Do you know what they are?" Eric asked.

He saw Anatoli give him a pointed look. He felt he was inadvertently digging a bigger hole for himself and couldn't quite get at why.

"You have my number if you need to go anywhere. I'll be working from my room today," said Anatoli as he was getting up.

Eric saw him drop his napkin onto the table, in a manner that Eric couldn't help but interpret as similar to the dropping of a medieval knight's gauntlet or the glove of some eighteenth century duellist.

"Thanks." It was all he could manage.

He felt better when he arrived at the conference room and saw Ray pouring herself a coffee. Today, he hoped he'd make a breakthrough.

"Have you heard?" she asked him.

"No. What?"

"Someone tried to take out Isadora. Sniper shot her as they were taking her out the jet. She's in intensive care. Not interviewable for some time, I fear."

"Everyone else okay?" he asked.

"Yeah. They eventually found where they'd shot from but they must have fired and ran."

He realised he'd tensed at the idea there had been more shooting. Ray was looking at him.

"You know it's okay to have a soft spot for your boss," said Ray, "but it's probably best not to piss off the man she's going to marry."

And there it was. Ray, and, he saw now Anatoli, had figured out what even he hadn't. It wasn't going to make the apology any easier. He chose to ignore the comment.

"I have sheets that Enya found on Isadora. I need to make copies to send to her."

Ray was pointing at the scanner in the corner of the room.

"Technically it's wireless. In practice, use the cable."

He nodded pleased to be moving beyond her insightful comment.

He looked at each sheet as he laid it on the scanner bed. The phone numbers would be what he'd start with. But the Vostok hotel invoice could be useful too, especially if it was where this activist course was held.

Finally, the list of targets needed more context. Should he alert the navy about their location being on the list, or would Enya do that through her friendship with Senator Torres? He'd ask in the email.

It was lunch time when he looked up from his laptop next. The canteen alert had rung about an hour ago without him noticing. The network of intrigue was now dense with overlapping information and connections. He shut the laptop down after the security protocols and sat back on the chair. At some point during the morning Ray had gone back to her office. He'd not even noticed that. The conference room seemed very big for just him. Even if it turned out to be for one day, he'd try and get an office, but hopefully what he'd just sent off, would be enough to get him recalled to Weddell City sooner.

Late to the canteen, he'd ended up with the least favourite meal on the menu and eating on his own. Half his mind was still working through the layers of information so he'd barely registered Ray sitting down opposite him.

“I think you should ask Colin to arrange a meeting of the Greens, and you should talk to them,” she said.

“Why?”

He didn't think it was such a bad idea, but he was interested in the reasons Ray thought it was a good one.

“Firstly, to see who doesn't turn up. If we're looking for factions, only one will be there, the moderate Greens that Colin is involved with. Secondly, I've heard you talking, you've Green sympathies, they'll listen to you.”

"Nothing wrong with thinking things could be done better. I'm not crazy on some of their wilder ideas, but yeah, the AFS could move faster in other directions."

"Good. I'll set it up."

He could tell she wanted to say something else, maybe about Anatoli, but thankfully she didn't. He wasn't ready. Instead she had got up and left, and he poked the remains of the stew about till he realised he wasn't hungry anymore.

The Confessional was busy that evening, Colin waved them through to a back room, which had about twenty people in it. Eric reckoned the citizen population would be close to the four thousand mark, and everyone here would be a citizen. Nearly one in four of the total AFS population were non-citizens. The changing relationship with the UN had initially brought a flurry of citizen applications to the state, but there were fewer now as the ease of travelling between the UN and the AFS increased.

Eric wondered how many had come to the AFS because it was less restrictive and had no eco-damage fines? He'd always thought some sort of penalty would be a worthwhile start. Nothing to make them less competitive, just more careful. He'd never been to Kunlun, but he'd heard a few stories about the mining operations there. Especially stories from the early days, when there was a mad rush to exploit the rare earth metals.

He recalled the list of targets. There was no other way to think about the list. And the fact that some of them were definitely in Kunlun. Maybe he'd be visiting there sooner than Weddell City.

Colin had brought the meeting to order, Eric had introduced himself and there had been a low murmur and a few glances at the door. He'd reassured them, and then explained what the Team thought had gone on and was going on. He asked them for their vigilance, assured them the state did not have anything against Green ideas, just a lot of bureaucratic inertia, which got a laugh at least. The meeting broke up and a few of them stayed on, drinking in the bar.

Colin came up to him.

"Good talk. It's nice to know some of those working for the state are roughly on the same path."

"Thanks," he said, "Who was missing? Ray thinks those are people we need to worry about."

"Well Adil Choudrey for one."

"We interviewed him. The Hotel Juniper receptionist."

"Yes. And two more, Lukas Brandt and Perry Coia. I haven't seen Lukas for months though, but Perry's always at a meeting. I can't believe she's been radicalised. There must be another reason."

Eric looked at Colin, the guy was so keen and naive, but he did know these people, maybe he was right.

"We'll check on her first thing tomorrow."

"Thanks."

Chapter Thirteen - Liana

Jonathan Blackbird Renner much preferred to be called Blackie, but the only people who called him that were strangers on social media who didn't know any better and Thierry. Since school, Thierry had been his friend, always helping him make decisions and looking out for him. Even back then he'd reciprocated the only way he knew how.

He'd come close to killing someone for Thierry before, in the heat of the moment, but the woman at the greenhouse was the first time he'd set out to do it and it hadn't been as hard as he'd expected.

He believed in Thierry's vision of an ecologically responsible AFS, one where the environment came first, not last, and the impact on the whole planet, not just the ice sheet, decided policy. Hearing Thierry talk it always made perfect sense at the time, but afterwards when he tried to recall the details, it was never as clear in his mind.

Blackie knew that was just him, the way his mind worked. Thierry had explained why the vine was important but Blackie had forgotten everything except the specific instruction to leave a torn piece across the woman's body.

She'd been light, he'd almost lifted her off the ground when he'd got the garrotte around her neck. It hadn't taken more than a few seconds to snuff out the vitality in her struggling limbs. She'd tried to grab his hands, but like always, he was too strong. Then he'd wiped down everything he might have touched. Thierry was very specific about that too, and he'd understood why. Then he'd left on the snow mobile.

It had been a long ride up to the ice sheet greenhouse: it would be a long trip back. After the big storm a few days earlier the weather had calmed down. A ridge of high pressure was pushing out from the pole and the temperature had plummeted. He was thankful for the heated seat on the snowmobile, but the heat simply didn't reach his face, where the narrow exposed strip between visor and suit now stung and a part of him imagined it so raw it could be bleeding. He tried to think about other things. The ship wide search that had been a 'drill' nearly a week ago had made him very jumpy.

Someone knew about him. Should he go back to the Mercer at all? He'd been gone for two shifts and the intervening rest period, having persuaded someone to cover for him, but his absence would now have been noticed by people he couldn't convince to ignore it.

As he came down from the glacier alongside a moraine line, he could see the glow from Progress. Thierry had given him an address to go to in an emergency, so that's where he'd go, get in touch with Thierry and find out what to do next.

It was early morning, Ray was in one of the two helicopters heading up to the illegal site where the spotter had seen the heat signature. She'd got the message after getting back from the Confessional: it was consistent with the kind of lapses that had occurred previously at small, battery-powered, illegal greenhouses, so she'd felt it would keep overnight.

With her visor down she could see the lighter snow swirling up as a paler blue than the background ice sheet. It had stopped snowing overnight but there was plenty of fresh stuff to stir. The helicopters shone their searchlights down into it as they landed.

Usually, the greenhouses they found this way had been abandoned, but the police never took a chance. The gangs who ran these outfits were very lax on the Code, even up here on the ice sheet. Maybe they'd come back for some reason and they wouldn't want to get caught. She let the squad go ahead of her into the building. It really was excellently camouflaged, she thought. With her visor down she could only see the leaks from the door, and overnight a lot of that heat had dissipated leaving a fading, pale green.

One of the squad came out and she heard him over the visor.

"There's a body."

Shit, she thought. Another one. Next time she wouldn't let it keep overnight. Bodies were becoming a feature of life at the moment. She headed to the door.

The inside was lined with silver reflective sheeting, the officers had cut the lights to every third panel and it was still bright. One of them was waving her over to the back of the room. She passed along the walkway, most of the plants seemed to be cannabis, always a favourite. Then she saw some trailing liana and began to put body and liana together. This would indeed be of interest to Eric.

She reached the body. It was a young woman, early to mid twenties, the same age as Eric probably. Short brown hair, cut in a practical way. She still had her survival suit on, but there was a red mark around her neck, and bits of plant were loose across her body.

“We’ll need one of the helicopters to go back and bring someone from Forensics, Pathologist Ricci and the Anti-corruption guy. Nobody move anything in the meantime.”

“Boss.”

Having taken some preliminary photos, she tried to discern if it was message, and if so, what it was, while the officers checked out the rest of the greenhouse, disappearing into a side room.

She’d perfected the art of slouching while standing and thinking; it had only been one shuffle from leg to leg before she heard them asking for her over her visor.

The side room was the cook lab. There was a bench full of chemistry equipment, half of which she’d forgotten what it did. There was a fridge, of all things, at the far end of the small room. The officer who’d called her was next to it.

“What d’we have?” she asked.

“Fancy names, but maybe it’s what you were after a few days ago?”

She peered into the fridge and saw some small, sealed test tubes, and they did indeed say, 'Pancuronium' and

'Tubocurarine'. Some of the others said, 'Scopolamine' and 'Atropine'. Sheena would know what they did.

It was difficult not to link these supplies with Isadora Ley. There was another dead body and the feeling that there was indeed a message being left. But Ray was very aware there was nothing concrete to link them currently. They'd need to keep an open mind on what had happened. It could just as easily be a gang on gang hit. Though, that had never happened in Progress before, but pressure was growing on Vostok gangs and they were expanding. She shrugged. She'd know soon enough.

She heard the helicopter land and saw Sheena and the forensic officer come inside, Eric bringing up the rear as usual, looking around.

Watching as the forensic officer started to work on surfaces, she gestured to Sheena and Eric to follow her. She brought them to the body.

"There's no ID on her," she said.

"I'll make sure I identify her as a priority," said Sheena, kneeling down and beginning to examine the body.

"Looks like she was strangled. Not sure about the vine," Sheena continued.

"I'll leave you to it, but I've got a fridge in the cook lab I'd like you to take a look at later," she said, seeing Sheena nod without looking up.

She gestured to Eric as she walked into the cook lab, and went to the fridge.

"Our drug cocktail ingredients, plus something else."

She watched as Eric peered inside the fridge.

"Scopolamine, either they believe in the truth drug shit or they're cutting it with other substances, and Atropine, I've only ever heard of that as part of an antidote to Sarin. What the fuck were they thinking of getting into?"

"How'd you know so much about this?" she asked.

"Professional interest," he replied.

"Sarin is a nerve gas, yes?"

"It's banned, that's what it is," he said, "And remains banned, across every UN state. I can't imagine we don't ban it too."

"You don't know?"

"Detective, clearly you don't either. As police we know the important stuff and how to look up anything else, yes?"

"Fair," she conceded.

"Is this all there is?"

"Yes. You wondering if they've got facilities for Sarin production?"

"Wouldn't you, if you found the antidote in an illegal greenhouse?"

"Maybe it's being imported?"

"That's worse. And what would the target be?"

"I thought you had a list of targets, taken from Isadora?" she said, without even thinking.

"Kunlun," said Eric.

A chill ran down her back. She'd never been to Kunlun, but like every school kid, she knew it was built inside a mountain, though people mistook it for underground. But what it was, was an ideal target for a Sarin gas attack. Enclosed, networked, with few escape routes. The population of Kunlun itself was about ten thousand, and you could wipe most of them out from a few locations.

She saw the same thoughts cross Eric's face.

"We need to get back, let the Agency know. We need to know who this dead woman is as soon as possible," he said.

"Sheena's good. And fast," she said as reassurance.

She left Eric at the fridge and went off to see how Sheena was getting on, and to make more arrangements.

They sat facing the body, which was strapped across the back seats of the helicopter cabin. Ray sat between Sheena and Eric. Eric was looking out the window, though she knew there was nothing for him to see and Sheena was busy tapping on a small field laptop. Ray stared at the body, willing answers from it.

Imagine, she thought, that I'd not noticed the puncture wound on Steve Jung, and he'd been mistaken for Pat, maybe based on some dodgy identification of the body by a Green activist. Would Pat Gallway still be dead? Probably, she thought. If Enya was correct, and he had been blackmailing someone, then that someone was ruthless. After all they probably had Isadora on the payroll.

But would this woman be dead? She'd been working in a chemical lab attached to an illegal greenhouse. It was a lot of investment to abandon, and she would be highly skilled, maybe too good to lose. Ray had to assume this had happened because of what they'd uncovered in Progress already, as part of some tit for tat between the factions. Which suggested they might be running out of time to stop it escalating further.

The sample amounts, in the test tubes they were bringing back from the fridge, were surely not sufficient to protect an attack force dispersing the amount of Sarin necessary for ten thousand people?

That was a question: how much was enough? The quantity would determine where they looked for the Sarin and the rest of the Atropine. And they should look immediately at the list of targets, get in touch with the authorities in Kunlun and let them know.

She wondered, now that Isadora was in intensive care, whether Enya and Chris would be back? She didn't think Eric was ready for them. After she'd confronted Eric with her suspicions about his feelings for Enya, she'd realised he'd no idea that's where his problem with Anatoli had come from. However, she'd not seen any change in his attitude towards Anatoli as a result.

Anatoli, she had to admit, wasn't helping. But then again, she could sympathise. It was easy to sympathise with Anatoli, like almost any other positive feeling would be easy to direct his way.

Maybe that was Eric's problem, he didn't want to like Anatoli because he was easy to like. Pretty twisted, she thought. Going with the flow was a big part of how she lived her life. She'd drifted into the police force because of someone else. She'd been swept up into working with the Anti-corruption Team in much the same way. Why would you want to go against the stream?

They'd got back to the office three hours ago. She reckoned Sheena would be in touch shortly. Eric had spoken with Enya, who'd already identified the non-Progress locations on the list as all places in Kunlun or the wider Massif area. Enya was going to contact the authorities and make them aware of a potential attack.

Ray saw Sheena through the glass approaching her office. She called Eric to let him know and Sheena had just sat down when he arrived. Turning her screen round so he could see the pictures, she nodded at Sheena to begin.

"Well, firstly, I have a positive identification. She's a local, Persimon Coia. Time of death around six yesterday evening."

Eric interrupted, “Colin said she was missing last night from the meeting. There was nobody at the door when uniform went along this morning.”

“Well,” continued Sheena, “now you know why. She was strangled, not with the vine, it was a steel wire about three mill in diameter.”

“The liana’s another message then,” said Ray.

“The breaking strength of a single vine isn’t enough to strangle someone. Three or four entwined, yes, but it wouldn’t leave the same marks,” said Sheena.

"The liana strand *must* be a message. Perhaps they knew they didn't have a lot of time when she would be alone?" said Ray.

“That would explain why it was abandoned. Whoever was coming to relieve Perry saw her body and ran. I hope Forensics come up with something,” said Eric.

“There was something under the fingernails, we've sent it for DNA analysis. Stomach contents, pretty standard winter meal. I’ve pointed out the interesting bits, but I’ll have the final report sent over in an hour. Just waiting on blood and DNA results.”

“Thanks, Sheena.”

She watched Sheena leave, thinking through the report.

“It couldn’t have been Isadora,” Eric said, interrupting her thoughts.

"The message is retaliation for Steve Jung, yes?" he continued.

"Certainly looks like it."

"I'm wondering if we should interview Adil Choudrey again, he wasn't at the meeting either," said Eric.

"I'd like to know the whereabouts of Jonathan Blackbird Renner too," she said, "I'm not quite sure who's in which faction, and I'm getting the feeling that's by design."

There was a knock at her door: she'd not even noticed the officer approaching.

"Boss, we've been inside Ms. Coia's apartment."

She saw the officer had two evidence bags, one with a laptop and one with a mobile in it. He was putting them down on her desk.

"Thought you might want these as soon as possible. Report will be with you shortly."

"I bet this phone is on your list," she said to Eric.

She saw him check his phone.

"Finally," he said, "got the rest of the list matched to names. Let's see if Persimon Coia is there."

She took the phone out of the evidence bag.

Chapter Fourteen - Profit

Rafael Dupont was in his senate office. Originally it had been designed by its first occupant, Senator Clarissa Roth, a founder of the AFS. Its next occupant had been the now disgraced Christine Frome, and as a result it still felt a very feminine room to him, despite his attempts to minimise the decor.

Clarissa had commissioned a mural when the Senate had been built and it was a piece of protected AFS culture. So there was little he could do about the mosaic. An idealised procession of AFS citizens, in shades of red survival suits, with the tools representing the exports of the continent, surrounded by adoring children, trooped across one wall.

He'd installed dark mahogany bookcases on the opposite wall and he'd placed his desk facing the bookcases so he sat with his back to the procession. He'd seen the interior of Gordon Murcheson's office and it'd had a big impact on him. Sourcing a lone leather armchair, he too now kept his whisky on the bookcase, despite thinking it tasted vile.

Rafael Dupont had long ago realised the importance of looking the part, and, as long as you ignored the procession on the wall, he felt his office said exactly what he wanted said about himself.

Sitting in his leather chair, musing on the cut crystal pattern on the decanter, he was thinking just a week ago he'd been very happy with his progress towards the Presidency. He'd successfully infiltrated the newly coalescing Green movement; to the extent his people had been influential in organising an activist training meeting in Vostok. That had been just over two months ago, and they'd managed to fire up more than a few of the activists to a more destructive line of direct action. The increased flaring at Progress had actually had an impact on the commodity price for Ethylene. Everyone at the Planetary Cooperation Group had congratulated him on that. Such a small nudge, he thought, for such easy profit.

Then someone had killed the activist, the flaring had reduced and he'd had to try and find out what had gone wrong. Worse, Pat Gallway had sent a blackmail demand. Of all the sneaky, under-hand things... and he'd been ready to absorb that when Pat had also turned up dead. He'd got worried at that point.

Doubling his security he'd asked Adil to find out who had killed Pat and was surprised to find out it was a foreign eco-assassin. Some woman from Lower Saxony, quite the reputation by all accounts. Clearly she knew enough about his network amongst the Green Movement to be a danger, but then he'd had an anonymous phone call letting him know the assassin had been captured and was being brought to Weddell City.

He now wondered at the source of that phone call, but it was beside the point, the sniper he'd asked Karl to arrange hadn't done the job properly. The eco-assassin was behind several layers of security in intensive care, out of reach, but worse, one of his greenhouses had been found, along with a dead activist. He was feeling targeted and was scared he might be next.

The activist, Perry Coia, had shown promise, she was an excellent chemist, with a hard-line attitude to activism that was entirely of her own making. She'd had some great ideas. His slight nudge of the Ethylene price had shown him what was truly possible, and a larger scale event in the mines of Kunlun had seemed like a worthwhile enterprise for him to invest in. They'd discussed it in emails and he wondered how far along the scheme had got? But he also wondered if his role had been uncovered? He could only continue to invest if he felt safe. He called Karl.

Senator Valentina Torres was in her senate office. It was highly unusual for her to be in during normal working hours. The office had been her father's and he'd had it decorated with a ceramic, relief map of Antarctica. It was one of the few places Valla felt at home, and she needed to feel that just now.

Martin was still at the hospital, having scans and tests, and she didn't want to think about that. So she'd come to work and thrown herself into things she'd been happy to leave for a week: before the simple idea of a week with Martin had fallen apart into this mess.

She opened the mail from Enya, and felt her heart sink. It wasn't improving. What Enya was suggesting; it couldn't possibly be construed as Green to do that?

She wasn't sure. They always sounded quite reasonable in tv interviews, but less so in direct conversations. Or at least, some of the debates she'd been part of where Thierry Vonne had been in the chamber.

He didn't seem to understand the delicate balancing act that the AFS played in the world these days. They simply couldn't shut off the supply of raw materials. For a start what would they trade for food?

He always seemed to suggest that the AFS, as holders of the world's largest fresh water reserves, would be fine. But that had shook her more. Water was basic, it wasn't a thing to trade. They already collected and shipped at cost, sending it to equatorial and desert states, it would be immoral to add profit to that cost. It would be against the Code. But the more she heard from Thierry Vonne the less she felt he had any respect for the Code, nevermind a desire to stick to it.

She'd arranged a meeting with Nikau Burns, wanting another head to strategise with, and it was no bad thing to have one so close to the President. There was a knock she recognised and Nikau popped his head around the door.

"Hi. How are you doing?"

He had shut the door and taken the chair on the other side of the desk.

"As well as expected. Thanks for coming."

"I'm always free to meet you, Valla. You know that?"

"Yes. I do. Until lately I've been fine, the navy's running itself and Veronica's a smart and capable deputy. I really thought I could sit back a bit."

She heard Nikau laugh, seeing a wry smile creep across his face.

“I know,” she said, “I should have guessed.”

“How’s Martin?”

“I think they’re saying he’ll make a full recovery. You wonder if they’re being entirely honest sometimes, but I dare to hope.”

She leant towards him across her desk.

“What do you know about the Greens, specifically Senators Dupont and Vonne?”

She watched his face as she asked, and could see he had something to give. Nikau didn’t play poker and famously never tried to hide the fact he knew secrets: he relied on his strength of will to not divulge those secrets. Just because she could see it, didn’t mean he would tell her, but it was obvious, he *was* torn. It was time to toss in the hand grenade that Enya had supplied in her email.

“I have information that some Green activists are going to target Kunlun with Sarin gas.”

She watched him physically recoil from her. Nikau had an extensive network of informants and he clearly had no idea about this.

“You’re sure?”

“Enya’s team have found a Sarin antidote at an illegal greenhouse where a Green activist chemist was murdered. They’re investigating factional in-fighting amongst the Greens but they've already got a link back to Rafael Dupont. I know," she said, sitting back again, "that you and Mariko were watching Rafael two years ago."

She'd let just a hint of threat enter her voice with the last sentence. Because if she found out Nikau and Mariko had any hand in bringing Isadora Ley to the AFS she would exact revenge on them, as surely as on anyone else who'd been part of it. She could tell Nikau had recognised the unspoken threat.

"Yes, we've been gathering evidence on Rafael. It's no secret he's part of the Planetary Cooperation Group, but we can't afford to have any attempt to take him down fail, so we've been waiting."

"If he's behind this, then you'll not have to wait much longer. It's treason and terrorism rolled into one. What about Thierry Vonne?"

"We've got less. He's definitely smarter than Rafael, and more likeable. As a result it's harder to get people to question his Green zeal. Which to be honest, I think is genuine enough, but also dangerously close to treason sometimes."

"Enya's here in Weddell City, Glenn and Alison are back today. I'd like us to data share tomorrow. The authorities in Kunlun have been made aware they may be targeted in an attack, but I'd much prefer we found the stuff before it got anywhere near Kunlun."

She saw Nikau thinking. She'd forgotten how good he was and she really missed working with him.

"It may already be there," he said.

Her blood ran cold and she shivered. It made absolute sense.

"Early autumn," he said, "move the stuff to Kunlun, store it somewhere till it's forgotten about. It'll be stable as two components for a long time, then you have all winter to choose your moment to mix it, when support or evacuation is difficult and maybe almost as dangerous."

"Bastards. When I find out who's behind this I *will* volunteer to be in the firing squad."

Chapter Fifteen - Data Sharing

Alison watched the daylight disappear as though time had sped up during the flight. With three hours till they landed, the sun had dipped below the horizon and though it was one o'clock in the afternoon it might as well have been midnight. She felt a weight descend, and then she felt Glenn's hand reach out and squeeze hers.

They'd heard the news about Martin, and about the murders at Progress. Terrorism was a fresh concern for the AFS, another unwanted import from the UN. Valla had asked them to come to a meeting the following morning. It was plenty of time to readjust to AFS time from Lima time, she thought, only two hours difference.

"It'll be all right," he said.

"I could hear, there were details she didn't want to say. I'm concerned about those."

"We've faced worse."

She looked at him, aware he was saying things he didn't believe.

"You don't believe that."

She saw him properly look back at her, and saw for the first time small lines at the corner of his eyes.

"No. But I've reached the stage where I want it to be true."

"We'll get through this," she said, "And that is something I believe."

“Agreed.”

Karl Leyden knew he was good looking and had an intensity that was especially attractive to the women who joined the Green movement. It was fair to say he'd used this to the movement's advantage. Tonight in a harbour bar on the outskirts of Weddell City, he was using it once again to save himself from the AFS forces and bring to fruition his most ambitious action yet.

"I don't know," she was saying.

She, was a wiry, red haired woman, who owned a fishing boat, The Girl Alice, who'd already confessed Green sympathies, while they drank the small beers, which he'd been paying for.

"It's just for a day, I'll bring it back I swear, you can name your price."

Watching her eyes, he saw his implication settle home and watched a smile grow.

"All right, tomorrow night, back here."

She passed him a small bunch of keys, conveniently marked.

"It's a promise."

The Girl Alice was an inshore fishing vessel, it needed something more substantial to get round to Saylon on, but she was perfect to go out into the Ronne Sea and locate the stash of Sarin antidotes. Heading to Kunlun to set this off himself; he wasn't making it a suicide mission.

Already in the harbour area, he scouted for a reasonable vessel, and spotted The Boy Ameel, a little less well kept. Climbing down onto its deck he noticed the owner appeared to rely on the harbour security gate, leaving the keys for the vessel onboard. Hopefully The Boy Ameel wouldn't need help to run.

The wind whipped at his face as The Girl Alice left the shelter of the harbour, navigating solely on radar in the darkest night. There were only a few illuminated buoys to keep him off rocks and within the deep channel. Pulling up the zip on the survival suit he brought his head back inside the small wheelhouse, and lay his phone on the instrument panel, opening the map showing where the stash was located. The boat motored ahead on the map towards the stash icon.

Dropping anchor off the small rocky island, he looked from the boat to the rocks and wondered how to get off the boat and onto the island? It was only a few metres of freezing sea; the survival suits were supposed to be good for fifteen minutes in the water: he shrugged, this was simply one more calculated risk in a lifetime of them.

The shock hit his chest as he dropped into the water making him take a deep involuntary breath. His whole body was now shaking. Kicking to get moving, hauling his arms over his head, one by one, he concentrated on swimming and not on his body's reaction to the frigid water. It took a few strokes to get within reach of the rocks, grabbing a hand hold and pulling himself out of the low swell, he stood, shivering violently. With a shaking hand, he pulled down the zip to access the inside pocket for the phone. The freezing drops of water fell from his gloved hand, moving slowly and deliberately inside the suit, careful not to drop his only means of finding the antidotes. The wind stole the heat from his exposed throat and chest. He zipped back up as fast as possible.

Stumbling over the uneven ground in the poor light from the phone's torch function, working his way to the stash location on the map, he could see it was thrust in a narrow gap where the sea had eaten into softer rock. He realised he'd been lucky, if it had been high tide it would have meant a return trip.

His hands were numb even through the gloves as he tried to pull the stash out of the tight fit, already beginning to think about the return swim to the boat, but the package would not come free. He breathed in, then out, trying to stop his shivering and examined the crevice with the torch function. The top of the package had been colonised by mussels spread from one side of the crevice to the other. Peeling them off one by one, their threads snapping, the pack was free and he stowed the stash inside his suit. Crunching on the discarded mussels, he crossed the rocks to the water's edge and clambered back into the sea.

So fixated on retrieving the stash, he'd forgotten to leave a rope down; swimming round to the stern he looked for something left hanging.

The Girl Alice was a well maintained boat, not much was out of place, but it looked like a rope had shaken loose on the far side of the vessel. The swell slapped with more force on this side, the boat rocked up and down, and as it came down he kicked up trying to catch the rope. It nearly slid through his frozen hand. His whole body felt beyond control with the shaking. He pulled. Forcing his arms to obey, climbing aboard, he lay panting on the deck, aware of the urge to rest and the heat flushing through him.

Before arriving in the AFS he'd researched what the effects of hypothermia were, and as he crawled towards the wheelhouse, there was the image of Adil Choudrey, at an abandoned research station beyond Weddell City in his head. Adil lying out on the snow, without his survival suit.

They'd agreed to meet after the activist had been interviewed by the police at Progress. Karl had had his doubts about Adil after the training course in Vostok. Seeing him at the research station he knew for sure, Adil had changed sides.

In an attempt to find out as much as possible, Karl had over-powered him and stripped him of his survival suit. It had been within reach, but Karl needed the information from Adil first. He'd been surprised that Adil hadn't given in, and, at how quickly it became unimportant, as he watched, fascinated, as the steps of hypothermia unfolded. Adil had stopped begging and become disoriented within twenty minutes, he'd died within the hour.

Karl shook himself free of Adil's face in its final moments. He was still shivering, scattering drops of seawater inside the wheelhouse. Motoring back into Weddell City harbour, he berthed the Girl Alice and headed for The Boy Ameel.

Onboard, after starting the vessel up, he'd discovered it was low on fuel, meaning a risky stop somewhere along the coast to blag some fuel. He was out of cash, and cards would be traceable, but at least they'd have to find him along a large stretch of mostly uninhabited coast, which should keep him one step ahead of the authorities.

They'd be heading for Kunlun too, but he'd been careful to only send emissaries to the activists there, and never the same one. The activists there didn't know anything, even less than Rafael, but there was no doubt Rafael would give up everything he did know: the man was spineless.

Earlier, Rafael had called to let him know Perry had been found dead, sounding panicked and more worried than he should have been. Karl had had to persuade him to calm down and stay put, but he'd already decided Rafael was past being useful.

It took three hours to find a small inlet along the coast to anchor in: the pressure to sleep threatened to overpower him. Going down into the engine room, setting an alarm for two hours, he reckoned the heat from the engines would keep the ambient temperature above ten degrees for at least that long, and he'd had plenty of experience operating on snatched hours of sleep.

Chapter Sixteen - Dirt

Alison recognised the meeting room this morning, as the same one she and Daniel Ektov had used to negotiate with the UN ambassador. Being back in it, she half expected Daniel to come through the door, but he'd been dead now for two years, shot in an attempt to assassinate President Gordon Murcheson. Sometimes she wished Daniel was alive and Gordon was dead, but the AFS would be a very different place if that had happened. Maybe a worse place.

Glenn was over at the side table pouring the coffee for them when Valla entered the room, followed by Enya and Chris Saraband. She heard Glenn clink more cups down and continue to pour.

"Alison," said Enya, "so good to see you, and thank you for bringing Glenn back in one piece."

She could see a broad smile on Enya's face. Glenn had indulged in some light teasing of Enya, before they'd left for Lima, suggesting he'd take the opportunity to go climbing.

She saw Valla and Glenn bring the cups of coffee over to the large conference table. The door opened again and Nikau Burns came in, followed by a familiar figure.

"James," exclaimed Enya.

Alison saw James give his usual shy wave to the room. It seemed two gold medals hadn't gone to his head in the slightest.

"Hi. I came back as soon as they'd let me. They were a bit unhappy I wasn't hanging around for the final ceremony, but I did point out it was getting serious back home."

He was sitting down on the other side of Enya from Chris. Glenn had pushed a coffee his way and had got up to pour two more.

"So," said Nikau, "can I ask Enya to start."

Alison knew the time for catching up was after they had sewn together as much as they had of the full picture. And Enya started with the details Alison had sensed were lurking in Valla's communications.

Alison couldn't believe someone would decide to use a poisonous gas to kill the ten thousand inhabitants of Kunlun, even if they believed that mining was bad for the environment. She thought there must be more to it.

The factional in-fighting interested her, it suggested manipulation somewhere higher up the chain. People had a natural tendency to put aside smaller concerns when they shared a big picture, but outside forces would always be able to use those small concerns, build them up to become apparently fundamental issues.

Someone was benefitting from the in-fighting, and she realised whoever that was would benefit from poisoning the main mining centre for the AFS. When Enya had finished, she said as much to the room.

She saw Valla nod, and Nikau typing something into his phone.

"I've not quite finished though," said Enya, "this morning we managed to access the information that was on an apparently blank sheet. It was a list of names, we believe it to be the attendees at a course held in the Ice Diamond Hotel, in Vostok two months ago. One that Isadora used a fraudulent AFS ID to attend, also attended by, Adil Choudrey, the Hotel Juniper receptionist, now missing having flown to Weddell City, Steve Jung, murdered, Pat Gallway, murdered, Persimon Coia, murdered and a guy called Karl Leyden who visited Progress three weeks prior to this all kicking off. There's two names we think are Kunlun based. We're still waiting on the Department of Citizenry to give us the details on Isadora's ID. But I think we can safely say she's in the opposite faction to Steve Jung at least."

"Still waiting?" asked Valla, "When did you put it in?"

"Two days ago," replied Enya.

Alison saw Valla look hard at Nikau, and Nikau tap furiously at his phone. Then it was Valla's turn to look at her phone.

"Jonathan Blackbird Renner has gone AWOL from the Mercer. He was last seen two days ago."

"He's Thierry Vonne's enforcer, has been since school," said Enya.

At this point Alison thought, she would have used her sharp mind, the biotech implant that had nearly killed her twice now, and had been surgically removed after the second time. It was only in moments like this that she missed it. Instead she concentrated her honed and original Special Stranger abilities; what she knew about people, how they thought, why they acted the way they did.

"Someone profited from what Steve Jung was doing. Is it possible to find out if the price of Ethylene went up, and if so who in the AFS would make money from that?" she said.

"Rafael Dupont and his friends in the Planetary Cooperation Group," said Nikau. "The whole ethos of that group is to profit from crises."

"Well," she said, "he could make a lot more from eliminating the mining at Kunlun."

"We have some dirt on Rafael already," admitted Nikau.

"Do you now?" said Enya pointedly, "And why doesn't the Anti-corruption Team have that dirt?"

"We were saving it up," said Nikau.

Alison saw Nikau would not look at either Valla or Enya.

"We?" asked Valla.

Alison saw Nikau continue to look at his hands and knew he wouldn't elaborate further on who the 'we' were. Did it matter she thought?

"What's the dirt?" she asked.

"He helped Christine Frome by arranging the disposal of Arnaud Cheung's body in the harbour," said Nikau.

At least he made eye contact with her.

"The cleaner admitted it was Rafael Dupont. I always wondered why he wasn't brought to the stand. I thought it was just his naturally slimy abilities. You may find yourself the subject of further enquiries, Nikau Burns," said Enya.

Alison heard the cold determination in Enya's voice, the tone that had made her legendary. She also agreed with Enya, Nikau shouldn't have allowed Rafael to continue.

"We needed enough rope to properly hang him. As you rightly point out, he's a slippery one."

"There's that 'we' again, Nikau," said Valla "I just want to make it clear to everyone else, I'm not part of the 'we'."

Alison felt the cohesion of the group unravelling. They needed brought back together.

"So, we have enough to reel in Rafael now?" she asked.

"We can pull it together in a few hours, yes," said Enya, who was looking at Nikau.

Alison saw Nikau finally look up.

"Yes," he agreed.

"Thierry Vonne," said Valla, who was looking at her phone.

Alison heard the flat tone of Valla's absolute emotional control.

"What?" asked Enya.

"He got Isadora Ley her citizenship ID. I'll kill him."

Alison looked around the table, and saw Chris, James and Glenn were all watching Enya.

"Wait," said Nikau.

Alison thought it was a particularly brave thing to have said at that moment. She watched Valla and Enya eye him like dinner.

"The two part components of the Sarin are most likely already at Kunlun. We should be very careful how we defuse this situation. Are we quite sure Rafael is behind it?"

She saw Valla breath in deeply, and Enya sit back.

"You have a man in his organisation, don't you?" asked Valla.

"We do."

Alison saw Valla had figured out something from that acknowledgement.

"Then you should find out. In the next few hours," said Valla.

"And," said Enya, "the State should be making plans to evacuate Kunlun. I know they've been alerted but we haven't said we think the stuff is already there. When we tell them, we need a plan ready to roll out."

"I can already bring in Renner for desertion," said Valla, "that will put pressure on Thierry, and if he is behind Isadora, then he doesn't have his assassin either."

"We have to find Renner first," said Enya.

"He's got to be in Progress. You've got people there?" said Valla.

"I do."

Alison watched Valla enter full General mode and wondered how she could still manage it.

"So," continued Valla, "as soon as we have proof Rafael gained directly from Steve Jung's activities we bring him in. He can't be left loose longer than necessary."

Alison saw Valla look directly at Nikau who nodded briefly and then got up from his seat.

"I'm going to have to leave you now for another appointment. I'll be in touch."

Alison wondered if he did have another meeting? Or perhaps, more accurately, he was leaving to set one up.

When he'd left the room, she turned to Valla.

"So who is the 'we'? I saw you'd worked it out."

"He works with Mariko Neish. He suggested she should stand for the presidency and they were pretty thick two years ago when Rafael eluded the repercussions of Christine's trial."

Enya agreed, “Yes it makes sense. It was Mariko’s people who were waiting for Arnaud’s body to be moved.”

“The President is withholding evidence?” asked Alison.

“Same old, same old,” said Glenn.

Alison was disturbed that there wasn’t more indignation in the room. Clearly corrupt presidents were considered almost Antarctic.

“It’s great to be home,” said James, smiling.

Enya burst out laughing. Alison and the rest joined in. The tension had been broken.

“Honestly,” he continued, “I was getting utterly fed up with only being asked what it was like to be black in Antarctica. Like they didn’t expect me to somehow survive here.”

Alison recalled that the Olympics had been held by the supra-state collective called Cascadia, a mix of ex-Canadian and US states on the North American continent’s western seaboard. It kind of made sense they would think like that. Poor James, that could only have been interesting the first time it was asked.

“Do you have your medals with you?” she asked.

“They’re quite heavy so I only brought one. I knew someone would ask.”

Alison could see he was looking at Enya with a mix of pride and concern as he stood up and began to fish inside his suit.

“I was rooting for you all along,” said Enya, patting his back.

Alison continued to watch Enya; she was clearly still preoccupied by something.

James passed his medal to Alison. It was heavy. Heavier than she’d expected. She looked at the design, the medal had a low relief of the Cascadia Mountain Range overlain with the six Olympic Rings, Antarctica’s ring hanging below the original five. On the reverse was another low relief of a rifle crossed with a pistol. She passed the medal to Glenn, and took the opportunity to get up and refresh her cup, heading back to sit in the chair James had vacated.

“What’s up?” she asked Enya quietly.

“I’m going to have to send Anatoli and Eric to Kunlun, immediately. How can I keep him safe?”

“He’s sensible, he doesn’t take unnecessary risks, and I think some of us are going to have to join him anyway. Don’t you?”

“Yes. You’re right, I suppose.”

Chapter Seventeen - For The Greater Good

Rafael Dupont heard some noise in the outer office, wondering momentarily what it was as the door to his office opened with more force than his secretary usually applied. Two uniformed police officers entered and approached him. He felt a slight panic, but fought down the feeling. This would turn out to be a misunderstanding he was sure. He had friends, some of them quite high up in the Police force now.

"Senator Rafael Dupont?"

"Yes."

"I'm arresting you on the charges of perverting the course of justice and conspiracy to destroy state assets."

The officer came forward and gestured for him to put up his survival suit and then his hands out. He shrugged himself into the arms of the suit and zipped it halfway up his chest, feeling the chill of the handcuffs, the weight on his wrists.

Deep inside the panic continued to fester. They sounded pretty serious charges, ones that were unlikely to have harmless alternatives for a misunderstanding to arise from. His mind was immediately thrown back to the phone call over two years ago, with the specialist cleaners.

He'd contracted them to forensically clean Christine Frome's flat and remove the body of the assassin, Arnaud Cheung. The lead cleaner was in Denam prison for life, the other was out on parole. What more might they have divulged since the trial two years ago? Why now? And what was destruction of state assets? It sounded very close to treason.

“Call Karl,” he said to his secretary, from between the two police officers, catching her nod before he was thrust through the door.

Being marched down the spiral ramp that accessed the senators’ offices, which in turn ringed the senate chamber, he could see people stopping and some were pointing at them. There was hushed whispering. None of this was going to help his ambitions, unless he could turn it to his advantage. Hopefully Karl could think of something.

His personal belongings had been taken from him before they’d put him in the cell, there was no way of knowing how long it had been since they’d arrested him and he tried to recall what the statutory time limit was. He had a feeling it was a long time, but it had been long enough so far, to think through what might have led to this. It was clear one of the cleaners had said something more.

At the time of Christine’s trial he’d been ready for arrest, but they hadn't come for him. Christine’s lawyers hadn't called him to the stand either and he’d put it down to some machination of Gordon Murcheson, but had never uncovered what Gordon had planned.

Now, the feeling in the pit of his stomach was suggesting it was someone other than Gordon, and their reasons were quite the opposite of protecting him. If someone had been waiting two years to ensnare him, they could easily have infiltrated his support over that time, despite his best attempts to be careful. Karl Leyden wasn’t known to many of his political supporters, only those who shared his commitment to bringing Global back to the AFS through the Planetary Cooperation Group.

River Sampson was now his number one suspect, a Lomonosov senior senator, however River wasn't the sharpest tool in the box either. But there were others, perhaps there'd be clues when they eventually bothered to question him. His stomach growled and he assumed from that it must be approaching late evening, his usual dinner time. All he knew for certain: it had been two in the afternoon when they'd arrested him.

Enya had all the evidence laid out on the table, including the latest from Progress. Eric had finally gained access to Persimon Coia's laptop and had found direct communications between Rafael and Persimon. That information had come through at half past one and had been enough for Enya to arrest Rafael. Shortly after, she received the evidence from Nikau that his inside man had met someone called Karl Leyden at an exclusive Planetary Cooperation Group event and, they had discussed how much money a small increase in the Ethylene price could net Rafael. Karl had apparently called it a trial run.

She'd decided to do a straight interview with Rafael first, and then let Alison at him. She could tell Alison was not convinced, but Enya had recalled Gordon's lawyer, Nancy Carter, from his trial. Nancy had annihilated the testimony drawn from the Global executive, Kutchner, by Alison's questioning. Kutchner had been a hostile witness, but she didn't think Rafael would be any more compliant and he had the credit rating to hire Nancy.

Alison had asked to view the interview remotely, thankfully not in the observation room, which Enya felt would've been difficult for some undefined reason she wasn't going to spend mental energy on.

She'd arranged to use the interview room with the wonky light. Years of using the interview suites had inured Enya to their particular foibles; the over-heated room, the wonky light room, the whining generator room, but they had their uses on subjects new to them.

She'd had Rafael sit in the interview room for nearly an hour, with the clicking and blinking light. She watched him from the observation room through the one way mirror. He'd shown signs of stress when he'd first arrived, and the tells were only increasing.

She entered the interview room. Rafael was chained to the desk, he'd had his head in his hands but had looked up when the door opened. She could see the panic behind his eyes, though it seemed he was trying hard to push it down. The fact he couldn't was only adding to his stress levels: it was a handy tool in these situations.

"Rafael Dupont, did you assist Christine Frome in the disposal of Arnaud Cheung's body from her flat?"

"I want my lawyer."

"For a senator you seem to have a poor grasp of the AFS legal code. Your lawyer can't stop me asking you that question. Or anybody qualified, asking you any questions, they can only suggest not to. Having one, however, at this stage, under AFS legislation, does amount to an implication of guilt in the charges laid before you. And any further charges that our investigations may uncover..."

She left the prospect of a charge of treason, punishable by firing squad, hanging in the air.

"All right, all right. Yes. I paid the cleaners. Because Christine asked me to do it and promised me the Defence Portfolio. I was young and naive. Christine told me she'd shot Arnaud in self defence."

"Do you trade via Interstate Stock Trading?"

She could see the question took him by surprise.

"Yes. That's not illegal."

Then she saw it dawn on him where the questions were going. He reddened: it was quite the tell. She felt one more question was worth it, even if he was now belatedly on his guard. The light flicked and clicked in quick succession for about ten seconds and then went back to its more random and lazier activity.

She'd seen him wince at it.

"Do you know Persimon Coia?"

She saw him pause. He was clearly working out the implications of admitting or not admitting his connection to her. He didn't seem to be coming to a conclusion.

She slammed the table, making him jump.

"Deny it, please. 'For the greater good'," she quoted from their email correspondence.

She could tell he was broken now.

"Yes, I knew her. Only through emails, I swear. She wanted to help with my Green policies."

Oh, thought Enya, not so broken he couldn't try a last slither. Well, once Alison was finished with him he would be properly crushed.

"We will be holding you pending further investigations for the next thirty hours. At which time any further charges will be brought and the decision on bail will be made."

She stood up and saw him look relieved. Alison had asked him to be moved to the warm room, an environment she said she preferred over the wonky light. Maybe he'd think he was being taken back to the cells. Enya smiled as she walked out the door.

Now she was concerned with chasing down the other members of Rafael's clique before they could do any damage. This Karl Leyden was someone she wanted as soon as possible. Apparently Rafael had instructed his secretary to contact him as he was leaving. A warrant was already out for his arrest but he seemed to have disappeared. There was a watch on the airport for him, which left only the sea as an alternative; harder to check, it also took longer to get anywhere.

She'd been in touch with Eric and Ray at Progress, and the Intelligence Agency at Saylon to alert them to that possibility. Those were the ports you'd fly to Kunlun from, but it remained a possibility that not only the Sarin components, but also the activists, were already there. Maybe the whole scheme was waiting on enough of the antidotes being produced.

She'd heard from Ray that they'd increased the spotting plane trips in the hope of finding more of the illegal greenhouses. Enya wondered if the official greenhouses both at Kwazi Station west of Progress, and in Progress itself were also worth a look at. The police chemist had estimated both the amounts of Sarin components that would be required for an attack on Kunlun and the antidote quantities per adult. It was a scarily small amount of Sarin, two pressurised tanks, the size of the average acetylene storage tank: they'd be easily missed in a cursory search of any mining facility. As for the antidotes, it needed more than they'd found at the illegal greenhouse. But it was entirely dependent on how many people needed to be dosed.

She was hoping that the antidotes were holding up the attack from proceeding. However, movements like this always attracted those who would die for the cause. There was no guarantee it wouldn't become a suicide attack.

She'd read up on the symptoms of a Sarin attack; starting with respiratory effects, it degenerated quickly into a loss of bodily functions. It didn't sound like an especially pleasant suicide, though quick: death ten minutes after directly breathing it in. The thought of ten thousand people going through that en masse was hard to imagine, but it was easy to see it would totally devastate mining operations for months if not years.

The door opened to the temporary office Enya had commandeered within the Weddell City Police department. Alison came in and sat down in the seat set to the side of her desk, looking tired.

“Coffee?” she asked.

“Yes, please. Though something stronger might not go amiss," said Alison, " I have bad news.”

Enya paused from calling for a flask of coffee and put her phone back down.

“It's not my office, but it can be arranged.”

“He’s not really in control of what’s going to happen at Kunlun, he’s more the financial backer than anything else. Not the mastermind, that’s for sure.”

Enya picked her phone back up and called Chris, asking him to bring some glasses and whisky.

“That doesn’t surprise me," said Enya, "Nikau’s inside ‘man’ is Victoria Beauchamp, she says Rafael was always mentioning a Karl Leyden, who we know visited Progress four weeks ago. She met him at a Planetary Cooperation Group evening.”

“It’s clear Karl didn’t consider Rafael particularly secure,” said Alison, “he doesn’t know details, but I did get some sense of the timeline, and I can confirm the components are already in Kunlun.”

“Shit,” said Enya.

The door had opened just as she'd spoken, poor Chris she thought, he always seemed to catch her rare moments of expletive.

"Sounds like I'm just in time," he said.

Enya declined a glass, but watched Chris pour one for Alison and himself.

"We need to get to Kunlun. If we can't catch Karl, we still need to try and stop the whole thing anyway. I'll get Anatoli to get Eric over there as soon as possible."

She checked the meteorological apps on her phone, the weather window provided by the ridge of high pressure was already collapsing. She rang Anatoli and told him to make the preparations. He'd insisted she called Eric separately. Whatever was going on between the two of them had apparently not yet resolved itself.

She found it difficult to keep the sharpness out of her voice when she told Eric he was going to Kunlun as soon as possible, with Anatoli. He sounded subdued in his replies, and she remembered that Ray McCarthy had likened Chris and Eric to a pair of loyal huskies.

She put her phone down harder than she had meant, and the low murmured conversation Chris and Alison were having stopped immediately.

"We need a charter to take us to Kunlun," she said curtly.

She saw Alison pick up on the unspoken tension between Chris and herself.

"What's going on?" asked Alison.

“Eric has a problem with Anatoli working in the Team, the general consensus is Eric has a thing for Enya, it’s frosty to say the least,” said Chris.

“Anatoli? Who *doesn’t* like Anatoli? Enya, you’ve got to sort that,” said Alison

“I had hoped they would do it themselves. But yes, team dynamic and all that. I will. However, who’s going to take us to Kunlun?”

“I’ll get on it,” said Chris.

She watched him proffer the bottle to Alison and saw her wave it away as he stood up and left the room.

“I’ve put Tolli in an impossible position," she said to Alison, "and I don’t know what triggered Eric at Progress because up until then I didn’t think there was a problem. Chris, Glenn and James are perfectly happy.”

“Well, yes,” said Alison, “Chris fancies him, Glenn knows the family and James likes everybody. I wouldn’t expect a problem there.”

Chapter Eighteen - Precision Cuts

Detective Ray McCarthy had been getting daily reports from the airport about passenger lists. She'd been relying previously on Eric Jordan, the Anti-corruption guy to sift through them, so it had taken her a bit of time to get into the habit of looking herself. Eric had been looking for Isadora, but the lists continued with nobody cancelling them after she'd been captured. She was looking back through them for Adil Choudrey, the Juniper Hotel receptionist that Colin had said was missing from the Green meeting two days ago.

Eric had had a big impact on the activists. Several had come to the station since, with little bits of information, mostly about Steve Jung. It had been gratifying to know they weren't so far gone as to turn their backs on the Code or the AFS in general.

She could understand their desire for change. A place like Progress was caught in the middle, and there could be more done to protect the environment. It wasn't like the AFS was short of cash, but everyone had noticed that when Global was kicked out nothing had really changed. She was scanning the departures for the day the meeting was held. The early flight to Weddell City: there he was, on his own travel documents, and why not? Back then they weren't looking for him.

She called Weddell City Police to speak to Enya and let her know. She got the latest update on Isadora, still unconscious. Enya read out the list of names uncovered on the blank sheet, Ray recognised almost all of them, except for Constance Mbeki and Yang Lau. She said as much, venturing they could be Kunlun based. Finally, they discussed the possible locations for Renner. Enya told her Valla was very keen to find him, though it was less of a priority than Karl Leyden.

It seemed to Ray, keeping Senator Valentina Torres sweet was always worthwhile. She arranged a team to sweep the other company accommodation block. The apparent lack of in-house management at the blocks would appear to be beneficial to those wanting to lay low in Progress.

Eric had arrived in her office later that afternoon with fresh updates.

"Adil Choudrey booked a snowcat out of Weddell City airport. They've not had it returned. Enya's arrested Senator Rafael Dupont: perverting the course of justice and conspiracy to destroy state assets."

"Not treason?" she asked.

"Not yet."

"I'm waiting on a report back from the accommodation block search for Renner. I expect he's been and gone, though. Any ideas?"

"We're looking at a minimum two factions, we've got Colin and a few onboard with respect to one, but Renner belongs to theirs. I'm not convinced Colin would willingly give up information on Renner."

"You want to bring him in again? That might be counter productive."

"No. His mate, George from the suit shop. He was very quiet at the meeting, slipped off straight away."

Eric's mobile went off. She waved him out of her office, seeing his face and knowing it was Enya's number. She was still concerned about the effectiveness of the Anti-corruption Team, spread between cities and with this widening crack in the dynamic.

She decided she was invested sufficiently in this case to keep at it whatever happened. Too many times she'd realised, she'd let things slip for a quiet life. A night in to watch the tennis did not out-weight this, and there was a real threat to the future of quiet nights in if she didn't find Renner, she was sure.

Her own mobile started to ring. It was the search team, they'd found evidence of occupation, snack wrappers and empty water bottles in a room at the accommodation block. It didn't look like anyone had been there today. She decided to head out and take a look herself. It had been a profitable move so far.

The room was identical to Pat Gallway's, but messier. High energy snack wrappers were now collected together in an evidence bag. The uniform officer had been picking the last few up when she'd arrived. The water bottles had already been whisked away to Forensics.

She received news the water bottle DNA was a match for what they already knew was Renner gained from Perry's fingernails. Before she seriously started poking around the room, she ordered George brought in.

It felt bad to be bringing in someone she went to school with, someone she'd always thought of as a good person. But you couldn't go against the Code and be a good person. She'd find out exactly who George was.

She got down on her hands and knees and checked out underneath the bed. She could see scrape marks in the dust.

"This wasn't you lot?" she asked the uniformed officer.

"No boss. We took photographs but we didn't disturb anything under there."

"He had an emergency kit to rely on. Someone put it there, or kept it up to date. I want the CCTV for as long back as possible, and I want everyone on it identified. Pay particular attention for George Tan showing up."

"Yes boss. We've already pulled the CCTV, it goes back three months."

She nodded. That should be good enough, she thought. She went into the en suite. Abandoned travel toiletries littered the shelf below the mirror. Renner clearly didn't care if he was identified as being here. His protector, according to Enya, was Senator Thierry Vonne, which could make you feel safe, she supposed. But it would also make you lazy. She went back into the other room.

"Did you find any scraps of paper, receipts?"

She looked afresh at the bag of snack wrappers. They were mostly waxed paper, but some were brown recycled paper.

"I'll take that bag, log it against my name, thanks."

Back at her office she tipped out the wrappers, there was the smell of sugar and preservatives from the crumbs of food still stuck to them. She picked out the brown recycled paper wrappers and smoothed them out, one at a time.

"Bingo."

There on a wrapper, was the imprint of a phone number. She called Eric.

"Ray. I'm on my way to the airport. Enya's told us to get to Kunlun. What's up?"

"Renner wrote a number down and I've got an imprint on a snack wrapper. I suspect it's George's but we'd have noticed his name on the list, so if it is his, it's under another name. I'm checking it against Isadora's list, before I speak to him."

"Thanks. I'll get back in touch when I get into Kunlun."

"Safe journey," she said, aware that Anatoli was doing the flying and you probably couldn't get safer than that.

"Yeah," said Eric.

She could tell, the irony that his life was in Anatoli's hands, had not bypassed Eric.

The number on the wrapper did indeed show up in the list. The name Achilles B was next to it. The AFS had a multi-cultural population, nobody would bat an eyelid at the name, but it was clear now it was a codename.

They'd merely brought George in for questioning, he would therefore still have his phone on him. Maybe he had two, but it was worth a try.

She entered the narrow interview room where George was sitting at the table. He looked up when the door opened and she knew he'd recognised her from school. He still looked wary. Her heart sank, he clearly felt he had a good reason for being wary of the police.

"Hi, George. You remember me?"

She placed her phone on the desk and sat down.

"Ray McCarthy, yes. I didn't know you joined the police."

"A few years ago now, George. You remember Henri Vogel?"

She could tell he did. Henri had been good looking and a little wild. Nobody was surprised he'd dropped out of the police course.

"Vaguely," he said.

Ray had no doubt that was a lie. Nobody vaguely recalled Henri, he imprinted deep in your memory.

She tapped her phone where she'd had the mobile number ready to call. In synch with the rattled buzzing from her own phone she could hear the buzzed vibrations of a phone deep inside George's survival suit.

"Tell me George, what did you make of Jonathan Blackbird Renner when he called you?"

She saw him almost immediately discount lying, his face an open book.

"You going to tell me he killed someone too?"

"Persimon Coia. It's a bit of a Green thing. Is this how the global population is going to be reduced? One politically incorrect activist at a time?"

George Tan might have been five years older than her, but she felt at that moment, she was schooling a toddler about the harsh realities of the big, bad world for the first time. His face had fallen, he seemed to have lost all his confidence.

"Perry? No."

"I have to tell you worse, she wasn't an angel, George. She was found up at an illegal greenhouse, cooking up Sarin antidotes."

"The nerve gas?"

He was shaking his head. She felt sympathy, it was hard to believe people were that fucked up. Big, bad world and all that, she thought.

"Yes. It's believed to be in bits at Kunlun. Ten thousand people, George, dying a horrible death."

"Renner isn't involved with them. He said he was trying to stop the Planetary Cooperation Group from infiltrating the movement."

"Well, taking out Persimon Coia was a start. We need to bring him in, before everything gets *more* out of hand. Where is he, George?"

She waited. She always felt officers underestimated the importance of waiting to the interview process. They badgered and harassed and didn't always get all the information as a result. She liked to make precision cuts to an interviewee's resolve and wait for the secrets to spill out.

Chapter Nineteen - Promises

Valla received a call from Kairns while she was at the hospital. It was the last day of tests for Martin. After it she called through to Veronica.

"Hi Veronica. They've got a sighting of Karl Leyden, last night at the Long Haul Bar. A woman says she lent him her boat, but it was back in the harbour with the keys in the ignition. Once Intelligence showed up they found a deep sea trawler was missing, The Boy Ameel. Owner was a stupid fucker who always left his keys in the boat. He says the engine's unreliable but the AIS is switched off, whoever took it knew at least to do that. I want the Coulter and Alvarez to head along the coast to look for it, one inshore, one a bit further out. And I don't want anyone in Progress knowing why they're leaving."

"Valla. I'll send the order out as top secret. We've still no sightings of Jonathan Blackbird Renner, but the Progress Police assure me he's not left through the airport. They've asked for Intelligence to give them a hand?"

"I think we can arrange that, I'll speak to Kairns, Progress isn't quite in his remit, but everyone expects him to head up the Agency in a few years time, nobody's going to piss him off."

"How's Martin?"

"Much better, thanks. This is the last day of tests. He just has exercises to do at home now."

"I'm really pleased to hear that, I'll be in touch."

Valla heard the click as Veronica hung up. She liked the Larsen junior senator. Another couple of years and she reckoned Veronica would be able to take on the Defence Portfolio. Valla abhorred power vacuums, she'd done everything she could to stop Gordon Murcheson creating one and she was damned if she was going to be guilty of it herself.

She turned as the ward doors swung open and Martin came through talking with the neurologist. They were both smiling, she felt her mood lift in anticipation. For a brief minute or two she wouldn't be planning on how she was going to nail everyone involved from Thierry Vonne downwards for their part in this. She saw Martin look over and she stood up to join them.

"Good news?"

"Yes," said Martin, "they're seeing lots of reconnections in the latest scans."

"I want to say, Senator Torres, the prompt actions of the medic at Mellor Station and yourself have played a crucial role in Martin's recovery."

"Thank you Doctor, I'll pass on your comments to Philippe Moussad, I'm sure he'll be pleased to hear them."

The neurologist was patting Martin on the back as he turned to go. She saw Martin looking at her.

"What's up?" he asked.

"They've got a lead on Karl Leyden. But nothing on Renner."

They were walking towards the lift, and she punched the button with some force.

"That's good about Leyden, isn't he the one who's involved with the Sarin?"

The doors opened and they got into the empty lift.

"Yes. He should be the priority. But, Renner gets us Thierry Vonne."

"Darling, the expert in battle is not moved by the enemy."

"You're right, as is Sun Tzu, but it's hard for me."

"You know as well as I do, what the right thing is," he said.

She saw him press the button to stop the lift, and looked to see why. He had one of his smiles that made his eyes twinkle. She pressed the restart button and kissed him.

"I do, and I will restrain myself in that regard."

She saw him smile again, and deep inside some of her darkness dissipated.

It was much later she got a text from Veronica letting her know the ships had sailed from Progress. Hopefully they wouldn't be missed until the morning. She put the phone on silent and turned over to press against Martin, holding him as if he would crumble without her arms around him.

The MS Alvarez and the MS Coulter slipped away from Progress with only the glow from the lights on the chemical plants to give them away. It had been days since the last flare at the Ethylene plant, so the complex had appeared as subdued as it was possible to be, with only the gantry lights snaking up the towers, and the occasional flood light activated by the movement of a night shift worker.

Captain Liam Kelly of the Alvarez called his counterpart on the Coulter over the phone.

"Ian? Hows things?"

"Liam. Good. I just get onboard and there's some secret shit going down. What do you know?"

"Well... You know how boring Progress is? It got a whole lot more interesting while you were on leave. Several murders, all Greens, as is the guy we're looking for. Word is Valla has dug out her Art of War quotes, and you know what that means."

"I do. I heard about Martin off the Mercer. Who'd have thought, eh?"

"Yeah, whatever you're thinking though, you'd best keep to yourself."

He heard Ian laugh. With all the navy ships in Progress, the news that Martin Kostov, XO of the Mercer was in a relationship with Senator Valentina Torres was the worst kept secret in the AFS. But it had hit them all hard to hear he'd been injured during the hijacking of the Torres jet. Martin had been well respected amongst the tight knit community the navy had developed into, over the short span of two years.

"I propose we take turns out wide. Veronica has suggested two miles. We've got to get her out on a trip sometime so she knows what she's talking about."

"Ah, Liam cut her some slack, she's just new. Yes, I'm good with swapping in and out, gives us a bit more search coverage too. Is that you volunteering to be first?"

"Give you time to get your sea legs back," he said.

"You just let me know when it all gets too much for you," said Ian.

He heard the click as Ian Khan, captain of the MS Coulter hung up. He called the bridge and ordered his XO, Nicola Larsen to take them out into the deep swell of the Southern Ocean. It wouldn't be comfortable but it was unlikely The Boy Ameel was going to be out further than them, given what he'd been told about the state of its engines.

He'd posted extra lookouts on the bridge and told Nicola to come a little inshore in an hour's time then head back out for another hour. They wouldn't find it this close to Progress but it was worth getting the crew used to the search format and the sea conditions. They and the

Coulter had also disabled their AIS, but with nothing to help find The Boy Ameel he was trusting to luck one of them would run across it.

Karl awoke shivering and checked his phone, still ten minutes till the alarm was supposed to go off. He was stiff. Stretching, he tried to bring some heat back into his body. It wasn't as effective as he'd hoped. Deciding to ignore it, he looked around for how to start the engines. Along the way, he'd picked up knowledge about all sorts of things; sniper rifles, aeroplane controls, the intricacies of radio frequencies and antennae but ship's engines were not, so far, on that list.

There was a greasy box, wire-tied to a supporting pillar directly ahead of him. At one point the box had come loose from its weld and presumably had been hanging from the thick but now slightly stretched wire that snaked up from it before being wire-tied. There was a large green button. Hopefully that would start the engines. What he knew about engines was that some engines needed primed, some of them needed coaxing but some of them required something akin to a three hour spa treatment. The Boy Ameel didn't look high maintenance, but it had also seen its share of abuse, there was a chance it simply wouldn't start again.

Pressing the green button, somewhere behind him, in the machinery, something coughed and turned. Once. He tried again. Another cough, a more hopeful sounding turn, then, an annoying whine, and another turn. The engine caught, it began an unhealthy sounding and low frequency, penetrating purr. He patted the support column and headed up to the wheelhouse.

The instrument panel was dead. When he'd cut the engines at the wheelhouse control panel, it appeared all the power had been cut. No back up batteries or maybe dead back up batteries. Rebooting the panel, he watched snatches of code appear and disappear on the screen. Then it was back. He was winning.

The sea was choppy close to the rocks and the swell constantly pushed the boat towards them. He manoeuvred the ship further and further out, till the coast was just visible. The wheelhouse was freezing compared to the engine room and it felt like it would be a long time before he felt warm again.

The cold dragged memories up to replay in snatches.

First, arriving in the AFS as a small child with his family. Refugees from Nederland, they'd been lucky enough, according to his father, to have got official places. Help with passage, help with employment. His father had made it sound like a dream come true, but Karl had hated the place; the dark, the penetrating cold and eventually, everything else about the AFS.

Then, leaving the AFS at seventeen, going back to Utrecht, becoming a rising star in the Green movement, he'd found Nederland wasn't what he'd hoped for either. It had created a feeling that he had no home, something he'd learnt to use.

And then there'd been Enid Decourcey, Isadora Ley's real name. They'd met in Utrecht, hitting it off immediately. It had developed into an incendiary relationship: he couldn't help but torture her battered psyche, and she seemed to draw out his ruthless streak.

Again, he saw her through the scope of the sniper rifle at Weddell City airport, being carried between the agents, and then the older memory it had triggered.

The reason he'd hesitated, and what had probably saved her life. Now he had mixed feelings about that. They'd chosen different paths to the same ends. Maybe if she survived they should call a truce, but he thought Enid enjoyed the fight too much.

Six hours later his phone rang. The ship had a sat link and the phone had connected automatically after the instrument panel rebooted. It was Rafael's office; cursing, he answered. It was Rafael's secretary, she sounded very upset. When she told him what had happened he understood why.

He hung up and disconnected the phone from the ship. Damn. Rafael Dupont had been a risk since the beginning, and all his misgivings about him had come true. The slime-ball had managed to get arrested. Karl had to decide now, whether to try to leave the AFS, or continue to Kunlun.

He'd always advocated a radical approach to activism, often arguing that there would have been no major ecological changes without the disruption of the Carrington events. Events that had led to the breakdown of civilisation, the deforestation of over half the remaining trees across the globe. Events that had required a serious Green agenda to be enacted. His argument was: if the AFS was to change its ways, it required as catastrophic an event, or events. Change, real change, he said, needed blood.

It was Kunlun then, somehow; either himself or via a message to his current emissary, Lukas Brandt. The AFS needed to see there were consequences to their actions. Mining was perpetuating the old technologies, when they needed to be rebuilt new. The AFS mines kept the Global mines going elsewhere in the world, hopeful of a profit, especially when the Planetary Cooperation Group was involved. He paused in his train of thought with a pang of guilt about his association with the PCC, his association with Rafael Dupont. But the end justified the means, and they would get what was coming to them. Rafael maybe sooner than the rest.

Chapter Twenty - Currents

Karl sailed on, heading north out of the Ronne Sea and into the Southern Ocean proper. The small trawler moving more violently in the increasing swell, it meant closer to shore was worth the risk. His stomach didn't feel right, and his head was beginning to feel heavy for some reason. After two hours of increasing discomfort he went looking for a first aid kit. Eventually he found something stashed in the small galley, it had one sea sickness pill, two months out of date.

The Boy Ameel was getting low on fuel, but Karl reckoned there was enough to reach Kwazi Station despite having stopped already. Kwazi was a small supply and loading point for the commercial greenhouses there and sometimes for those at Progress. If he couldn't steal fuel there, then it was worth risking paying by card. It felt if he could just keep his momentum, he'd stay safe.

Captain Ian Khan of the MS Coulter was sitting on his bridge. It was four in the morning, he'd just relieved his executive officer, Nicola, and to keep a sense of day and night, the bridge lights were low. It was the Coulter's turn to be out wide, twelve miles offshore.

The ship had been converted from a large, pelagic trawler but the swell was deep and long, and rolled her like she was half the size. The swell was part of the remnant circumpolar current that tried to re-assert it's full flow round Antarctica in the winter. Ian had heard climate scientists say when it gave up all together there would be a big increase in the temperature in Antarctica with an attendant increase in ice loss.

He was less sure the current would switch off in winter, the darkness of the polar region seemed to him a sufficient mechanism to keep the area cold enough to fuel it. After all, he thought, the demise of the North Atlantic Drift had been much heralded for over a century and had never come to anything, even if it wasn't what it once was.

Looking down to the radar screens, one close in and one at maximum extent, he could see they were nearing Kwazi Station, a day's sail out of Progress and the supply base for the vast commercial greenhouses. It was the only refuelling point between Weddell City and Progress. He called the Alvarez, and heard Binh Mitchell answer.

"Binh, is Liam around?"

"He's just gone to his cabin, I can put you through?"

"Please."

He waited, hearing the phone ring and then found he was reconnected to Binh.

"I'm sorry Captain Khan, he must be in the shower, can I take a message?"

"Yes. Ask him to confirm with Intelligence that The Boy Ameel was low on fuel. It seems to me we could simply wait for it to show up at Kwazi Station."

"As soon as he's free I'll let him know."

"Thanks."

Neither of them would have their AIS transmitting, so they'd just look like supply or freight vessels on the radar as far as anyone on The Boy Ameel would know, and if it *was* low on fuel, it would have no choice but to come in to Kwazi. Nobody chose to lose power in the Southern Ocean.

Twenty minutes later he got a call from Liam, agreeing to the idea, along with some continued ribbing about sea legs. He didn't mind Liam's joking, when it came time to be serious, Liam was more than capable. Their ships were built to survive in the conditions of the Southern Ocean and his crew of twenty, including a commando force of four, were all experienced sailors. But he saw no need to put them and his ship at risk when an opportunity to catch this Karl Leyden alongside, presented itself. He called ahead to Kwazi Station and let them know what was planned and what they should do.

They were six hours away from Kwazi Station when the solar alert sounded on the bridge, accompanied by the alerts from the mobiles of those on the bridge. Cursing his luck; it made things harder, but not impossible. The ships all had shielding for sensitive instruments and point breakers on everything else. The radio might work to a degree, they'd just have to be careful what they broadcast. But it did mean they had no secure way to call for back up, or to inform anyone if they were successful or otherwise.

Blackie was asleep, curled up in a ball oblivious to the wind huffing outside the tent. Thierry had set it all out for him. Take the grab bag from under the bed, head off on the snowmobile. It had fuel and batteries, enough Thierry had said, to get to the greenhouses at Kwazi Station, and then Thierry assured him he'd arrange passage on one of the service boats and Blackie would be gone.

He woke, not sure what had caused him to. Listening, all he could hear was the noise of the wind, buffeting the tent material. It was seven in the morning, according to his watch, but the lack of any light made time of day simply random numbers. Feeling refreshed, he decided to move and, after carefully stowing everything into the grab bag, he began to dismantle the tent.

Half an hour later he was cutting across the ice. It was at least forty eight hours travel time to the greenhouses and he'd only covered a quarter of the distance. The headlight of his snowmobile showed the scattered ice crystals picked up from the surface by the wind. They hit his cheeks, stinging. The feelings from coming down from the illegal greenhouse on the ice sheet, came back to him.

It hadn't been as bad as he'd imagined, but he'd be red and raw again from this journey. Thierry had promised he'd get a new identity, finally have a name to be proud of and he'd settle back into his comfortable life in

Weddell City; going to the pub, watching the football. Till the next time Thierry needed him.

The pattern of his current existence repeated itself; setting up the tent when he got too tired to concentrate on driving, moving on when he woke up. Finally, there was a glow reflected on the low clouds, the yellow light of greenhouses. He felt nothing. It was just another step in the journey.

Setting up the tent at the ice sheet edge, it was close enough to see a vessel approaching through binoculars, but at a distance no one would notice him if they were outside the greenhouses. His phone chirruped: it was a solar alert.

A ship would carry on in these circumstances, he thought, but a brief tinge of panic fluttered in his chest as it dawned on him, there was no way of communicating with Thierry. Now, it all came down to waiting.

The Boy Ameel wheezed into Kwazi Station harbour on fumes and Karl knew he'd been lucky. The swell had been picking up along the coast and he'd been forced to move further offshore rather than spend fuel battling the inshore current's desire to push him west. Further out, he'd found the fast remnant of the circumpolar current moved him in the needed, easterly direction.

He hadn't dared try to get more sleep, dozing fitfully in the wheelhouse till the solar alarm had gone off and after that developing a heightened alertness. What would happen when that wore off, he wondered?

The boat had shielding on its critical systems but he was still glad to reach the safety of Kwazi Station harbour, to drop anchor, and have the excuse of the solar alert for not contacting the harbour master.

It was eleven in the morning, but not so as you could tell. The harbour lights were still dim. Presumably they lit up more when something was scheduled to arrive. The whole place felt abandoned, generating a feeling between his shoulder blades. Switching off the lights in the wheelhouse and shutting down the engines, he zipped up, moving slowly out of the door.

There was only the slap of the waves on the side of the boat. He pulled down his visor and scanned the shore. There were no signs of people, turning, he caught a flash of yellow heat signature in the water. Looking again, there was no trace. It could have been marine life. A seal perhaps.

His alertness was wearing thin, his body clearly thought he was safe, but his mind was less sure. He pulled out the knife he kept on him. Guns ran out of bullets, they were loud and drew attention to your location. Knives were the weapon of choice amongst most of the radical activists. Crouching down, he moved to the harbour side of the boat.

The tide was in but there was still some height to reach the harbour level. It would need a torch to find the ladders spaced out along the wall. He lifted his visor, setting the torch function on the phone down low before switching it on, seeing the ladders just at the bow. He pushed his phone back inside his suit and headed forward in the blackness. There was a creak. He stopped, fairly sure it wasn't him but aware that tiredness could increased your paranoia.

Who knew he was here? It wouldn't be difficult for anyone to guess where he'd head for if someone knew he'd taken The Boy Ameel. But who could get here fast?

The navy. His adrenaline surged, his arms shook with it. Should he make a run for the ladders and the quayside, or turn and search the boat?

He pulled down his visor and turned, finding himself facing the pale yellow strips of a face less than two metres away. His instinct was to throw the knife, but before he could raise his arm fully, there was the crack of a gun.

A searing heat pierced the top of his arm, making him drop the knife in pain. His instinct was to jump in the water, but he wouldn't last with only one good arm to pull himself out again. He put the good arm up in the air instead.

More yellow striped faces appeared and his arms were pulled behind him, the pain of his wound reached a fresh intensity as that happened. He was too tired to plan anymore. Finally there'd be sleep, but he was confident there'd also be a way out. It wasn't the first time he'd been shot or arrested. And, he thought, his back up plan was already in motion.

Captain Ian Khan had been watching from the bridge, although most of what happened had been obscured from his view. He was relieved to hear the confirmation they'd got this Karl guy, and had radioed the harbour master to switch on the harbour lights, and saw for the first time, the quarry they'd set off to catch.

Through his binoculars the man looked slight. Ian could see blood, a hot trace of red in the thermal imaging. He let the medic know they would be needed. Then he called over the radio to the Alvarez. Over the crackle of solar particles' signatures, he let Liam know they'd been successful and were now heading out for Weddell City.

Liam had chosen the short straw in this engagement by being the later arrival and the Alvarez was going to tow The Boy Ameel back to Progress. Liam confirmed he'd be in Kwazi in two hours.

Chapter Twenty One - Kwazi Station

Blackie saw the lights from a small boat as it approached the harbour from the left. It seemed too small to be either a supply boat or a freighter coming to take fresh produce away. Smuggling was a way of life and he'd no desire to get involved in any gang activity. Thierry had no sway with the gangs, while they, reportedly, had a few senators in their pockets. He didn't strike camp but continued to watch through his binoculars.

The ship had entered the harbour now and was half hidden by the tops of the fuel tanks that lined one side of the harbour: low, wide, conical shapes, most of the tanks' bulk was below ground helping to keep the fuel warm. The binoculars fell onto his chest but he drew them up almost instantaneously, after noticing a movement to the far right of the harbour.

Another ship, but only the port and starboard navigation lights on, and bigger, based on those lights. Not a supply boat or a freighter, the lack of lights made him wary. Something was going on in the harbour, maybe gang on gang, but worse for him, state on gang. If one of those ships was a navy vessel, he could be in trouble. Hopefully all the action would stay in the harbour, but he decided to strike camp and be ready to leave just in case.

A shot echoed out from the harbour. The thermal imaging on his binoculars wasn't good enough at that distance to see and he'd nearly started up the snowmobile but stopped himself: that noise might travel. Right now, whoever had fired the gun was concentrating on the harbour, and, if they then left having done what they came to do, it was highly possible Blackie's escape lay in whichever one of the boats was left.

All of a sudden the harbour lights came on to full brightness and he raised the binoculars back to his eyes, watching as four figures hauled a fifth up onto the quayside. They were heading round to the far side of the harbour where he could see the larger boat, now well lit, and make out the small cannon mounted in the bows. Navy. It was right to have been cautious.

He'd heard Thierry talk about Valentina Torres, the Defence Portfolio holder and knew Thierry didn't like her, but was always careful not to antagonise her either. If Thierry had a plan for Valentina, he hadn't shared it with him.

He waited till the navy ship was moving off before starting the snowmobile, shivering from waiting without the protection of the tent. The heat from the seat took some of the chill away once he got going, but tiredness was beginning to take its toll.

Stopping briefly at the chainlink fence surrounding the harbour complex, he drove alongside it, away from the buildings, looking for some cover to stash the machine.

Close to the shore there was a mound of big boulders, part of the sea defences. Parking the snowmobile, he used the tent to camouflage it, securing it all down with smaller stones which the sea had plucked off the boulders already. Standing back, it almost looked like another boulder. His shoulders ached from the effort, and there were hunger pangs from his empty stomach. The rations ran out ten hours ago, and there was no indication of when an all clear would come through. He was moving and thinking on automatic now.

The harbour lights had dropped in intensity, presumably to normal daylight levels. They still threw deep shadows off the stacks of empty crates and the drums of unknown contents that were scattered along the quayside. He cut a small hole in the fencing with the bolt cutters from the grab bag and carefully squeezed through, checking his suit for any tears and making for the nearest shadow. Having worked his way towards the small boat, he was finally able to drop down to it's deck from the harbour wall. The tide had already turned and it was a big drop. He rolled as he hit the deck, and crawled for cover, ignoring the jarring in his legs.

The continued solar alert hadn't yet been cancelled, no-one would come for this vessel until it did. There was an unknown amount of time to either hide here or use it to escape. There must have been a reason the boat was brought here, he thought, and it was probably smuggling. The navy was primarily concerned with that.

He found the hatch down to the engine room, but once inside, the flinty smell of hot metal was nearly overwhelming. It wasn't a good smell. The engines needed lubrication, which might be a problem for him. He got closer and found the main control panel. Most of it seemed to have been bypassed, but the fuel indicator was at zero. He followed the cabling to a wire-tied box with a single button.

He sucked in his breath over his teeth and sighed. If this boat started up it would be a short lived miracle. His heart sank and his aches and pains intruded again into his thoughts. It was only good for hiding out on. Finding a corner in the engine room to settle down in, he tried to get comfortable on the greasy, and rapidly cooling deck.

Ray had ordered the helicopter when it became clear Renner probably still had the snowmobile that George had mentioned during his interview.

It was obvious that Renner would run for Kwazi Station. Even in the winter, ships came and went from there. Renner's friend, Senator Thierry Vonne would also have plenty of influence to arrange transport, but leaving immediately in the helicopter meant they could arrive just a couple of hours behind Renner.

The solar alert had been a pain. The helicopter was small, only carrying five, including pilot and co-pilot and once they were all in the shielding covers it felt like it would burst at the seams. They kept going. Then the second alert went off. They'd have to come down lower, the pilot said, but he agreed not to turn back.

As they approached Kwazi Station, she could make out a vessel arriving. They touched down on the harbour helipad.

After repacking the covers, she turned to the two officers from Progress.

"He's come here on a snowmobile, see if you can find it. It must be relatively close."

"Boss," replied one, as they turned and headed towards the outer fence for a perimeter check.

Fifteen minutes later, the ship was now alongside and she recognised it as one of the converted trawler, navy vessels from Progress, two people were approaching.

The man was small but compact, older than her, the young woman was clearly deferring to him as he thrust his hand out and Ray took it in a handshake.

"I'm Captain Liam Kelly, MS Alvarez. We're here to tow The Boy Ameel back to Progress. What's your rush?"

She saw him nod at the helicopter as he asked.

"Detective Ray McCarthy, Progress Police. We're following a fugitive, wanted for murder. He's here somewhere. Before you take this vessel we'd like to search it."

"Let's do that together," said Captain Kelly.

"Okay," she agreed.

"We'll use our commando team. Do you know if he's armed?" he asked.

"Probably, but I don't know. He's capable of violence, but we need him alive."

She saw the captain turn to speak to the woman who'd come with him. Then he turned back to her.

She was worried this was getting out of hand. Did she trust some navy commandos not to get trigger happy?

"I propose, if you agree," said Captain Kelly, "to send my four man team onboard. The team from the Coulter has already successfully apprehended a fugitive, Karl Leyden from the same vessel."

She looked at him, he seemed confident they could take Renner alive. But something nagged at her.

"I'd like to go with them," she said.

Inside a part of her was asking why she said that, and what happened to the 'go with the flow for an easy life' attitude? In answer, she knew that Renner wasn't Leyden. Renner looked to Thierry Vonne for direction and when put in a sudden stress situation he was going to react very differently to Leyden. She hoped her police negotiation training wouldn't be needed.

The captain nodded his consent to her and turned to wave at his ship. She saw four figures, jogging with small arms held to their chests. She tried to imagine what all this sounded like to someone hiding out on The Boy Ameel.

The helicopter and the engine of the Alvarez couldn't be rationalised away as normal activity. Renner would be hyper-alert to every sound and he'd hear them coming onboard, for sure. He'd be making snap judgements and she didn't think that was his forte.

Chapter Twenty Two - Salvage

The lead commando was climbing down the ladder to the deck of The Boy Ameel. Ray couldn't hear anything from his movements. They'd already swept the deck from the quayside using their visors. If Renner was onboard, he was inside somewhere.

Ray had a habit of thinking of people in terms of animals and Renner, felt to Ray, like a rat. There wasn't a single habitat in the AFS that didn't have rats. They scavenged from people and sometimes even derived precarious protection from them. But cornered, they attacked.

She was third down the ladder, and tried not to make a sound as her suit boots met each crusty rung. She touched the deck with one foot then the other, slowly moving away from the ladder. She could see one of the commandos in the wheelhouse, the other seemed to have disappeared, then she saw in her visor, the escaping interior heat showing pale yellow at the edge of an access hatch in the deck. Moving deliberately and as quietly as possible she went to the hatch and opened it. Flicking her visor up quickly, she looked in. It was visibly dark, yet thermally there was the background fading heat from the engines, now a yellowy green on the deck.

She hoped there'd be a light to switch on: seeing facial expressions was very important in gaining the trust of someone who might be on the edge mentally. Sweeping her gaze round the area she'd stepped down into, most surfaces were showing pale blue but there was a door with a brighter green edge. She could hear a voice. She moved as quickly as she could to the door, opening it and seeing the engine room laid out in pale yellow blobs and greener backgrounds. She spotted two figures, from their facial heat she could tell one was the commando, he had yellow strips between his suit and visor. The other must be Renner, colder for having hid out for however many hours onboard, his cheeks were almost as faded green as the background metal in the engine room. She knew he must have seen her on his visor.

"Jonathan," she said, "I'm Ray. We'd like you to come with us. Nobody needs to get hurt."

Weapons could be a problem for visors unless they'd recently been discharged or had fresh blood on them. She couldn't see anything, but knives were often such thin slivers of blue you'd be mad to discount them. She had to assume he was armed, as she expected the commando had already. She'd also no idea if the commando was aiming at Renner right now. Something she knew would be a concern for Renner too.

"I've done nothing wrong," said Renner.

His voice was somehow disembodied from the thermal spectre she was looking at.

"Well, now, Jonathan, that's not strictly true, is it? But I'm sure you want to get your side of the story across?"

There was a noise above them and she saw Renner's green striped face rise up. The commando threw himself at Renner's torso. Ray could see there was a spurt of red as the bodies met. She didn't know who's blood it was, but the visors were all calibrated to show temperatures around thirty six degrees celsius as red. Renner went down with the momentum of the commando's lunge.

The commando didn't get up. Shit, she thought.

There must be an effing light in here somewhere. Before she could look, she heard another set of feet behind her and the click of a gun. There was the spectrum equivalent of a bright flash. She lifted her visor to see a wide-beam torch now lighting the scene. Renner was standing, holding a bloodied knife, the commando was still on the floor. To her left was a shadowy figure of the commando holding the gun and torch.

"Jonathan, please, drop the knife and move away from the body," Ray said.

She saw Renner was shaking his head, the movement travelled down his arm to the knife.

"Accident."

She could hear real concern in his almost childish voice, and watched him raise the knife to his own neck. She put her hand flat towards the commando, asking for her to wait.

"No, Jonathan, no. Don't do it," she tried for the right balance of command and pleading.

She saw him pause, she hoped he'd drop the knife.

"Didn't mean..."

Then she saw some new thought cross his face and suddenly he was sweeping the knife across his throat in a deep cut. Blood started to flow in furious pulses. He'd cut his carotid artery. The knife clattered to the deck, quickly followed by the body of Jonathan Blackbird Renner.

The commando ran over to her comrade and Ray could hear her calling for the medic over a static laden radio. Ray knew Renner was dead already. She felt drained. All they had without Renner to question, was evidence that he was a friend of Thierry Vonne. Nothing so far had proved Renner was under orders from Thierry.

More torches now illuminated the main space of the engine room as a medic and another commando entered. Ray felt superfluous and headed up on deck. Her stomach was in revolt at what she'd just witnessed and she was glad of the hit of freezing air when she got outside. Still, she felt she needed to lean over the side of the boat for a minute or two, just in case. Bodies were one thing, suicides quite another.

She couldn't see anything in the dark, only hear the slap, slap, slap of the waves against the boat. A slow hand clap, she thought. She shook herself. It was what it was. She climbed back up the ladder and stood on the quayside. The harbour lights had brightened slightly.

She looked around at Kwazi Station. There were low buildings ahead stretching along to the side of the harbour that the Alvarez was tied up to. To her left was the low tops of the fuel tanks, looking like flattened volcanoes. She could see the torchlight from the officers searching for Renner's snowmobile just above them. She hoped something could be salvaged from this.

The woman who'd been with Captain Kelly when they'd first met was coming towards her.

"Detective McCarthy, I'm Nicola Larsen, the executive officer from the Alvarez, I need a statement from you about what happened, for our report. Captain Kelly thought it'd be easier onboard."

"My team's out there searching for the snowmobile, someone'll need to let them know where I am."

"I'll get someone to keep an eye out for them coming back."

She walked with Nicola Larsen, towards the Alvarez in a deepening daze as the whole situation seemed to crystallise.

Captain Kelly's cabin was about the size of Ray's office, Ray marvelled at the use of space that allowed a desk *and* a bed in the same amount of room. He offered her coffee and the idea of something warm and caffeinated had never sounded so welcome. She described the events that had occurred on The Boy Ameel, well schooled in the art of reporting.

There was a knock on the closed door and the captain called out, 'enter'. There was a sailor with a vacuum flask and two mugs. They were set down on the desk, after a space had been cleared.

"Why do you think he did it?" asked Captain Kelly.

She took the proffered mug and sipped, feeling the heat drop down her throat.

"He probably panicked, worried maybe about how this would reflect back on Thierry. Maybe he thought he'd give something away when questioned. I'm pretty sure he did it to protect Thierry Vonne."

"That's serious loyalty," said Kelly.

"I understand the senator is very charismatic and, from what I've found out so far, Greens are capable of anything."

There was another knock on the door, and Nicola the XO entered without waiting.

"They found this on him," she said.

She saw an evidence bag containing a mobile phone in Nicola's outstretched hand.

Maybe, she hoped, there would be something on it which would make up for this.

"And they've found his snowmobile," said Nicola.

Chapter Twenty Three - Grounded

Anatoli landed at Mellor Station with considerably less hassle than the last time, though the conditions were already deteriorating towards the usual background winter weather of squally snow showers. He continued to check what the weather was at Kunlun. Enya had indicated it was urgent someone from the Team got there.

He wondered what they hadn't been telling the authorities at Kunlun? Of course, now he was sticking to the role of charter pilot he was not asking the usual questions, and Eric was certainly not telling him anything. Anatoli knew communication was key to safety and he didn't like the situation, but felt lost about how to pull it around. Chris Saraband was the person in the team who did that, and Chris was with Enya.

They clipped to the line and headed towards the station to meet up with Roy, Philippe and Poul. He'd had time to load some of the supplies they'd promised to get last time, despite still have the junk that Ray had left behind. The supplies included the whisky now nestled inside his survival suit and by the time they'd got through the airlock it was in his hand.

"You remembered," said Roy.

"How could I forget? You sent a list. There's more stuff onboard. But we can't stay longer than refuel time."

Roy was nodding and shrugging on his suit arms.

"Yes, Sir," said Roy with mock seriousness.

The five of them were sitting in the cabin, while the line outside pulsed fuel into the jet. The bottle was being passed around, and Anatoli noticed Eric was occasionally joining in. He wasn't sure whether that would turn out to be a good thing or not. He couldn't recall ever seeing Eric drunk. He saw Roy look at his watch.

"Probably should check now."

Anatoli headed into the cockpit as Roy went outside to check the fuel line. He saw the gauge registering almost full. He called Roy over the visor comms.

"Disengage. And thanks for everything."

He headed into the cabin to say goodbye to Poul and Philippe, who were already standing: Poul with the whisky bottle, now half empty. There was the usual back slapping and promises as they headed out. Bringing up the steps behind him, he checked the weather one last time. His arrival would be behind a squall line, thankfully, and, an hour out from Kunlun, he'd be able to access the more detailed local conditions in the Massif.

The Progress Massif as it was now known had once been simply a dome in the ice sheet, hiding a mountain range called the Gamburtsev Range. Now it was a series of peaks exposed above the ice and worked from within. Every AFS child knew there were other mines elsewhere in Antarctica, but they also knew the Massif was key because of it's rare earth metals.

Anatoli had a bad feeling about why they had to go to Kunlun. He could always pick up from Enya when she thought he was in danger, and her concern laced everything she'd said in her last call. It wasn't the assassin, because he'd heard she'd been shot, so it was something new. He could also sense a deepening change in Eric's mood. It felt to Anatoli like he was past sombre and into the 'might not make it out alive' mood, possibly with help from the whisky. He hoped Enya was coming soon to sort it all out.

He finished the pre-flight checks and let Eric know to buckle up over the speaker, taking off within minutes. He reached cruising altitude and saw a sliver of daylight at the horizon.

He loved flying. Every aspect spoke to his soul, from the technicalities, the sensations, the danger, through to the stunning views. Countless times he'd tried to get that across to people who asked him why he wasn't in politics like his father. Only Enya had got it first time.

They were half way to Kunlun when he heard the solar alert. The rule required pilots to make the shortest journey to safety, and they would continue to Kunlun, but he still let Eric know there was a shielding cover folded up under his seat. Some people were extra cautious about solar radiation. If the alert stayed on and generated a follow-up, he too would put on a shielding cover, but its bulk made him delay.

The covers were based on the technology built into space suits from before the Carrington events, and had found a new lease of life while the space race went into hibernation. There were people back in space, but only recently. Before then all the efforts had gone into getting the satellites back up and running and fresh solar trackers in place.

Half an hour later with a continued alert, Anatoli was fighting his way into the shielding cover. Kunlun knew he was coming, so they'd still have the runway cleared as much as possible and everything functional, but he knew once he'd landed nothing else would, not until the all clear. Somewhere, Enya would be grounded. Either still in Weddell City or at Polar Station. More delays.

He saw aurora start to snake across the sky. A red glow at first but then the rippling green curtains as he began his long slow descent, both colours from excited oxygen atoms. The green was very bright and the snow covered ice sheet reflected it back into the sky. He could now make out the dark peaks of the Massif ahead. He checked the local conditions. Downdrafts at the runway seemed slight, also minimal cross winds. He hoped the aurora would continue to shine a bit of light for him. There was nothing more disconcerting than landing on instruments and the projected simulation, knowing that a sheer drop was either side of you.

He was on approach, the sides of the exposed peaks loomed above him from both sides. The valley was faintly lit by the aurora. He could see the runway edge ahead visually and reassuringly it matched the projected simulation. He concentrated solely on the landing. His mind emptied of all the other concerns. He'd expected the slightest slide to the right and had already corrected for it as the jet touched the runway and he moved smoothly forward, braking, as he followed the runway lights. There was only the darkness of Kunlun's opening into the mountain, but as he approached, floodlights, gaining in intensity came on, and he could see the ground crew directing him towards a side hangar space.

As he descended the steps of the jet, following behind Eric, he looked out to the opening and saw only the eerie glow of the aurora above the dark mountain peaks. All the landing lights had been extinguished. There was a feeling in the pit of his stomach, and he suddenly felt very alone in the densest habitat of the AFS.

Enya's phone had gone off with its alert at the same time as the others, a chorus of various alarming noises. They'd only flown half an hour out of Weddell City by that point, en route to Polar Station. Officially they should have turned back, it being the shortest route to safety, but they'd agreed with the pilot, everyone signing waivers, to continue in the event of alerts. Every aircraft in the AFS had to have basic emergency equipment, for crashes, for ice stranding, for landing in water and for solar flares. They all struggled into the bulky shielding covers.

The covers were always too large for Enya, and she was swamped inside hers. She saw James trying not to laugh. It was ridiculous no matter how serious the current situation was, and she smiled at him in return. They returned to the discussion of planning the safety of the population of Kunlun.

Half an hour later when the continued alert chorused across the phones, the conversation dried up. Enya could see through the window the red glow, building in intensity from behind them. The light got brighter as they flew across the edge of a green aurora curtain. She tried not to look and pulled her head back inside the hood of the shielding cover. The particles ejected from the sun could fall straight through things, but the aurora was proof they didn't always and hit with enough energy to send an electron into a heightened energy state, only for it to release light as it returned. All perfectly safe for oxygen atoms and not so good for the complex organic molecules making up life. Hers in particular. She hoped Anatoli was already on the ground and safe.

They had left the shimmering curtain of light behind, over an hour ago, and she felt the pressure change in her ears as they came down quickly to approach the Polar Station runway. The pilot was good, though to be fair, mediocre pilots didn't last long in the AFS.

She wondered whether she should use someone other than Anatoli? Was she relying on his willingness to get involved, even though she tried to avoid asking him? Maybe, subconsciously. Then for a moment she was angry with Eric. Who was he to set her limitations? But quickly realised, it wasn't Eric's fault.

She tried to look at the problem from the outside. It was true what Alison had said about the others. What if she made Anatoli an official part of the Team? And why did she feel so strongly against that?

She felt the bump, as the jet made contact with the blue ice runway, felt the fluttering of the flaps transmitted through the fuselage and the rumble over the net beneath her feet as it came to a halt. The floodlights came on and she could see the low complex of buildings sprawling to the side.

Soon they were inside, shedding their shielding into a large box, the jet identifier, WD459, written on a card held in its display slot. There was nothing to do now but wait. And think about things she'd been putting off for almost two years.

It began to dawn on her, the ambiguity, over Anatoli's status in the team, was the reason why nothing about their wedding had been planned. Tolli had even stopped mentioning it. She felt bad. She'd never considered moral cowardice one of her traits, but this felt pretty close. He really couldn't be their charter pilot once she married him. And she did want to marry him. Trouble was she also wanted him to be their charter pilot. Now, it was obvious what needed to happen, she felt a weight lift from her shoulders.

"Hey Boss. Want to join the game?"

James had broken through her reverie and she looked up at him from her chair in the public lounge. He was pointing towards the nearby canteen doors. Through them she could see the back of Chris' head and half of Glenn's face.

"Sure. For old times' sake."

James gave her a big grin, and she felt happier. Her huskies, as Ray had put it, were a great team. Even Eric.

Chapter Twenty Four - The Densest Habitat

Anatoli stepped through the airlock doors into Kunlun proper. He was stunned by its size. He'd expected something spacious but this was enormous, maybe ten times bigger than any mall he'd ever been in. He looked up until the brightness of the lights stopped him. They were as effective as any artificial-day lighting he'd seen, yet in the cavernous space, it felt like Kunlun had trapped a mini-sun inside.

"Quite impressive? Eh?" said a voice.

Anatoli looked back down, and kept going a bit further than he expected to. The man was in his late sixties, salt and pepper hair swept back. He was sitting in a tracked contraption, his hand sat lightly round a joystick on a small control panel attached to the arm of the seat.

"I'm Jim McAndrew, the mayor of Kunlun. Welcome. I was led to believe there were more of you?"

"Mayor McAndrew," said Eric, "Yes, there's more coming, but the solar alert has delayed them. I'm Eric Jordan, of the Anti-corruption Team."

Anatoli saw Eric proffer his hand to Mayor McAndrew. Then he noted the lack of introduction of himself, and saw that the Mayor had noticed it too.

"You are?" Mayor McAndrew asked, looking at him.

He recognised the look and, based on the age of Jim McAndrew knew what was coming, people always had to ask to be sure, because his colouring was different to his father's.

"Anatoli Dale. Charter pilot."

"Ha ha, I knew it. You're the spitting image of your dad. How is Arne?"

Anatoli sensed Eric stiffen.

"He's fine, still working."

"I'll bet. Well come on, let me show you around."

Mayor McAndrew was pushing the joystick with expert control and the tracked chair turned on it's own circle, speeding away at a brisk walking pace. Anatoli and Eric had to jog briefly to catch up.

"This is the main hall, as I'm sure you can tell. All our retail and public spaces are within it."

Anatoli saw him wave his other hand forward into the mountain and to the left and right as he spoke. Suddenly the chair turned, nearly hitting Eric who was on the opposite side to Anatoli.

"That's the central lift we're heading for. We've got service, emergency, mine and residential lifts as well. There *are* stairs, but I don't recommend them."

Anatoli heard him laugh at the end of that. He tried to recall if his father had ever mentioned Jim McAndrew. Something vague came to him. A mine accident and an exo-skeleton suit were about all he could remember of any story. It must have been a very long time ago.

The lift was big enough to take a snowcat vehicle, and quite full. It had waited for them to arrive and get inside before the operator had closed the doors. There was a mix of people; a few children in school uniform, people in cloth business suits, casual indoor wear and the rest in workwear. Nobody in what Anatoli had heard referred to as Basics, the underwear that he'd been told the miners often stripped down to in the heat of the deep mines. He also noticed he and Eric were the only ones in survival suits.

The lift opened and Mayor McAndrew began to move, so Anatoli did too. He turned to see Eric coming up behind, clearly not sure which side of the Mayor to walk on. He almost felt sorry for Eric, realising for the first time, just how young he was. He moved to the side to open a space between himself and Mayor McAndrew, which Eric moved towards but didn't fill, continuing to hang back. Anatoli wished Enya and Chris were here already to sort this out. He'd never needed to develop any people skills beyond his natural affability.

An automatic door opened ahead and Jim swept into a large office, dragging Anatoli and Eric in his wake. He could sense the tension between the two of them, just as easily as if there was something physically there. It surprised him, Arne had always been able to put people at their ease, and his son didn't strike him as terribly different. And the boy, Eric, didn't seem to have the confidence for his position. Teamwork was important, a lifetime working in the mines at Kunlun had taught him that. It was one of the reasons he was still alive.

He nodded to Carole his secretary in passing as another automatic door opened into the more subdued lighting of his own office. The inner sanctum of his world. He moved behind the purpose built desk and settled back, ready to dig out all the truth that he knew had been kept from him so far by the Anti-corruption Team.

"Have a seat," he said pointing to the two chairs placed in front of his desk; they were a delicate balance between comfort and formality. He watched them sit, Eric still nervous, Anatoli very at home.

"Now," he said with a sharp tone, "What the fuck's going on? A Sarin nerve gas attack? Is it here already? Nobody seems able to tell me."

He saw Eric flinch slightly, saw the weight of responsibility settle on his forehead. Good, it looked like the boy could step up when required.

"We now have information that two tanks with the precursors to Sarin nerve gas were brought here in the autumn," said Eric, "We've been tracking Green activists who might try to get here to mix them. Our concern is that the original plan, whereby they would have immunity from the gas, might be ditched for a suicide mission. We're as worried about deaths from an evacuation as we are from any actual attack."

Jim saw this was news to Anatoli, but credit to the senator's son, you'd hardly tell. He sat forward, resting his elbows on the ends of his chair arms. He'd suspected the Sarin was already here, the peculiarities of Kunlun made it an obvious target. He'd been having the water and air treatment plants checked over regularly since being alerted, but looking for two specific compressed gas tanks in a city with hundreds of such things was going to be harder than it sounded. And then, there was the information Yang Lau had given him today.

"I can get manifests from around autumn checked. Do you have any suspects?"

"We're especially interested in a Karl Leyden, it's unlikely he's here now, but the names of who he visited, if he did come here, would be very helpful. I can send all the information we have on him once the all clear comes in, but for now I have a picture and some details."

"I'll be up front with you," Jim said, "we do have some home grown Greens, and I'd like to think they'd never get involved with shit like this, but they're young and stupidly naive. They'd have to be, to live here, and think you could make this an ecologically sound enterprise."

He continued, "You'll want some local manpower. I can't offer you much, we have a few police officers, some decent militia"

"I'd like to work with the militia," said Anatoli.

Jim caught Eric's response to Anatoli's interjection. The boy did not like Anatoli, and Jim couldn't figure out why. He'd seen this sort of thing in mining teams before, if it wasn't dealt with it would eat into morale like acid into rock.

"I've already had a word with a local, shall we say, import business contact, they've suggested such tanks might have been decanted into smaller containers already."

He looked from Eric to Anatoli and back again.

"So we're looking for flask sized containers? Does your contact know where the original tanks are?" asked Eric.

"I can find out. I'm going to ask for the return of the flasks, I trust my town to do the right thing."

He saw Eric shaking his head.

"Well if you've got a better idea, present it to me by seven tomorrow morning. Carole will get you accommodation sorted."

He waved a hand at them to get up and get out and saw Anatoli rise immediately, Eric following. He checked his phone and saw the solar alert was still valid. He felt under pressure in a way he'd never experienced before; somewhere there were fatal risks he couldn't make safe yet. He knew, you could only protect so much against human error, and very little against errors of judgement. He asked Carole to find Yang Lau. He wanted to find out why Yang had suggested the stuff had been decanted, maybe she knew more than she'd already told him.

As he exited the Mayor's office, Anatoli remembered what Glenn had once said about Kunlun, how things were discovered here and refined in Vostok. Glenn had been referring to Freddie Tran, and he knew the story about the SASER trial in the Innonnox Mine: at least as well as anybody able to piece together the rumours and near legend. But he'd seen for himself at McMurdo and the research facility near Melchior, the result of the device Jean Mirales had wanted to be a safety alarm, which Gordon Murcheson had taken and turned into a gun. Not all refinements were good.

Carole, James' secretary had passed them onto a young man, who'd introduced himself as Conn. Conn had led them back to the main lift. Anatoli took the opportunity to shrug off the arms of his survival suit. The ambient temperature must be about twenty degrees, just a bit too much for the suit to cope with. He saw Eric do the same out the corner of his eye.

It felt like Eric was trying very hard to be out of Anatoli's eye line, but the tiredness from the flight was now catching up with Anatoli and he didn't care. He just wanted something to eat and to get some sleep.

"This secure accommodation, Conn, it comes with food?" he asked.

"I can get something for you, pizza's very popular. What would you like?"

He saw Conn turn back to include Eric.

"Margherita for me," said Eric.

"Sounds good, mine with mushrooms too, thanks."

He watched Conn pull out his mobile, and caught his eye with a questioning look.

"There's a city wide LAN, we're protected by the mountain from solar radiation. Check your local connection options," said Conn.

Anatoli was pleased to know they'd have some instant communication available whatever the circumstances outside. He could have a good look around the city's virtual spaces and hopefully become useful to the local militia. He had no doubt the Mayor would make an announcement tomorrow regardless of anything Eric said.

Anatoli had recently been promoted to lieutenant in the militia: the highest rank he could achieve given his flying commitments but he didn't want to be a leader anyway. He'd rather be working with the militia than Eric.

The lift opened, having only travelled one floor according to the indicator lights, yet it felt to Anatoli they were much higher up in the city. Conn had turned left and Anatoli saw a sign in red neon up ahead, it read 'State Accommodation'.

"Here we are," said Conn, "your rooms are either side of a shared space. It's all guaranteed bug free, I'll be back at six in the morning. Mayor McAndrew is an early riser."

Anatoli looked at his phone, it was eleven at night already and he had lots of research to do. He entered the room, dropped his bag and flopped back onto the bed. Before he could worry about closing his eyes there was a knock at the door which presumably opened into this shared space Conn mentioned.

Opening the door, he saw Eric sitting at the table, starting on a slice of pizza. Anatoli headed over and opened the other pizza box, looking around for something to drink. There were carafes of water and a coffee machine on a sideboard.

"Want water or coffee with that?" he asked.

"Water, thanks."

Eric sounded tired too, Anatoli could see the night becoming fraught, and hoped it wouldn't end badly. He sat down with a coffee and began his pizza.

"So," said Eric, "Militia?"

Anatoli listened to the tone, it wasn't quite conciliatory but it couldn't have had any worse descriptions hung on it. He felt Eric was trying. He tried to imagine Eric as a new captain in the militia, someone who might need a lieutenant. He decided to treat Eric as a training exercise himself.

"I'm a lieutenant, I can be useful."

"Hmmm. Do they do a lot of search training?"

"Yes, they have treasure hunts, scavenger hunts, and they do hide and seek too. What did you think the training was like?"

"Marching, I suppose. I went straight into Police Training from school, never been in the militia. We did marching."

"It has to be fun, people have to want to do it, otherwise nobody would turn up, and fun can still be instructive. You wouldn't believe the scavenger hunts I've been in."

"So we could ask them to scavenge for Green Manifestos, or syringes full of antidotes?"

Anatoli ignored the comment.

"Old flasks, or something like a leaf. Doesn't have to be real, but never underestimate how legitimate a crime can become in your head when you're not caught at it. I bet you someone brings us a real cannabis leaf, from a friend of a friend. That's how we'll find the illegal spaces."

"Is there a prize?"

He could tell Eric didn't believe a scavenge hunt could work, but Anatoli recalled some of the items his fellow militia brought to the attention of superiors during previous scavenger hunts, and how torn some of them had been about what to do with the information they provided.

"Usually a bottle of booze, but it's the prestige of beating your comrades. You've no idea how competitive it can become."

He saw Eric look at him, as though Anatoli was being appraised in the light of new information, but before he could think further he heard both his and Eric's phones chime with an all clear.

"Thank fuck," exclaimed Eric.

Anatoli's mobile began ringing, it was Enya.

"Hallo," he started, but was wiped out in a barrage of questions from her.

"Yes. Yes. We're fine. Yes. When will you get here?" He managed a question of his own while she paused.

"Good. Do you want to speak to Eric?"

Eric had looked over at his name, Anatoli had seen his face, there was no doubt about Eric's feelings. Enya had declined, in answer to Anatoli's question.

"I think you should," he said, handing his mobile to Eric.

He was too busy with the thought of Enya arriving at five in the morning to bother eavesdropping on Eric's answers, but was interrupted by a nudge from Eric handing him the mobile back.

"Thanks," said Eric, "I think we need to get some sleep and plan once she arrives."

Anatoli watched him head towards his room door. He heard it shut and the lock snick in place. He continued to sit, savouring the brief phone conversation, no longer feeling as alone as he had earlier.

Out in the Southern Ocean, the MS Coulter was steaming towards Weddell City, as the all clear chorused through on the phones. Ian called the Defence Office and got put through to Valentina immediately.

"Ian. You have our man, in one piece I hope?"

"I do, Senator. He's got a bit of damage to the top of his knife arm, hopefully a permanent disability in that regard. But he'll be able to talk, as long as you can keep Intelligence away from him. I've heard about their protection."

"Captain Khan."

He heard the warning in her voice, perhaps he was on speaker, and someone from Intelligence was in the room. Shit. Oh well, it was said now.

"Senator."

"I've got Regional Controller Kairns of the Intelligence Agency and Senator Veronica Tambor here, with me. Do you have an ETA?"

"We expect to take just under two days to get to Weddell City. I can confirm an ETA closer to the time."

He heard a male voice. Kairns, he thought, unless Valla had been economic with the room's occupants.

"We'll be taking the precaution of interviewing Karl Leyden onboard the Coulter. I expect a copy of your security protocols for that. Ahead of arrival."

Shit, he thought, him and his big mouth.

"Yes Sir," he replied.

"Well done, Ian, please pass on my thanks to your crew for a smooth operation."

"I will do, Senator."

The line was cut. He sat back in the chair, and breathed out, not realising he'd held his breath for the last seconds of the call. He called Binh, who should be up ready for a night shift, and let him know they'd be discussing their security arrangements as soon as he arrived on the bridge. He might have dumped himself in the shit, but it didn't mean he couldn't cover himself in something else over this.

Chapter Twenty Five - Hidden Things

Enya watched through the windows trying to see if there was any hint of terrain in the dark. She pulled her visor down and instead of black got a relentless blue instead. All of a sudden she felt the bump of the wheels touching ground. She'd heard Anatoli describe landing at Kunlun, and she tried not to think about the sheer edges at the side of the runway, as the jet slid slightly from side to side before straightening.

Lights came on and she caught glimpses of a cavernous space with walkways, ladders and open stairs. The jet came to a halt and she undid her seatbelt. The pilot, a young woman with short cropped hair, came through into the cabin from the cockpit.

"Wow," said the pilot, "That was exciting."

Enya tried to recall what Chris had told her about the charter pilot. A name came to her, Chick. Must be short for something else, she thought. Chick looked a couple of years older than Eric. It was all beginning to make Enya feel old, but she was still impressed with the woman's abilities.

Chick had stayed apart from them at Polar Station, she'd disappeared almost immediately on landing and had only turned up again when the all clear had come through. Enya wasn't sure how she felt about that. On one hand, it was a clear cut divide between team and charter, but on the other hand, she liked to get to know who she was working alongside, it made her feel safer.

The steps to this jet were similar to the Torres Mining jet Enya noticed, hydraulically operated and stowed within the fuselage. It was a higher spec'd jet than Anatoli's. She came down the steps last, watching Chick and the others disappear into the rock hewn structure, hearing the steps retract behind her. Then she saw Anatoli coming towards her, and she smiled. Despite all the horrible reasons for being here, she was happy, and it was entirely down to seeing him again.

"You didn't need to be here, I'd have found you," she said.

She saw him smile and then heard him laugh.

"I've no doubt, but I thought this was better."

They hugged, her arms were at his waist, she let her head rest on his chest and breathed him in.

"Who was flying?" he asked, as they separated and began walking towards the doorway in the rock.

"Somebody called Chick. Chris organised her. What did you think?"

Anatoli's opinion of their current charter was a deal breaker for Enya.

"Not bad."

They entered the room where there was some basic paperwork going on. She saw Chick turn round from the counter and spot Anatoli.

"You're Anatoli Dale, aren't you?" Chick asked.

"I am," said Anatoli.

Enya thought he sounded wary, and wondered what reputation preceded him with the other pilots.

"Oh, gosh," said Chick, "I'm Chick, sorry, Charlotte Ewing. I've heard so much about you. You're a bit of a legend, especially landing in cross winds with a chewed up net at Mellor Station."

Chick was gushing at Anatoli, but Enya thought it was a professional kind of gushing.

"Well, thank you. I didn't expect anyone to have heard about that yet."

"Roy's a terrible gossip on the radio," she said.

The clerk behind the counter coughed and Chick turned back round. Anatoli was shrugging his shoulders at Chris who was looking askance at him and Enya saw that James and Glenn looked less surprised than her at the gushing.

"You've all been booked into the State Accommodation by Mayor McAndrew..." started the clerk.

"Oh, that's ok I have a friend here, haven't seen them in forever, I just need directions," Chick interrupted him.

"Right," said the clerk, sounding to Enya a bit put out, "Fatima will show you where the State Accommodation..."

This time it was Anatoli who interrupted, "It's okay I've just come from there, I can show them."

Enya saw the clerk rolled his eyes, but he was at least smiling.

"Well then, Fatima can show you to where your friend lives," said the clerk to Chick.

"Super," said Chick.

The team left the office and followed Anatoli towards the lift.

"She's terribly enthusiastic, " said James, "I like her."

"I watched her land, she did okay," said Anatoli.

Enya saw Anatoli press the button to call the lift, and was amazed at the size of the inside when the doors opened. The lift was empty except for the operator who asked them for their destination and closed the doors.

"We have to be at Mayor McAndrew's office at seven, so there's just time for a freshen up," said Anatoli, "Someone'll come for us. I get the impression they're used to newcomers getting lost here."

Enya saw the operator sneak a smile.

They arrived at the next floor and got out following Anatoli to the left. She heard the lift doors slide shut.

"Mayor McAndrew seems to think the tanks have been decanted. He wants to announce an amnesty for them this morning. We were thinking of suggested to the mayor we run a scavenger hunt with the militia instead," said Anatoli, "A list of items including the flasks, give them twelve hours, say."

"Let's hear his reasons and decide from there," said Enya, "he knows his own people better than we do. All we've managed to bring was enough antidotes for ten people, it's all that was available at short notice, so we've got to find the flasks safely."

She saw the red neon sign for the accommodation. She wasn't comfortable with such an obvious location, but reckoned secrets were fairly difficult to keep in a place like Kunlun anyway. It was why she was worried. People would be keeping these flasks secret: how effective would Anatoli's scavenger hunt turn out to be? But how dangerous would calling an amnesty be if they didn't recover all the flasks?"

Anatoli had shown them into what he described as the common room between his room and Eric's. Eric was waiting for them, Enya could see his face was a sea of different emotions. From the initial anger it had quickly morphed to happiness, then it had moved to worry, and back round to irritation. Everyone had sat round the table, dragging two armchairs from the corners of the room to join the four chairs already there.

Eric started, "Mayor McAndrew has been checking on the water and air filtration plants. He suggested the tanks had been decanted into flask sized containers, something about an import contact, clearly a smuggler. This is apparently why he thinks an amnesty would work. Anatoli want's the militia to run a scavenger hunt."

She heard the grudge in his voice, it was time she felt, even though everyone was tired, to finally sort out what was going on within the team.

"Thanks. However, as well as our ongoing concern about the Sarin, I have been dealing, or perhaps more accurately, not dealing with another matter. But we're all together again and I think it's time to clear the air."

She looked directly at Eric as she finished, then she took in the rest of the team and finished her sweep at Anatoli.

"First I want to apologise to my fiancé, it's my fault I've not kept work and personal life separate, and he's suffered because of that."

She saw Anatoli shake his head and begin as if to say something then stop.

"Secondly, I want to apologise to my team, to all of you. I've muddied the waters, without realising I was doing it. We all worked so well together, I never noticed some of you had issues with the way we were operating and I've relied on others to be smoothing them over, which was properly my responsibility."

She looked at Chris, who smiled back at her.

"I've made some decisions," she continued "We'll be continuing to use Ms. Ewing as our charter pilot, and I know I speak for the whole team when I thank Anatoli for everything he's done for the team."

She paused as Chris started clapping and the rest joined in. She watched Eric, he was clapping but she didn't think he really agreed.

"Right," she said and the clapping stopped, "Next, I'm recommending Eric is promoted to a position in the

Intelligence Agency. I sent a request while we were at Polar Station and Regional Controller Kairns has agreed."

This time she paused deliberately and was pleased to see Chris take the hint and start clapping. The rest joined in. She did not look at Eric.

"Finally," she said, "I'd like to invite you all to my wedding, which will take place on August the eleventh, at some venue to be confirmed."

She was smiling and looking at Anatoli, seeing his wide grin.

"That's less than a month away," said James.

"I think he's waited long enough," she replied.

"So," said Glenn.

She heard his tone draw a line under her speech.

"This scavenger hunt, are we sure it's going to access every part of Kunlun?"

"Indirectly," said Anatoli, "but we should try to systematically search for illegally carved out spaces. The equivalent of smuggler warehouses if you like."

"Presumably, if the mayor has already been checking out the water and air plants, he'd have been alerted to anything suspicious near to them," said James.

Enya nodded.

"I get the impression he's going to call for an amnesty whatever we say to him, what do we do if we only get a few or even only half the flasks back? " asked James.

"Something to discuss with the mayor," said Chris.

She noticed Eric was very quiet. Tough, she thought, it wasn't a punishment, but it was operationally, the best solution.

"I'm going to freshen up," she said looking at her watch, "Meet back here in fifteen minutes, for our pick up."

Chairs pushed back from the table.

"I'll show you where your rooms are," Anatoli was saying to Chris, Glenn and James.

She closed the door in Anatoli's room and leant back against it. That had been hard. She understood now why Valla and the Intelligence Agency used psychological evaluations rather than a gut feeling. She knew Kairns in Intelligence would find the right place for Eric, he was an excellent investigator after all.

They were in Mayor McAndrew's office. She'd taken Glenn with her to the meeting and told the rest to find out what had been happening in Progress, data share and think about likely locations for illegal tunnels. The mayor had the city militia captain there and she outlined the five items for the scavenger hunt.

"Forgive me, Inspector Zhao," said the mayor, "It's an excellent idea, and I'm happy if the militia want to run it, but I'm still going to announce an amnesty for the return of the flasks. The estimate is ten catering flasks per tank. Till we get them all back, civilians will be told to stay at home, I can't have people making themselves a target."

She looked at the militia captain, who nodded.

"Let's just call it a search for the non-returned flasks and be done with the games," said the captain.

"Fair," said Enya, "How long will you give them to return the flasks?"

"It takes forty minutes to walk from one end of Kunlun to the other, side to side, less if top to bottom. They don't need long if they're serious. An hour. After that, total lockdown, and the militia keep searching. But, we need to keep the mines operating."

There was a knock at the door and the mayor's secretary popped her head round. Enya saw the mayor nod at her and the door closed again. Enya wondered what that was all about. She saw the militia captain just as curious.

"I'll let you get started, I have an amnesty announcement to prepare," said the mayor.

She recognised dismissal when she heard it. Clearly whatever the knock had been about was the next thing on the mayor's agenda. She and Glenn left with the militia captain. The captain nodded to the mayor's secretary on his way out, but there was no one else in the room. Enya's curiosity was piqued and she caught Glenn by the arm, slowing him from keeping in step with the captain.

"I want to see what happens next, that knock was suspicious."

Glenn was nodding.

"Over there," he was pointing.

She saw a shadowy space between support pillars.

They watched. After a minute or two, a woman entered the outer office. Enya reckoned the woman would know they were hiding and watching. Mayor McAndrew hadn't struck her as a big fan of subterfuge so it was the woman with something to hide. Enya didn't like that immediately. They were searching for hidden things. She nudged Glenn.

Back in the meeting room she outlined what she wanted to happen. Glenn had been of the opinion that the woman they'd seen was the mayor's smuggler contact. Another Freddie Tran in the making, she thought. She put Eric onto finding out who she was.

Anatoli was with the militia already, but the rest of them were to wander as aimlessly as possible while covering the city in an efficient manner ahead of what she considered an inevitable lockdown. There was no way all the flasks would be recovered.

Glenn had said he was going to start with his cousins. It was the first she'd heard that Glenn had relations other than Gordon Murcheson. She decided retrospective psych evaluations and background checks were long overdue. Not because she thought they'd uncover anything detrimental, but she realised not having the full picture of her team was unhelpful. If Glenn had family here, was he going to be able to remain clear headed?

She had given each of them a set of antidotes. Now they were making waves, it was safer to have some protection should it panic someone into action. She wished she had something on the Greens here rather than the vague assurance from the mayor they were mostly harmless.

Chapter Twenty Six - Back Road

Yang Lau left the mayor's office with a lot on her mind. When she'd first been contacted by the mayor she'd been suspicious. She had a few small greenhouses, on illegally excavated tunnels, and she'd been told when the tanks had shown up they were spare supplies of Ethylene, a vital component in artificial ripening. It hadn't seemed weird to see them being decanted into the catering flasks a few weeks ago and she'd paid it no attention. Then Jim had told her they contained Sarin components. She'd revisited the location but the tanks had been moved.

Now she'd thought back she realised she knew one of the girls decanting the tanks, it was Cassie Galados. Yang knew the girl was trouble already. Cassie had tried to get into the cannabis greenhouses more than once and Yang had needed to pay a visit to her in person. Yang could tell it hadn't changed Cassie's ambitions, only the number of broken ribs the girl had recovered from.

The growing Green movement had already prompted Yang to infiltrate it in Kunlun. Along with one of her trusted enforcers she'd attended a workshop in Vostok. She'd been shocked by the discussions. Now, knowing Cassie's willingness to be a martyr to the Green cause and that she had access to Sarin components, Yang was as close to terrified as she'd ever been.

She glanced over at the pillar where she'd been watched by two people, whoever they were, they'd gone. It was an added complication. Too much attention was now being focused by the state on Kunlun, which had usually been left to its own devices in the past.

The militia search was underway, and the mayor's announcement had just been made. It was one hour and counting. Anatoli could feel the tension as he walked the corridor towards the state accommodation. He'd been asked to use his outsider perspective and given free rein by the militia captain. He knew, like Vostok, the smuggler places wouldn't be on any official maps, which meant excavated tunnels not known to the authorities. The easiest way to find them would be a ground penetrating radar. The mining companies must have such equipment or at the very least you must be able to hire it here.

He found Glenn in the meeting room looking at a map of Kunlun.

"Trying to navigate?" he asked.

"It's a rabbit warren, I never grasped the metaphor till now," said Glenn.

"I can help. Your cousins, they're miners?"

"Yes, they own two small mines. Why?"

"I need ground penetrating radar. I'm looking for unofficial excavations, I reckon that's the best place to stash stuff."

"I was going to visit Reuben first. He's on tenth, at twentieth apparently. But I don't see a floor ten on the map."

"Ah," said Anatoli, "it's not quite that simple. It's to do with utilities. Tenth is an area not a level. But, if you download the app it'll make it much easier to find."

"There's an app?" asked Glenn, "Of course there is."

They exited the small residential lift, and Anatoli rubbed his ears at the pressure change. He saw Glenn do the same. A man approached them, the double of Daniel Ektov, Glenn's maternal grandfather.

"Glenn," said Reuben, "I haven't seen you since we were boys, that one time at McMurdo. Was it a birthday party or something?"

Anatoli watched them embrace and Glenn pull back to look at Reuben. He felt awkward at being there, but Reuben had already seen him.

"Who's this?"

Glenn introduced him as a friend and colleague and Anatoli felt a small pang of sadness that he'd not be working with the team after this. They'd all keep in touch but they would have less in common, no new shared moments of danger. The stories when they met up again would not always include him. It was the first time he'd really felt angry towards Eric, even though he knew Enya would have changed charter once they'd married.

"Come on, meet the family, what brings you to Kunlun?"

"It's to do with the flasks of Sarin, Reuben, I wish it was better circumstances. Anatoli'd like to use a GPR kit, he wants to find tunnels that aren't on the maps."

"Oh," said Reuben, "I didn't realise you worked for the government. Yes, I don't expect they'll get all the flasks back. It's a worry, but Mayor McAndrew knows what he's doing. I can get you some ground radar, no problem, we keep our own kit and rent it out as a sideline."

"Thanks," said Anatoli, "I really appreciate it."

"I might even be able to suggest a good place to start looking too. Here we are," said Reuben as he opened the door.

Two small children ran towards Reuben, shouting 'daddy'.

"Let me introduce you to Katya and Olga."

Anatoli had little experience with children, but even he recognised this pair were the epitome of cute. He wondered how Glenn would be feeling right now, knowing they didn't have more than ten vials of antidote available to them. Added to the environmental suits the mining firms and militia would have, it was still a tiny fraction of the populace who would survive a hit on a main utility from the flasks' contents.

He looked at Glenn and could see emotions play across his face.

Reuben continued talking to his children, "This is my cousin, Glenn. He's come all the way from Weddell City to see you but first he's going to talk with daddy."

Anatoli saw the girls stop jumping around and look more seriously at Glenn, then they ran off further into the apartment. Reuben was opening a door next to him.

They were sitting in Reuben's office and drinking something he'd called brandy, but Anatoli had his doubts about its production process. It was certainly alcoholic, however.

"When I heard the announcement I could hardly believe it," said Reuben, "How much Sarin are we talking about?"

"The components were in two acetylene tanks originally. I know the Mayor has direct evidence it was decanted into catering flasks, but I don't know how," said Glenn, "We estimated ten flasks each. It depends if they decanted it all."

Anatoli understood Glenn's need to be frank with Reuben. Since the announcement, the whole complex of Kunlun had felt more tense, but he'd seen no signs of panic or vigilantism. The Greens here, like everywhere in the AFS were people's sons and daughters, friends and lovers. They weren't outsiders like Isadora Ley or Karl Leyden, and people were clearly still getting to grips with the idea some of them were prepared to poison the town.

Of course, he thought, some of those with the flasks might not know exactly what it was they were holding. The components wouldn't be active till mixed together. They could have been told anything.

It was the gamble that Mayor McAndrew had taken: that most of them had a conscience. But Anatoli knew there were fanatics like Steve Jung and Perry Coia who would continue with the plan, and now they had a heads up everyone knew about it. Would it speed them up?

"The mayor has a relationship of sorts with Yang Lau, our local crime boss," Reuben was saying, "I bet she knew the stuff was decanted, but I bet she didn't know it was Sarin components."

"Why?" asked Glenn.

"I've met her once. She not stupid, just what you could call an alternative businesswoman. Anyway, let's talk about the GPR. I have two kits, which I'm willing to hire to the militia for basic maintenance fees."

Anatoli looked directly at Reuben to check he was serious. There wasn't a hint of mischief in the face looking back at Anatoli. He turned to look at Glenn who was less successful. The pair burst out laughing.

"How can you joke about this?" he asked, annoyed.

"Sorry," said Glenn, "it's an Ektov thing."

Anatoli thought back to the many times he'd met Senator Daniel Ektov. The joke seemed less surprising in light of that.

"You'll have to meet my wife, Abby, but then I'll take you to the storage, we'll pick up the kit, quick operational run through and I'll show where you might get lucky," said Reuben, throwing the remains of the generous measure of 'brandy' down his throat and slamming it on the table in a way that made Anatoli half expect it to be chucked over his shoulder. Anatoli didn't join him in finishing the drink. But he noticed Glenn did.

They were at Reuben's storage area, much lower into the mountain than the residential district, closer to the mine shaft heads. It was considerably warmer. Reuben had just finished overseeing Anatoli's use of the GPR kit.

It had a small screen on the handheld that attached to one stick, but it could also link to a visor. Anatoli was seeing about two metres into the rock face of the storage area, if he turned the dial he could extend the range to just over ten metres but with a drop in resolution. The whole kit was more or less a knapsack and two sticks; heavy and slightly unwieldy sticks, but he reckoned he could manage.

"Thanks for this," he said to Reuben.

"Thank you for going looking. I'm presuming you've got some sort of protection if you find them and they're prepared to mix the stuff?"

"We've got antidotes. You got suits?" asked Glenn.

"I have two, with twelve hours airtime each," answered Reuben.

"Here," said Glenn.

Anatoli saw him pass two syringes to Reuben, the antidotes, Atropine and Pralidoxime. An adult dose would cover both girls. But Glenn would now be without.

"I can't take this," said Reuben.

"You can, and you will, for the girls," said Glenn.

Reuben had grabbed Glenn in a bear hug. Anatoli concentrated on stowing the sticks in the webbing harness that the rest of the electronics on his back supported. When he looked up, Reuben and Glenn were at the door.

"C'mon, let's go find some some tunnels," said Reuben enthusiastically.

Anatoli felt like levity was Reuben's main coping mechanism, and he forgave the earlier joke completely.

Reuben had led them deeper into the mountain but not lower into it. They passed a few shaft heads, proclaiming the names of the mine and it's owners. Anatoli had been pleasantly warm in his ordinary clothes back in the residential district, but now he understood exactly how basic, 'Basics' would probably need to be in the mines.

The sweat dripped down the sides of his face. He saw Reuben stop at a large metal door and then slide it open, the wheels it hung on squealing on the metal rail. Inside was a rough hewn tunnel. Reuben gestured to them to come inside.

"It's called the Back Road," said Reuben, "it eventually gets up to the old residential area, sometimes it's a bit of a climb, but I reckon, your best bet to find illegal tunnels, is somewhere off it."

"How come the militia aren't here?" asked Anatoli.

"Because most of them have things here they don't want found either," said Reuben.

"Ah."

"Good luck," said Reuben.

Anatoli heard the door wheels squeal behind him and switched on the torch, seeing Glenn just ahead of him with his torch, shining up the tunnel.

"We should let Enya know where we are before we disappear," he said.

"Good point," said Glenn, "but I haven't had a connection since we passed the last mine shaft."

"I'll start up the tunnel, you go back, let her know. I'll not move off the main tunnel, if there's a fork I'll stop."

He saw Glenn come back past him and watched the dim light of the main tunnel appear as the door squealed open. It went darker again as it shut. He had to presume the door was often opened and shut. If lots of people used this back route to stash stuff it felt a reasonable assumption. He switch on the GPR and started to probe the tunnel sides.

He'd gone about fifteen metres up the tunnel when he thought he'd picked up something odd. He still wasn't sure what a cavity would look like, much less a larger, secret tunnel, running parallel or away from this one. He moved another metre, and saw the same pattern of colours. He decided on a larger sampling interval. If it was a parallel tunnel, it would still be there two metres later, but if it was the end of a tunnel running away at angle it might not.

He heard the door squeal faintly. The tunnel must have curved as he'd moved along it. The door sounded very far back.

Chapter Twenty Seven - Manifesto for a Green World

Cassie was in the kitchen when she heard the announcement. The old cripple they all seemed to adore, was appealing for something. She was only half listening, until she heard the word Sarin. Her heart started thumping and she felt sure her mum would notice. She tried to calm down and headed for the front door, picking up her satchel on the way. Inside it was a catering size flask with one of the components for making Sarin.

As she strode away from the apartment towards the residential lift, she already knew who amongst the so-called activists would cave and hand in their flasks. And she knew who she could rely on to stick with the plan: Only Evan Redbarn was guaranteed, sadly the rest were not. And the guy who'd arrived recently from Progress, she struggled to recall his name, Luke or something like that, would be trying to take charge.

She remembered meeting him; a cocky little guy. Lukas, that was it, Lukas Brandt. He seemed to think he was a big deal, kept dropping names and then apologising because nobody knew who they were. But she *had* heard of Karl Leyden. She'd read his Manifesto for a Green World, and knew from that, exactly what was required to get it too.

It wasn't like she'd miss anyone from Kunlun. She hated her mum and her obsession with making enough money to buy the latest gadget. Their house was full of useless contraptions, never used after the novelty wore off. It was so much waste. Sometimes when she thought about it, it made her feel physically sick.

She had stashed her other flask in a small tunnel off the Back Road, but she didn't know where Evan had put his.

She envied Evan, his mother was always out, or asleep and he had the run of their apartment. He'd even been able to offer Lukas a place to stay. She decided to head towards his apartment. Then she realised it would be better if they weren't obviously together at this moment. She could call him, decide if they needed to meet. She knew right now, what she needed was anonymity, and staying at home was not it.

God, her mum could gossip, it was a wonder she had any privacy, and it wouldn't be long before her mother would begin to piece something together. She'd already heard about Lukas staying with Evan.

Her mother didn't like Evan. She called him the 'coarse boy' even thought it was more a comment on his mother's occupation than on Evan himself. Cassie felt the things Evan's mother did for money were less damaging to the planet than what her own mother did. From Cassie's point of view, they were perfectly acceptable.

Cassie's father had died in a mine accident. They'd lived on the insurance payout quite comfortably, until there'd been an increase in state and city taxes. Her mother had grumbled about it, but, Cassie had read the taxes were to create a basic kind of insurance. The very thing Evan's mother hadn't been able to rely on, his father succumbing to lung disease in a Global Corporation mine.

It had been too late for Evan's mum. She'd slid into a life that Cassie, who'd met her once, thought she was now resigned to.

Cassie was determined never to resign. She was going to be active. She was going to make things happen. Make the AFS sit up and listen to its young people. They wanted changes like the ones the UN had introduced; environmental damage fees, mining taxes and real protection for the existing wild spaces, but she'd go further; not a state by state solution. It needed a global attitude, and she'd introduce population management and eventually, depopulate the Antarctic. People shouldn't live here, she thought. Not if you wanted to control the climate and get it back to where it should be.

She was willing to do what was necessary and Evan would too. Evan liked her, a lot, but she didn't want to get involved. There was a whole chapter in Karl's Manifesto on the dangers of getting involved with fellow activists. It was a weakness that could be exploited.

She was now near to Evan's apartment and called his number. The backlight from her phone decreased in brightness to match the poor lighting. Evan lived behind the commercial district, in an old residential area carved out during the earliest version of Kunlun, when they'd excavated wide rather than high. A few bad faults to the north of the mountain had put an end to that idea.

"Evan?"

"Cassie."

He sounded excited not scared.

"Cassie, Lukas says we need to hit the air plant for Second, it covers a lot of residential areas. The announcement said everyone needed to stay in their own apartments. Nobody is going to be in the commercial districts."

"Does he?" she said, "Well, I have to go to the Back Road to get my other flask. I'm not risking coming all the way back to there. I'm going to hit a big mine. Aren't we here to do economic damage as well?"

"But Lukas says..."

She cut him off, "I don't give a fuck what Lukas says. He's a short-arsed shit, who thinks he knows everything and we're all bumpkins. Fuck him. You do what you want, Evan."

"He's got guns and we're going to shoot our way into the air plant. Everyone is going to hear about that. They'll cover up anything you do, 'n' just say it was a natural accident."

"Don't care. I'm picking the biggest mine. There's no way they've shut down production. If I poison the whole shaft, I'll have taken it down for weeks. Let's see them cover that up."

"Lukas says he has antidotes."

Cassie considered this. She had relied on her forward momentum not to ask the question, but now the chance of staying alive made her ask it. Just how desperate was she? Was she willing to die in the act of mixing the Sarin flasks and dropping them into the shaft?

"Cassie?"

She could hear the pleading in Evan's voice. It was pathetic, she thought. It stiffened her resolve.

"I'm going to be all right. Enjoy your shoot out."

She hung up.

Though, she realised, the logistics of how she was going to mix the flasks and send them down the shaft together hadn't yet been worked out in her head, but, where she'd stashed the other flask there was more equipment, something would work, she was sure. She'd always been able to turn her mind to making things: a legacy of all the discarded gadgets.

Karl was supposed to send somebody with mixing equipment, when the time was right and she'd thought Lukas had it when he'd turned up, but Lukas had been very vague about his reasons for arriving. She didn't believe he had antidotes either, that vagueness had sounded like there was no plan and he was just on the run from somewhere else. Probably something had gone down in Progress; his own cock-up she presumed.

She reached the entrance to the Back Road at the edge of the old apartments on the commercial level. Nobody lived this far back nowadays. The opening broke through from a room in an abandoned apartment. The light had faded to nearly nothing and she switched on her head-torch before shouldering the door open.

She wasn't the only person who knew about this door. Plenty of Kunlun had things to hide, or stash. Rubbish they couldn't officially recycle, illegal stills or greenhouses. But her tunnel off the Back Road was all her own.

Evan had 'borrowed' an excavator over a few nights and they had cut a long, thin tunnel heading down towards the mine head level. They'd made a bulb shaped space to stash the equipment they felt would be useful to disrupt the mining activities. That was, until Perry Coia arrived.

It was Perry who'd inspired them all to think differently. As a result they'd abandoned the tunnel. They'd never even showed it to her, much less mentioned it to Lukas. It had been Perry who'd first mentioned Sarin. She'd explained how chemicals could cause disruption that would make the authorities behave in a more Green way. She'd been the one who'd given Cassie a copy of Karl's Manifesto for a Green World.

It had been a complete eye opener. What the AFS taught about the Carrington events and its aftermath, had always focussed on the creation of the Free State, and less about the strengthening of the UN and its subsequent introduction of ecological laws. Karl had explained in his Manifesto how the latter had relied on the former. It made perfect sense.

She was sweating, the canvas of the satchel rubbed into her bare shoulder. She'd wrapped her shirt around her waist and she tried again to shift the satchel strap over the strap of her vest for momentary respite. The flask bounced off her thigh leaving an ache she knew was a bruise and she had begun to hate Kunlun with a fresh passion. People weren't supposed to live inside mountains, or in frozen wastelands. They deserved an outdoor life, growing food in the fresh air, not in an artificial-ripening atmosphere. The animal and plant life of the planet deserved a stable climate to exist in, not one that was still running out of control. She realised in her angry frustration that it had been left to her to make a difference, and it was making her cry. Here, and now, she was going to make a stand that everyone in the AFS would see. She wiped her arm across her eyes.

Finally, she saw the rock markings that denoted the beginning of their tunnel. She took the satchel off her shoulder, feeling a wetness that couldn't be all sweat and squeezed into the narrow opening.

Enya was once again pinned down behind cover. Not by sniper fire for a change, but the automatic gunfire of a young man with little regard for life. She could hear, but not see his accomplice busy dragging something sounding like an oil drum. She guessed it was being dragged towards the humidity regulation component of the Air Handling System. The next step would be emptying the components into the drum, maybe mixing it if they could, but by that point Sarin would already be evaporating into the air ducting and be on its way towards the residential area served by this plant.

When they'd got the call through from the militia guarding the plant saying they were under fire, Jim McAndrew had told her the plant served three thousand homes. She couldn't let them begin to empty the flasks. She called James over the LAN on her visor.

"Can you get the guy with the oil drum, or the boy?"

"Not yet. I'm still trying to get into position. How much ammo does that little ... have?"

"It's not infinite, but it doesn't need to be."

The boy was alternating between the assault rifle being fed from the box at his feet and an automatic gun she didn't recognise. The guy moving the drum was clearly in charge, the dragging noise had stopped briefly, and after that the boy had slowed down from the onslaught unleashed when they'd first turned up.

Enya could see some of the bodies of the dead and injured militia who'd been caught unawares. She could see one slowly trying to crawl to cover. She risked a few shots at the boy with the automatic weapons, forcing him to concentrate on her location.

Chris was providing cover for James to manoeuvre into a position where James could get a shot at the drum guy. She could hear Chris' shots pinging off the machinery mostly, but between them both, she thought the boy was being kept occupied enough not to figure out what was going on. They could get him once the flasks were safe.

She heard a voice in her visor, the distortion on the signal made it difficult to recognise who it was.

"Enya... got... penetrating rada... Anatoli... Back Road... tunnel..."

The signal turned wholly to static. She realised it must be Glenn. She'd not heard from him, or Anatoli for nearly an hour. Any militia were on their way here or already guarding the other vital utilities. It had looked like the target was the air plant, but what if there was a secondary target?

"Eric," she called on her visor over the LAN to reach him at the Mayor's office.

"Boss?"

"Do we have any other missing Green activists we should be worried about?"

The connection was crystal clear, even over the gunfire she could hear the rustle of papers.

"Cassiopeia Galados, she's the one who was seen decanting the components. Her mother said Cassie left the apartment during the announcement."

"Shit," said Enya, "Find out what the Back Road is and how to get to it. Glenn and Anatoli are there. There's no signal. If it's nothing, get them back here."

Chapter Twenty Eight - Gut Instincts

Eric was walking towards the main lift from the mayor's office, with a route mapped on his phone to the Back Road, but his mind was somewhere else entirely. He could feel the thread of his decisions stretching back to the confrontation with Anatoli in Progress. But it went beyond that, to his first meeting with Enya Zhao at Weddell City Police Department, and further back to when he'd first heard about her. How could he have been so blind to his own feelings?

He'd always wanted to do the right thing. He couldn't stand the feeling he had when he made a mistake, it seemed to ripple through him from the pit of his stomach to the middle of his head. All his life he'd tried to minimise experiencing that. Perhaps, he thought, in order to avoid that, he'd pushed how he felt for Enya down into his sub-conscious and then convinced himself it didn't exist? Clearly it had found ways to manifest itself, and he'd rationalised it as a dislike first for Anatoli's position, and more lately for Anatoli himself. Even now, he could feel a small hard core that told him not to like Anatoli, a totally irrational thing.

He stepped out of the main lift at the commercial district level. It was deserted. A fresh sensation appeared between his shoulder blades, wiping out the earlier feelings in his stomach. His mind seemed to snap to attention and the thoughts about Enya and Anatoli dropped out of view. They had triangulated Glenn's call to a mine head location and, though his map had several entrances onto this Back Road tunnel, it had been clear they were somewhere at the base of it. He walked along the empty concourse to the mining lift. It had the same shiny surround as the other lifts, but as Eric approached he could smell the rock dust and metallic scents.

The lift had been down on the mine head level and took nearly half a minute to reach the commercial level. As the door opened there was a fresh wave of metallic odours and a swirl of dust escaped into the concourse. It was hotter inside the lift, he wiped his forehead with his arm and saw the scratched graffiti covering the walls. It was mostly names, but amongst them at the deepest layer were comments on the old mining corporations that used to operate here. On top of those were political slogans from the start of the AFS. The mines had been one of the places the AFS had started. The common dangers had united disparate nationalities, it could almost be said the Code was born in Kunlun and not on the snowfields. He wondered if that was another reason the Greens had targeted it?

The door opened, but there was no increase in metallic smell, his nose had already got used to it and there even seemed to be less dust. The extractors were humming overhead. He realised up above they must have turned the extraction systems down to the bare minimum, a vain attempt to minimise drawing anything through in Second. The light was dim down here, his sense of unease increased.

He jogged carefully along the tunnel, the Back Road was at the end of the mine head level, it was why the message from Glenn had been so broken up. He could see from his own phone the LAN strength dissipating to zero. Up ahead he could make out the end of the tunnel. The head torch the mayor had given him showed him, in bounced snatches, the metal sliding door, half covering a dark hole. The feeling between his shoulder blades intensified. He squeezed past the door and slowed to a walk inside the much rougher surfaces of the Back Road.

His shirt was sodden with sweat now, he took off his gun harness and then the shirt, wringing the moisture out of it and tying it round his waist. He slung the harness over his shoulder, making sure he could still access the gun with ease. He could feel the tunnel curve and rise as a result of his sensitive inner ear, the reason he didn't enjoy flying, and something he'd consciously covered up to take the job with Enya.

He tried his visor comms, if Glenn or Anatoli were nearby they'd pick it up, but there was only static in answer.

The dragging noise had stopped. It meant that the drum was in position. It was now or never.

"James?" she called over the visor.

There was no answer. She felt a moment's panic. If James was hit, their odds of success got smaller. She heard the crack of a shot, and breathed a sigh of relief.

"Shit, missed."

The boy with the automatic weapons had stopped firing. She risked a quick look to see what was going on. The boy was crouched down now, half hidden behind a gap in the machinery, still attached to his guns. The drum was indeed close to the humidity regulation unit, but there was no sign of the guy who'd dragged it there. More worryingly there was one flask lying on its side, next to the drum. She adjusted her visor to zoom in as much as possible. The top was definitely half unscrewed. Was the first flask already emptied into the drum? Or stashed somewhere with one of the activists? They couldn't risk the flask on the floor being punctured or opened whatever had happened.

There was a fresh crack as James took another shot. She watched the boy squeeze further into the small gap between the boxy machinery. He'd dropped one of the guns now. There was an answering shot from the other guy. She tried to work out where it had come from, searching with her visor.

She saw a movement. Higher up. James must have seen it too. There was another crack. Then clanging down through the machinery. She hoped it was a gun, and not an opened flask. Her view was obscured by the drum and the shadows cast by the machinery.

"Is it the flask, can you see?"

Chris answered, "Yes, it's opened, there's liquid coming out."

"Shit," she said, "Make sure you've got your antidotes handy."

She saw the boy edge forward from his spot. She fired at him, joined by shots from Chris on other side of the space. The boy pushed back into the gap. She had to reload, there was a pause from Chris too. Just as she finished reloading she looked over and saw the boy running forward beginning to fire wildly at the drum and the flasks, lying within a metre of each other. Then there was a crack from James' rifle and he went down. Enya focussed on the flasks, she could see beads of liquid and dribbles seeping from a myriad of holes along the capped one and the puddle from what had been in the uncapped. The Sarin was being created as both liquids vapourised.

"Take the antidotes, now!"

She fumbled in her clothes for the inside pocket containing the antidote syringes. She tried to resist the urge to sniff as her nose started to run.

"Don't sniff," she reminded them, as she jammed the syringe with the Atropine into her arm and pressed the plunger down. Her chest already felt like it was on fire. She coughed, unable to stop herself.

Her hands were shaking. Her arms began to ache. The second syringe slipped from her hand. She willed herself to stay calm. She picked it up with a slow, considered movement and pushed it into the same arm. She heard her breath rasp. Slowly she felt some stabilisation occur.

"McAndrew," she called over her visor, "you've got to shut down Second. There's Sarin in the ducting. It's incompletely mixed but it's there. You have to evacuate as per our plan."

She made her move. The other guy might only be injured, he could have antidotes, but she had to stop the continued mixing before more Sarin got into the system.

She made to move from her position and fell to her hands and knees.

Crawling towards the flask that had been punctured, pulling at her shirt, she ripped a strip off, wrapping it across as many of the punctures as possible and then pressed the flask, most holes down, into the ground. She saw James and Chris staggering out from their hiding places. James heading to where the other activist had been while Chris came towards her. She saw him pick up the cap and flask that had clanged down and screw the cap back on, shaking his head as she looked at him hopefully.

She looked down at her hand pressing on the flask. She could see the shirt material darkening as it wicked up the component.

"Chris," she coughed, "Is there a lid for the drum?"

She looked again at the drum, checking what she could see of it for bullet holes. Miraculously, it seemed unscathed. She crawled round to check the other side.

"Found it."

"Bring it here. Chuck the other flask in too."

She knew they were all covered in Sarin vapour, and that of the components. They needed to secure the remains of the components and stay apart from each other. It was the only thing she could think of doing now.

Dropping the wrapped flask to join the other one now in the drum, she watched Chris put the lid on and then they both shoved it as far away from the plant machinery as they could. The eerie silence told her that the plant had been shut down.

James had reappeared dragging the other dead activist and had dumped him next to the boy. They both looked so young, she thought. How did they get to this stage in such a short amount of time? What was going wrong in the AFS that the Code no longer held?

They checked the militia for signs of life. Enya went to the guy who'd been crawling for cover earlier but there was no pulse. He could have caught a stray bullet from when the flask got punctured. She hoped so anyway, better that than the Sarin. She saw James and Chris shake their heads as they checked the other bodies.

She felt sick and wasn't sure it had anything to do with the chemical cocktail of Sarin and its antidotes. They hadn't stopped it. She began to cry. The bastards had managed to get the stuff into the air system.

She felt burning on her hand and saw red welts begin where she'd come in contact with the liquid from the flask. It would be a long wait till the decontamination team turned up since they'd be working on civilians first.

"We did the best we could," she told them. But she expected they'd hear her disappointment. She was already analysing what could have gone better. They were sitting apart from each other, James propped up against the wall near the door, Chris back close to where he'd taken cover, and she'd retreated to the machinery she'd used for cover.

She tried to recall what the active lifetime was for Sarin, but she knew the components were stable for longer, so they had to reduce the chance of more mixing. She could feel her eyelids drooping despite the throbbing pain in her hand.

"Boss."

James' voice jerked her awake.

"Boss, don't you dare," he said.

"Yeah," agreed Chris, "nobody here want's to explain to Anatoli what happened."

Her team, she thought and smiled. Who needed psyche evaluations? She'd done all right with her gut instincts.

Chapter Twenty Nine - Doing Something

Cassie had scrambled down to the space, sliding the last few metres. She didn't remember it being this steep but she wouldn't have been so tired and sweaty before either. There was less equipment too. She wondered if Evan had been visiting the tunnel without her? Maybe he'd showed Lukas what they'd stashed? Her anger flared again at the thought of Lukas. He couldn't be more than a few years older, but he'd tried to lord it over them. She'd show him.

She pushed amongst the tubing to uncover the other flask. There was no way she could get both into her satchel so she needed to find something else to carry them in. Something wheeled she thought. She didn't want any more bruises than necessary. She was sure they'd brought a hand truck down, they'd used it to bring a generator. She searched under a tarp finding the generator but not the hand truck. If Evan had taken it...

She spotted the handles of the hand truck poking up behind another tarp covered thing. She pushed the tarp off and found the hand truck was still under the mini excavator, up against the wall of the tunnel.

How? It was like it had been backed up on purpose to make the hand truck difficult to get to. Lukas must have been down here. What a dick, she thought. Clambering over the excavator, she tried to stand down between it and the wall but her legs only fitted down sideways. She pushed against the wall and levered her body against the excavator. It shifted slightly. Enough to turn her feet into the gap. She pushed more, using her feet, until the excavator shifted off the load plate of the hand truck.

Lifting it up she crab walked it out of the gap, wincing as the edge of the load plate swung back into her ankle.

Out of the gap, she bent down to check her ankle. A red line showed where it had hit, but thankfully the skin was unbroken. Down here she could get the virulent strain of tetanus, specific to Kunlun. They insisted on a shot with any cut, regardless of the state of your regular vaccinations. Another reason not to be living here, she thought.

Pulling the hand truck over the uneven surface, into the centre of the space, she placed the two flasks on the load plate. Something was needed to strap them to the back support. She started rifling through the loose materials, then stopped. There was a noise she was sure hadn't been her. It sounded further away, almost like it was through the rock. She scrambled up the steep path to where it became more shallow, then stopped and listened.

There was something. A scratching noise. It didn't sound like rats, it was too irregular. She tried to imagine what it might be and drew a blank. But it was certainly people. And it wasn't going to be Lukas or Evan, they were being all heroic at the air plant.

It would be easy to get trapped in this tunnel. There was no point in trying to hide. She'd need to get moving and risk the noise alerting someone. Whoever it was would back off if she threatened to open the flasks. It felt like she'd have the upper hand in any confrontation.

She found the straps under the tarp she'd tossed aside earlier. Tying the flasks on securely, she began to haul the hand truck up the steep incline, resting briefly to listen for the sound once it was shallower. There it was; a scratching, like something was being pressed against the rock but then slipping against the surface.

Dragging the hand truck behind her, she tried to jog up the tunnel, but it was only a few metres before she had to rest. Would they really back down if she threatened to open the flasks? Probably not if she was still in her tunnel, especially if they had antidotes. She had to make it out of her tunnel before whoever was doing whatever the scratching was, met up with her.

If she went up the Back Road, instead of down to the mine head level, she could get to the old residential level, where the negotiations might go better with living space nearby to contaminate.

It seemed like ages till she could see the narrow opening of her tunnel onto the Back Road, and she stopped one more time to listen for the scratching, hearing nothing. It was worrying. What did that mean? At the opening she realised the load plate was too wide to squeeze through with the flasks strapped on. It would need unloading, then the plate folded up while she squeezed through with the flasks, and she could then re-load on the other side.

She put the flasks down carefully and pushed the folded hand truck through. It fell to the floor of the tunnel. Shit. It sounded really loud. She stepped through the opening. There was a flash of torch light. She ducked back inside. Her heart was thumping harder than earlier and her body began to shake.

"I've got the flasks. Back off or I'll open them," she shouted through the opening, cursing the wavering in her voice. It made her sound weak. Like she wasn't serious.

"We don't want you to do that."

A man's voice; level, not the slightest quiver in it. He sounded like he was used to ordering people about. But not like Lukas. He sounded like people did what he asked, and he didn't sound like he was from Kunlun either.

Her mind was beginning to run through too many scenarios, too many what ifs. She didn't feel like she had many useful choices.

"What's your name?" he asked.

Why didn't they know about her? Was Evan right and they were going to cover it up? She'd make sure everyone knew it was her.

"Cassie Galados." She felt better about her voice this time. She ramped up the defiance. "I'm the leader of the Green Resistance."

"Cassie. Please, give us the flasks, just roll them out. Nobody needs to get hurt."

Oh, but they do, she thought. Only through the pain of loss are people moved to make the world a better place. Karl had shown her; countless times it had taken wars, famines, disasters, before people would come together and change things for the better.

It made up her mind. Even if it was just him and her, she'd have made a difference. Unscrewing the lid of the first flask she threw it out into the tunnel, quickly unscrewing the next one and doing the same.

"Shit!"

She smiled when she heard him swear. In the warmth of the Back Road, the liquids would evaporate quickly and the vapour would mix and sink to the lowest point. It would head more in his direction than hers. She heard another man's voice. They seemed to be arguing. Then, there was a third man's voice. She sniffed involuntarily as her nose began to run. Three was better than she could hope for at this point. She imagined them saying her name with their last breath.

Eric had run up the tunnel when he heard Glenn shouting. He had just got in sight of Glenn and Anatoli when he heard Glenn swear. He caught them in his head torch and scanned ahead of them. He saw the flasks. Opened. Glenn and Anatoli seemed to be wrestling and ignoring him. What were they doing?

"Glenn, Anatoli, antidotes," he shouted to them.

Glenn turned to him and he saw Anatoli punch Glenn in the arm, with the bottom of his fist. He didn't understand. Glenn was pushing Anatoli off. Eric ran to meet them.

"What the fuck?"

"Glenn gave his antidotes to his cousin. You need the Atropine straight away," said Anatoli.

"Was that yours?" he asked Anatoli.

"Yes," said Glenn, "and you better take yours now too."

Eric made a snap decision. He thrust his syringes at Anatoli and headed past them to the flasks.

"No."

He heard both of them shout, but he ignored it. They'd stop once they realised it was too late. He reached the flasks. His nose was running. Don't sniff, he remembered.

He wiped his nose along his arm. A movement caught his eye. There was a girl in a crack in the rock wall. She was coughing and she had the lids for the flasks in her hands. Taunting him with them even as another cough contorted her body. He picked up the flasks and threw them at the crack. She ducked out the way and he heard the flasks rolling down a slope.

"You..." she was coughing and doubled up, "bastard."

He saw her disappear after the flasks. He followed, picking up the lids she had dropped in her latest coughing bout. He could see the narrow tunnel but no sign of her until he looked down and saw her convulsing on the floor. He coughed, and spat what had been generated out onto the floor.

He couldn't see the flasks. He moved past her and spotted one flask lying against the rock wall. He got to it and screwed the lid on. His chest felt like it was full of needles. He turned and saw the other flask near to her feet. He dropped to his knees and crawled to the flask. His hands ached as he screwed the lid on, but it wasn't just his hands, his legs and arms ached and twitched. Breathing became torture. Dropping the flask, he concentrated on crawling for the opening. He knew what Sarin did. He knew it was unlikely he was going to survive, but he kept crawling because he had to do something.

Glenn felt his chest loosen. Anatoli had handed him the Pralidoxime syringe shortly after he'd injected Eric's syringes. Glenn had been prepared to run up the tunnel without the antidotes, but Anatoli had whipped out his syringe of Atropine and tried to use it on him. There had been no time to explain, and when Eric had distracted him, Anatoli had taken advantage. Now they were both dosed, but Eric was somewhere in the side tunnel, with nothing.

Glenn knew the chances for Eric were slim, but they had to try. He'd heard something amongst the static when he'd tried to contact Enya. It had sounded like gunfire. He didn't think anyone was coming to their rescue and to be fair, they'd be a liability to anyone without antidotes till the Sarin broke down.

He nudged Anatoli who was doubled up and Anatoli nodded, straightening up. Glenn pointed at the crack with his torch. They staggered towards it. Glenn squeezed in first. He immediately saw Eric on the floor.

He was at Eric's feet, as Anatoli came through the crack. Together they manoeuvred Eric out of the small tunnel and began stumbling slowly up the Back Road with him between them.

When he thought they were far enough away, he nodded at Anatoli and they stopped, laying Eric down. Glenn checked his pulse. He was still alive at least. He looked up and saw Anatoli leaning one-handed and hunched against the rock wall. He saw the wrack progress up from his middle, and watched as Anatoli crumpled further and vomited. The smell made him want to be sick too. He turned and retched.

They made slow progress up the Back Road, stopping to rest every now and then. Seeing the terrain with the hand held torches made the going difficult. Glenn checked Eric every time. He couldn't believe he was still alive. This time he saw Anatoli check his phone for the LAN connection.

"Anything?" he rasped.

"No. But we must be getting close to the top end. I think it comes out into a derelict area at the commercial level. At least there won't be anybody around."

"I"m sure I heard gunfire when I spoke to Enya, we have to assume not all the other flasks got handed in."

"Shit. We've got to get Eric antidotes as soon as possible if he's to stand a chance."

"I know," said Glenn, contemplating asking his cousin to make an impossible choice to risk finding them.

Glenn saw Anatoli nod for another stop, but he was surprised since it hadn't been long since the last one.

"There's a draught. Should check."

"You go. I'll wait."

All their speech was now staccato phrasing.

It seemed longer than the few minutes it was, before he saw Anatoli in a stumbling run, coming back down.

"There's a door... opens into a room... got a signal... let them know..."

He heard Anatoli wheeze and then have a long hacking cough.

They carried Eric through the door into the room now lit by portable lights and inhabited by enviro-suited human shapes. One came towards them and bent down to Eric. Glenn saw the syringes empty into Eric's dirty arm, smeared in blood, sweat and snot. He hoped it would be enough.

Chapter Thirty- Decontamination

James heard the footsteps coming from behind the door he was leaning on. He shouted through his visor that the room was contaminated, and heard an answering okay, with a request to clear the door.

He rolled to the side as the door opened and three people in enviro-suits entered, closing the door behind themselves quickly.

"We've come to do the preliminary decontamination. You'll need to strip and step into these suits."

James took what looked a lot like a hooded, heavy duty polythene bag from the outstretched hand of the nearest suited guy. He started stripping off, concentrating on trying to keep the 'bag' as clear of the floor and his clothes as possible. When he looked up he could see Chris was covered in his bag with only his face showing. Enya was in her bag, but as usual, was having to gather up spare capacity in her hand. She was smiling over at him. He smiled back.

"Has anybody gone down the Back Road?" Enya asked.

James could hear her anxiety, he'd heard her call Eric over the visor during the fire fight, and as far as he was aware they'd heard nothing since from any of them.

The suited guy nearest her shook his head.

"We've been busy trying to limit the contamination, only got on top of it now to come and get you. Is this a fresh site of contamination?"

"Probably," said Enya.

James could hear her voice quaver. It was the most emotional he'd ever heard Enya. She was normally so cool. When she swore, that was when you knew she'd got angry, but this was different.

They all heard the guy call over the LAN to find out if anyone had information on the Back Road but James didn't hear what the answer was, the guy had realised he was broadcasting and killed the local comms. They were ushered out of the air plant and another two guys in enviro-suits passed them going in with jet washers and hazardous waste bags.

On the other side of the door was a plastic tent with compartments. They got scrubbed down, checked over, injected some more and given fresh clothes. He was too tired to ask what was in the syringes, but he felt better.

He saw Enya collar a guy and demand he call Mayor McAndrew. He knew Enya hated to be out of the loop, and their phones had been taken for decontamination, but there was more than that to her demands. He went over to her, while the guy was getting fobbed off at the first stage of contact.

"Boss."

She'd turned to look at him.

"Where are they?" she asked, "What if there were more flasks in the Back Road? I need to know."

He saw a man approaching, he could tell Enya recognised him.

"Captain," she said, "there's a potential incident somewhere on the Back Road with Cassie Galados."

"We've sent a team to search. You need to stay calm, you're recovering from Sarin poisoning, elevated blood pressure doesn't help. Here."

James saw the guy pass Enya a mobile. He wasn't convinced it would reduce Enya's blood pressure but it would certainly keep her off the militia's backs.

He could see her pressing buttons, and saw her face fall when the call failed to connect. He put his arm around her.

He'd never have dared, never have thought there would come a time when he would feel he needed to, but he knew it was the right thing to do. He saw Chris look over and nod.

"You can only try every ten minutes. Okay?" he said.

He was shrugged off as Enya nodded at him.

James watched as they brought out the bodies of the militia who'd been guarding the air plant when the two activists had struck. They were in the same heavy duty polythene bags but this time without a gap for faces. It was going to be hard for the families, he thought. And then he remembered, they'd not been able to stop the components getting into the humidifier unit. He stopped a woman who was about to go back into the plant room.

"How many?" he asked.

The woman answered him without emotion, "Fifty at last count. We have some in intensive care, but they'll hopefully make it."

James let go of her arm and sat down onto the ground. Fifty. It was too many. He saw Chris come over and he stood up.

"Don't let her ask," said Chris, "not now, not till we know what happened in the Back Road."

"She's got the mobile, she'll be focussed for a while on that. Hopefully she gets an answer soon."

They both turned to watch Enya sitting cross legged on the gurney bed they'd recently been checked on.

Anatoli was lying face down as instructed, when he felt the buzz in his pocket. He lifted the phone and saw an unfamiliar number.

"Hallo?"

What he heard next was the most beautiful thing he'd ever heard in his life. It was Enya. She was alive. He let her talk, just happy to hear her voice. It almost didn't matter the terrible things she was telling him.

An enviro-suited guy came up to him.

"You'll have to hang up. We need to decontaminate the phones, and your clothes, and then you. We've got a unit coming in the next few minutes."

"I've got to go, I love you," he interrupted her, feeling awful as he did it. He didn't want to go. The electronic signal bouncing from his mobile to the LAN and down to her mobile felt as solid and real as if it was a rope and now he was going to cut it.

He hung up and passed the guy his phone. It went into a smaller bio-hazard bag, and the guy gestured to him to put his clothes into a large bag. Anatoli realised he was going to spend time in Kunlun beyond Basics.

He could see them constructing the decontamination unit outside the apartment. The same guy came to collect his bag.

"Will I get my stuff back?"

"Only the phone, this kind of decontamination is quick and effective but destructive."

They were in fresh clothes waiting in the decontamination tent. Anatoli had lost sight of Eric once they'd gone inside. He didn't feel able to interrupt the busy coming and going of the decontamination team. They'd clearly come from somewhere else, the suits had scrape marks and stains on them. With the information Enya had been able to relay, he knew there'd been civilian casualties. They might have stopped it from being a disaster, but they hadn't been able to stop it completely. He felt empty as he thought about that. He would have been able to see whereabouts the air plant serviced if he still had his phone. It was maybe better he couldn't see what was in the area called Second.

A suited medic came past.

"Up onto the bed and lie on your front," they ordered.

"The guy we had with us, is he okay?"

"We've got him intubated, but he's not responding well."

"Thanks."

The medic moved on and Anatoli looked around for Glenn. He spotted him lying on his front on a nearby bed. He walked carefully over: his body not fully under his control.

"What you doing off the bed? Didn't they say lie on your front?" said Glenn, his voice muffled across his arm.

"Yeah, yeah. I'm a pilot remember, I'm built for chemical intoxication."

He heard Glenn's laugh turn into a hacking cough.

"Seriously, I just asked about Eric, he's not responding to treatment."

Glenn had lifted and twisted his top half, taking his weight on one arm. His other arm reached out, his hand meeting Anatoli's shoulder.

"It was always a long shot from the moment he ran past us to the flasks," said Glenn.

"Why did he do that?"

"Same reason you injected me," said Glenn.

He looked at Glenn, his face appeared honest and open, but Anatoli still felt guilty. He wondered if he should have tried more with Eric?

"It wasn't your fault," said Glenn.

Anatoli felt less convinced he didn't play a part though.

He wandered back to his bed and lay down on his front. Whether it was the movement pushing the drugs faster through his system or plain tiredness, he felt his eyes closing and he let them, thankful for the oblivion that sleep would offer him.

Jim McAndrew was in his office, behind his desk, feeling helpless. He glanced over at the exo-skeleton standing in the corner. The man who'd built it for him had been dead for ten years and nobody in the AFS it seemed, was able to get it to move again. He was left with the tracked chair and right now he felt its limitations keenly. He'd been kept up to date as much as possible both on the LAN and the UHF radio the militia had been using. He'd been able to co-ordinate the evacuation as soon as he'd got Enya's message from the air plant serving Second. It'd been a hard decision, knowing that there were four flasks still missing. Where to pull back the militia from to help with the evacuation? What he never would have guessed though, was that the secondary target would be the Back Road.

When he heard that he was worried. It had been so close to the mine heads. And now he still had a missing pair of flasks, with no idea who had them, or where they'd been. The Greens who'd handed their flasks in, had, to a person, been genuinely shaken to find out they had Sarin components. He'd questioned them individually. They'd all fingered Evan Redbarn and Cassie Galados and a few had mentioned a new guy called Lukas Brandt, but he'd got no other names from any of them. His suspicions had niggled away at him. He made the call he'd been putting off.

"Yang?"

"McAndrew."

He never expected to get anything from Yang she didn't want to give him. But was there something in her tone? Or was he just a bit paranoid now that sections of his community he'd previously trusted had betrayed him?

"We're still missing a pair of flasks."

He listened carefully to her voice as she answered.

"That's not good. Would you like me to look for them?"

He felt sure she had them. Maybe a wayward Green thought she could be persuaded. Could she? Was there a price she'd accept?

"I'd really appreciate that," he said, "If it was found as soon as possible then we would be able to stand down the emergency level."

"*I'd* really appreciate that," said Yang, "Business isn't so good when there's an emergency level in operation."

The line went dead. He hoped she did have them and wasn't about to turn the place upside down looking for them. Yang Lau could, on occasion, be less than subtle.

Chapter Thirty One - Fruitcake

Thierry Vonne was tall and angular, with dark latin looks. Some said he had a temperament to match. Passionate, was what his supporters said. A bully, was what others said. He didn't care either way. He had an agenda and that was to see the AFS adopt the UN eco-laws, to see an end to plastic manufacture and a reduction in mining activities.

He wasn't naive, he knew the climate was beyond resetting, and that you couldn't shift four hundred, thousand people off the islands of Antarctica even if you had somewhere to relocate them to. Rising sea level had put paid to that idea anyway. Across the world relocation was already happening within UN states from their own reshaped coastlines, they weren't about to take on more.

He'd tried to do it the right way. He'd got elected to the Senate and on an openly Green ticket. He'd been genuinely surprised at that, and pleased. It had given him hope, which the Senate and its interminable sub-committees had crushed in the two years since his election. Then he'd got a tip off about Rafael Dupont.

Someone he'd thought was a Green ally, was instead working with Global Corporation to profit from environmental catastrophes. And crucially getting away with it too. It was then he decided the right thing needed to encompass some wrong doing.

He'd contacted some European Greens, sounded them out about direct action. Those inquiries had led to the contact details for what they described as an eco-assassin. He had stepped back at that point but then he'd been contacted by Maddy Clearbright. The Networking Coordinator for the alliance of the AFS' Green movements, had notified him of a course being run in Vostok. She'd seemed concerned, told him she didn't recognise any of the contributors, and when he pressed her, admitted she'd like him to dig into the organisers' backgrounds. Everyone was mindful of what had happened in the past to the Resistance, and no-one wanted the Greens to go the same way. The Families saw themselves as the only legitimate political associations and they didn't like competition.

When he'd asked Blackie to sniff around, he'd found out it was Rafael Dupont backing it. That was when he looked again at the eco-assassin. She was supposed to simply report to him on the Vostok course, and she had. After that he'd lost touch with her. He thought that was just how these things went.

Then she turned up in Progress assassinating Greens. Dupont was behind some of that, he suspected, maybe even the attempt on her life. Now, she was recovering in hospital under Intelligence Agency security. He'd heard the State Negotiator had already visited her, and that worried him. He'd heard how good Alison Strang was.

If he was going down, then he was determined to take Rafael Dupont with him. His best friend Blackie had died trying to put things right and Thierry's own part in this was bound to be uncovered. Dupont couldn't be allowed to wriggle out like he always did, and just because they'd arrested him didn't mean he was going to Denam. Look at how Gordon Murcheson had managed to evade the hardship of prison and end up under house arrest. No. Rafael would be dead, one way or another, because Thierry knew it was a firing squad that waited for him.

What he'd done was treason. He was under no illusion about that.

Sitting at home he was thinking it all through, having missed the Senate for nearly a week. How would he get to Rafael before they came for him next? People were already asking about his absence. The news channel was burbling in the background till he was interrupted in his thoughts by the TV suddenly trumpeting a breaking story.

Kunlun had suffered a terrorist attack linked to the Greens. Thierry felt his plan collapse around him. He had only one play left to make. He called Nikau Burns. His gut turned in revulsion, even as he heard Nikau pick up. It felt like selling out. Nikau worked for the President and Mariko Neish would expect something in return for saving him. However, he reasoned it was better to stay a Green Senator who owed a debt to the President, than to be a Green Senator who was shot for treason, if it meant he could take Dupont down.

Enya woke. For the briefest of moments she didn't remember, then it all came back and she felt the weight of guilt return. She should have investigated the Greens earlier. Should have looked into why Dupont didn't go to prison for his part in disposing of Arnaud Cheung. And she should have been keeping a much closer eye on Mariko Neish and Nikau Burns. People had died, both innocent and guilty, and the guilty had taken their information to the grave with them. Pushing her own guilt aside she filled the space with a determination to make those remaining give up all their secrets.

She got out of the bed, careful not to disturb Tolli. They'd finally all been allowed back to the State Accommodation last night, and she'd attempted a debrief session but it had become clear everyone was still processing. Voices were flat, beyond tired. She'd sent them to bed almost immediately.

No one had talked about Eric, but he was obviously on everyone's mind. Especially on Anatoli's, she had found out when they were alone.

He'd told her it was his fault and she'd argued with him, realising quickly she'd not get through right now. Everything was raw, and she'd have to wait for a more rational time to talk with him about it.

She got dressed, went into the common room and saw the coffee had been refreshed. She was sitting at the table with a cup when Glenn appeared.

"How's Anatoli?" he asked.

"Still saying it was his fault."

"Oh Enya, it was mine. If I hadn't given Reuben my doses, Eric would be fine. How does he think it was his? Do you want me to speak to him?"

"No, thanks. I think we all need a bit of time to pass. I was going to call the hospital shortly and ask after Eric, find out what the total is, and then arrange to meet with the mayor."

"I'll stay here, see what I can do to collect the information we have together, I managed a call through to Alison last night, she said she'd spoken to Isadora. But that can wait."

Enya sharpened at the name. Glenn was right, it could wait, and she fought the urge to change tack. She found the number for the hospital and the one for the mayor from the city information net, putting them both into the address book. She wondered when they'd get their own phones back.

The hospital rang for a while.

"Hello? This is Detective Zhao from the Anti-corruption Team, I'm enquiring about the status of Eric Jordan, one of my team?"

She waited while she was transferred and the ringing started again. She repeated her request, trying hard to sound neutral, the hospital would have been overwhelmed, she knew she should be more patient. But a knot was forming between her shoulder blades, she could sense something was wrong. The nurse who'd answered at the ward had asked her to wait and it was a man's voice she heard next.

"No... How?"

She saw Glenn looking worried at her. She couldn't stop the tears beginning.

"Thank you."

She put the phone down on the table, wiped her eyes and sniffed.

"Eric's dead. Tetanus. Cuts on his hands and knees when he was crawling in the tunnel."

"Tetanus? Doesn't that take days?" asked Glenn.

"Not here apparently. Everyone assumed he'd had a shot down at the decontamination site and when they found out it was too late."

She felt the heat in her eyes start over. Another thing to feel guilty about. She had offered him the job that had brought him here.

Glenn had stood up and come round to sit next to her.

"It's not your fault. He made his own decisions."

"He saved Anatoli..."

"Enya, " interrupted Glenn, "you said yourself we need distance. Call the mayor, let's get all the bastards who've led to this. Then we can look at our own roles."

She looked at Glenn, remembering how she'd helped him in the Environment Department building to search for Alison. He'd stayed focussed, and so should she.

She dialled the mayor's office.

"Mayor McAndrew," she started.

"I've heard from the hospital about your team member. My condolences to you and your team. I'm so sorry."

"Thank you, I just heard. Do you have a death total?"

"It's still standing at fifty. Everyone in hospital is expected to make it."

"Oh, that's good. I'd like to meet this morning."

"I agree, I'll speak to Captain Stanley."

"The militia captain, yes, but also Yang Lau. I understand that might be difficult. But she attended a Green course in Vostok, she has information we need."

"I'll see what I can do, but I have no control over her."

"Thank you, see you at ten."

She put the phone down checking the time. Half an hour. What was she going to tell Tolli?

"The deaths are still fifty," she said, "There's fewer in intensive care and they reckon everyone will pull through."

She heard the door open behind her and looked at Glenn for help, but then the outside door opened and Chris and James came in. Her team was all here. There was no putting it off. She waited till they were all sitting down at the table.

"Eric's dead," she said, "Not from Sarin. There was a mix up and they didn't know he'd not had a tetanus shot. I want you all to get shots. I don't care if you think you're all right. I'm meeting the mayor at ten. Hopefully Yang Lau will be there and we can get some info on the Vostok course."

She kept going, not wanting to give anyone a chance to speak, "Glenn has spoken with Alison, Isadora is talking. I want someone to get in touch with Ray at Progress. Someone to speak to Valla at Weddell City, I want info on Nikau Burns, the President, Rafael Dupont and Thierry Vonne. Glenn, get back in touch with Alison. Anatoli find Chick and get the jets ready to move. We're not going to sit here and wallow in what we could, or should, have done differently. Do I make myself clear?"

Sweeping the table in a look, she hoped it made her appear harder than she felt. Seeing them nodding back at her, she trusted them not to let her know if it didn't.

She left the room. It wouldn't take long to get to the mayor's office but she couldn't stay. It wasn't leadership. She knew that. But having relied on her gut feeling to build the team, she relied on it now. She had to leave them to work together.

Though it had never been a busy thoroughfare, the walk to the main lift was quiet. There was almost no-one around. When the lift doors opened there was only the operator. She checked her phone to see if the emergency level was still active and saw it was still in force. Maybe the mayor was being cautious?

She stepped out onto the main concourse, it had a few militia patrolling. She was approached by a pair.

"Agent Zhao?"

"Detective, but yes."

"The mayor is happy to see you now. If you'd follow us."

She fell into step with the two of them. They headed over to a shop front, which should have been closed because of the emergency level, but seemed to be unlocked. It struck her as too cloak and dagger to be the mayor. She expected she'd find Yang Lau on the other side of the door. She wasn't wrong.

"Yang Lau, I presume?"

She faced another Frederika Tran. There was definitely family ties there, she thought.

Another woman was in the room, but Yang didn't introduce her.

"Detective Zhao. I understand you'd like to know about the course in Vostok?"

"Yes. Do you know who organised it and if so, can you prove it?"

"I know it was Rafael Dupont. Proof is your job, is it not detective?"

"Fair. What was discussed?"

"There was talk of direct action. Almost all the delegates agreed. One or two were reticent about saying so at first."

She saw Yang nod at the other woman.

"We took notes, I've made you a copy."

She took the sheaf, and knew it was all she'd get from Yang, but she couldn't resist asking.

"What did you make of Isadora Ley?"

She saw Yang smile, as if she knew exactly how Enya felt about Isadora.

"Interesting lady," drawled Yang, "nuttier than a fruit cake, as my gran would say. Stay well away from her is my advice. But I can see you won't take it."

She turned away from Yang to leave.

"Half aunt. I'm sure you were wondering."

She turned to look again at Yang but there was no one in the room now. She left the shop. There was no sign of the two militia guys either. Arriving at the mayor's office, the militia captain, who'd seen her approach, was holding the door.

Chapter Thirty Two - Limpets

"Nikau, this is Senator Vonne. I was wondering, is it possible to meet? With you and the President?"

Thierry had tried hard to keep his voice neutral, as if this call was about something completely different from one which, he hoped, would save his skin, but he wasn't convinced he'd pulled it off when he heard Nikau reply.

"Senator Vonne, I'm presuming this is a delicate matter, to call me rather than the president's secretary. I am of course, well known for my role in delicate matters."

He changed tack immediately, Nikau was an expert negotiator, the best thing to do was to keep to his path.

"It is indeed delicate. I understand you have Rafael Dupont in custody and there is the matter of the Green activists involved in Progress and Kunlun. I make no secret of my Green credentials, I'd like to make sure the whole movement isn't going to be tainted by the acts of rogue activists."

He thought Nikau had taken the bait.

"I can call the President," said Nikau, "see if she has room in her schedule. She's aware the Green movement is very popular amongst the youth and I know she wants to involve them, make them feel their voices have been heard. Let me get back to you."

He heard Nikau hang up but didn't feel more secure. It felt too easy: he played the conversation back in his head and felt he was being set up somehow, but he couldn't be sure that the feeling wasn't just paranoia. He needed to make his appeal direct to Mariko and the best way was through Nikau, but it wouldn't stop him making a plan B.

Alison felt tired despite just waking up. Talking to Isadora had been hard going. She felt it was akin to prising a limpet off a rock; difficult to do, not good for the limpet and ultimately it would only be used as bait.

She'd realised she was still stressing about Glenn being at Kunlun and was concerned her techniques had had little impact on her emotions from both.

She was going to meet with Kairns this morning to discuss how to bring the evidence provided by Karl and Isadora together. They were quite the pair, she thought, already aware from Isadora of the history between them, if not the gory details.

She'd spent an anxious couple of hours after the gas attack news broke, till she'd heard from Glenn and she didn't want to experience that again. More and more, she knew, she was avoiding thinking about her feelings, and soon she would have to stop and fix that. If she just got Karl and Isadora out the way, she promised herself it would happen.

The taxi was waiting at the apartment block car park, taking her to the Intelligence Agency building where she hurried through the security. Kairns was waiting in the lobby.

"Alison, thanks for coming over so early."

"Don't worry, I didn't get much sleep anyway."

"You've heard from Glenn?"

"Yes. He couldn't tell me much though."

"They've lost an agent. Eric Jordan."

She gasped.

"You knew him?" asked Kairns.

"A bit."

She wasn't going to mention Anatoli now, there was no point.

"I'm sorry."

Kairns was ushering her into a ground floor meeting room. As she entered she saw Valla and a naval captain sitting at one end of a large glass table.

"Valla. I'm probably not surprised. How's Martin?"

It was out before she even thought about the unknown captain sitting next to Valla. Shit, I'm really not with it, she thought. She checked Valla's face to see how badly she'd messed up but got a smile in return.

"Alison, this is Captain Ian Khan of the MS Coulter. He assures me the whole fleet is keeping my secret."

She gave a small embarrassed laugh and sat down.

"Martin's doing well," continued Valla, "they said he'll make a full recovery. How's Glenn?"

"Alive. But I've been told they lost Eric Jordan."

Kairns had followed her into the room and was now pulling out a chair opposite her.

"Tetanus," he said, "a strain specific to Kunlun. Well, now we've done introductions, let's get down to business."

She saw him nod at her. She started.

"Isadora Ley, real name Enid Decourcey, a Lower Saxony native. Active in the Green movement since her mid teens, a history of childhood abuse before that, pretty nasty stuff judging by some of her reactions. She suspects Thierry Vonne sent her the citizen ID and invitation to the Vostok conference. She sent a report on the course to an anonymous drop box location. She's less convinced it was Thierry who contracted her to kill Steve Jung. She's not daft, and she's had plenty of time to try and figure out who set her up. She's pretty much decided it was Rafael Dupont, and she's certain Karl Leyden tried to assassinate her. But it's hard to separate how she feels about Karl and her train of logic there. I'd appreciate some clarity, if there is any, on that."

Kairns nodded.

"Karl Leyden, real name. Technically stateless, although he has both an out of date AFS ID and a fake Nederland passport. He's revealed he helped Rafael Dupont to encourage direct action amongst Green supporters, he claims it was to create a demand for change, as per his Manifesto for a Green World. He also claims Isadora wasn't paid by Rafael because it was Rafael who ordered the hit on her. He admits he was the sniper."

Alison saw Valla was looking impatient.

"Do they know anything more about Thierry though?" asked Valla.

"Karl said he made a point of avoiding him. It seemed he wanted to take Rafael down but not Thierry. He'd no idea about Jonathan Blackbird Renner. I'm sure of that."

"So," said Valla "Rafael Dupont was trying to stir it amongst the Greens, maybe make it difficult for them to realise they were being used by the Planetary Cooperation Group. We've got Rafael. What do we have on Thierry?"

Alison could tell Valla remained agitated, which was never a good thing.

"Thierry Vonne fraudulently obtained a citizenship ID for a person who did not merit one. He hired an internationally wanted eco-assassin. It's enough to arrest him for undermining the state, and then we can find out more," said Kairns.

"Treason," said Valla.

Alison saw Ian Khan look at his boss.

"Senator Torres," said Ian, "the lesser charge is the safer charge, and more can be added. Let's not forget Nancy

Carter's going to be able to finance several European holidays out of the impending trials."

She saw Valla soften.

"You're right Ian. Let's add the nails slowly. But I foresee a problem and I want to act in a timely manner. I don't trust Mariko."

Alison had already heard the idea that President Mariko Neish had withheld evidence in respect of Rafael Dupont. Now Valla was suggesting she'd protect Thierry Vonne too. What would Mariko gain, she wondered?

"I can get an arrest warrant today on what we have, for the lesser charge," said Kairns.

Alison saw him stand, heading to the far corner of the room on his mobile.

"We need the Anti-corruption Team if we're going to investigate the President," she said to Valla, "Glenn said Enya was keen to get back to Weddell City. What can we do to prepare for them?"

"I'll have a word with Nikau, remind him of his loyalties," said Valla.

"I'd like to talk to Karl, and to Rafael again," said Alison looking up at Kairns who'd returned to stand at the table.

"I have limited jurisdiction on the Coulter," he said, with a nod to Captain Khan, "But you're welcome to Rafael. He's mostly blabbered stuff we already know, but there was some useful information on the Planetary Cooperation Group, and we've arrested who we can."

Alison looked at him, "River Sampson, Victoria Beauchamp?"

"For the moment, yes. We don't need to show our hand yet," he answered. "I've just issued a warrant for the arrest of Thierry Vonne. If he thinks Mariko will protect him, I suspect he'll be in custody shortly." He continued, looking meaningfully at her, " You'll have to get to him before she does."

"Where? I'll be waiting."

"Stay here, make yourself comfy. I'll let you know."

She saw he was pointing at the coffee flask and a basket full of high energy snack bars. She smiled, knowing Kairns' fondness for the snacks.

"I'm heading over to the Senate," said Valla, "Captain Khan, continue to detain the terrorist Karl Leyden onboard your vessel."

Alison saw she was determined to hang onto Karl Leyden regardless of how it looked to the outside political world. It seemed Valla had lost her last shred of trust in the President. She watched Ian Khan nod and leave.

"Are you sure?" she asked, when he'd left.

"Yes," said Valla.

Alison knew better than to argue against Valla's one word answers.

She watched Valla and Kairns leave the room and settled down to wait. It was the perfect time to examine her feelings, but before she could delve inside, her phone rang. It was Glenn, they were leaving Kunlun shortly, via Slessor Station. He told her it would take eight hours, providing there were no interruptions, bringing them into Weddell City just after eight in the evening.

Anatoli was transporting Eric's body back in his jet, while the team were travelling in the new charter's jet. She felt for Anatoli and understood why he'd offered. Though, she knew from Glenn's voice, there were things she wasn't being told about what had happened. There was more than tetanus to this.

She sat back in the chair and let her mind wander. It shot straight to her worries about Glenn, and Enya's team in general. She teased at the hints and evasions she'd heard in Glenn's phone calls and even Kairns this morning. She knew whatever had happened to Eric was loaded with guilt for Glenn but Kairns had been more reticent about the loss.

Kairns wasn't Enya's boss, but Alison could sense he was going to make a play for the team to align more with the Intelligence Agency in future. She didn't think it would be long before Kairns was in charge at a national level. He had a bureaucrat's sensibilities with a spy's ruthlessness. She thought he'd be quite good at the job, but knew Glenn wouldn't agree. And, she was back worrying about Glenn.

The Murchesons needed to allocate blame, and they were quite sure once they'd decided on who, even if it was themselves, that they were right about it too.

Glenn's grandfather, Gordon, had the knack of never thinking he'd been to blame, while she knew from experience Glenn could take it on easily. Thinking about guilt she realised Anatoli had ended up in difficult position, and even she found it hard not to apportion some blame for that to Enya, but Alison could understand how it had come about.

She continued to work through her thoughts and feelings, weaving the minutia she'd picked up, analysing them into a framework she would hang the details on, when the team arrived in Weddell City that evening.

Two hours later, her reverie was disturbed by the opening of the door. It felt too little time for Thierry to be in custody, so she braced for bad news. She expected Kairns, but instead was surprised to see Nikau Burns come into the room.

"Alison, they told me I could find you here. I'd like to run something past you?"

She was even more surprised. Nikau was usually very assured in his decisions, she didn't think there was an ulterior motive at play though, he sounded genuinely uncertain.

"Yes. Should I be in State Negotiator mode for this?"

She heard him laugh, it wasn't a happy laugh.

"Probably," he said.

She watched him sit down, drinking in his body language. He was torn, both options looked like they were bad. She felt perhaps he'd lost his way working for Mariko Neish instead of Valla. She'd never thought there was much to the Families set up in Antarctica, but now she realised they did have their own distinct cultures. Maybe Nikau had spent too long in the Lomonosov culture for his own good?

"I heard there's a warrant out for Thierry Vonne. He called me yesterday evening wanting to meet with Mariko. I think he wanted to cut a deal and I think Mariko will make one with him. I can see why it would be good. I can see why it would be bad. I know Enya is coming for Mariko too, which is right, but also the worst thing that could happen right now. I can't ask Valla for her opinion because she can't see past revenge on Thierry."

Alison had known Nikau had a conundrum, but she'd never thought it was something as big as this. What she said now would impact to a deep level in AFS politics. More than anything she'd done as a Special Stranger or even a State Negotiator. She worked on the implications of each possible decision, the way a chess player thinks many moves ahead. She was searching for something that felt the right thing to do, and harder than that, something that would feel the right thing to Nikau too.

She saw him sit back in the chair as she continued to think. He'd seen her in action many times, she knew he would give her the time.

Chapter Thirty Three - Hubbub

The atmosphere in the team jet had been subdued, but Enya thought it would have been worse if Tolli hadn't offered to transport Eric Jordan's body back in his jet. She was worried about him though.

He'd been very quiet at Slessor Station while they'd been refuelling, it was a side to him she'd not experienced before and she felt at a loss to know what to say, so they'd just sat next to each other, holding hands quietly. It had been hard not to say something, her entire personality was about action, but it was also about doing the right thing, and something deep in her gut told her this was the right thing.

Now they'd landed at Weddell City and she was in the airport office processing the paperwork for Eric's body to be held in the local morgue till his family were traced. She'd called the police as soon as she could in Kunlun, only to find out he had no next of kin listed. She was determined to find out why and if necessary organising something herself.

The rest of the team had already headed to the Intelligence Agency building: Valla had said that was where they'd bring Thierry Vonne when they found him. Enya would've preferred it to have been Weddell City Police but she also sensed Valla wanted this arrangement and she wasn't going to argue with Valla, yet.

The time was coming however; Karl Leyden shouldn't still be on the MS Coulter; but she'd no desire to take on Valla and Mariko Neish at the same time, and she considered the President more of a concern than Senator Valentina Torres right at this moment.

She passed through the Intelligence Agency security and headed for the ground floor meeting room. Stepping inside, it felt more like an operations room than a meeting room. The table was littered in papers and opened laptops, an incomprehensible spider diagram sprawled across a whiteboard at the far end and she could see Valla, Kairns and Chris all on their phones in different corners. James and Glenn were head-down in their laptops.

She saw Alison look up from some papers she was reading, and wave her over.

"This looks serious," she said to Alison sitting down.

"Thierry has disappeared, there's obviously concern after Kunlun about what he might do," said Alison.

"But that was Rafael's nutters, stirred up to act."

"Try telling them that," replied Alison.

"Where do you think he's gone?"

"Nikau came to me this afternoon, said Thierry wanted to meet the President. He asked me what he should do."

"And?"

"I said Mariko would be doomed if she met with Thierry, the warrant was issued for undermining the state, she couldn't meet someone wanted for that."

"Too right."

"It looks like Thierry figured that out on his own, when Nikau tried to get back in touch, there was no reply. The airport and port are locked down. It comes down to how well connected the Green network is, and how much they'll do for him. Hence the..."

She saw Alison sweep the room with her hand.

"Is Chris talking to Ray?"

"I think so. She got access to Renner's phone while you were in Kunlun and there's evidence Thierry told Renner to kill Persimon Coia."

"Good. But where do you think he's gone?"

"Well, now he knows it's hopeless, I think he's going to do something spectacular, not destructive. He's aiming for martyrdom, a 'popular hero' level of death."

"Wow. Valla'll give it to him too. Have you tried to talk to her about it?"

"I was waiting for back up."

"We've got to get her to see that: before he's found. Know any appropriate Art of War quotes?"

She saw Alison smile, and beyond her, Chris was coming towards them.

"Boss," he said, "Ray's been speaking to Maddy Clearbright, the Green coordinator, apparently someone has found out where the office for the Planetary Cooperation Group is located, here in Weddell City. It went up on their social media accounts two hours ago."

"That's where he'll go," said Alison, "A perfect last stand. He'll probably take hostages to begin with. That allows him to make demands that have to be broadcast. They'll be Green policy changes. Then he'll release the hostages, and it'll end in a bloody shoot out. Voila, martyrdom."

"Where are the offices?" she asked Chris.

Chris came next to her and showed her his phone. There was a familiar pattern of streets, the beginning of Torres Boulevard out by the hospital. She saw the red flag marker on a block on the corner of Lomonosov and Jacobsen. She understood his unwillingness to say anything out loud. She nodded at Alison.

"Valla," said Alison above the hubbub in the room, "Got a minute?"

Enya saw Valla turn round, finish her call and pocket her phone. There was the familiar stride round the table to where they were both standing.

"Outside, I think," said Alison.

Enya was surprised that Valla complied without question, but she could see the curiosity in Valla's eyes.

"What?" said Valla.

Enya thought the tone was sharper than Valla had intended. She saw Alison give her a look.

"I'm talking as your friend now, Valla. You have to take Thierry alive and under no circumstances should he be allowed to go down a martyr."

"You know where he is?"

Enya could see Valla's anger hadn't blunted her perceptions in any way.

"We do, and we want to take him quietly. Trust me on this," said Alison.

Enya saw Valla soften more and wondered why Alison had waited.

"Okay. How?"

"You're good with this idea?" Enya asked.

"If you and Alison think this is best, then it's clear I'm letting my emotions get the better of me."

And Enya had her answer.

"Let's go back in and let the boys in on the deal," she said.

When they went back, the hubbub died instantly. All eyes were on them.

"Would you like to share?" asked Kairns.

Enya walked up to the whiteboard, and wrote the address down.

"As of a few hours ago this address was posted on the Green network as the location of the Planetary Cooperation Group offices. Alison believes this is where Thierry will be. She also says he's willing to martyr himself, and use us to do it. He's going to stage a hostage situation and demand Green policy changes. We cannot allow this behaviour. It would be an open invitation to any disgruntled group in future. Nor can we make him a martyr. So, gentlemen, how are we going to do this quietly?"

She looked directly at James Wylie as she finished.

"Why's he not taken the hostages already?" asked Kairns.

"Because he has to be seen to be provoked at every turn. It's basic martyrdom rules," replied Alison.

"Oh, they made me do it, I'm just a victim?" asked Glenn.

"Exactly."

"If only we had a willing Green activist," said Enya, thinking of a few back in Progress.

"Thierry must know most of the ones in Weddell City, but he wouldn't know many in Progress to see," said Chris.

"Colin?" she asked.

"George would be better."

"So someone's going to pretend to be this George character, arrived from Progress, and try to get close to Thierry at the Planetary office? Where he probably is already, waiting to act." said Valla.

Enya felt she was unduly harsh on the evolving plan, but had some fair points. There needed to be a reason for Thierry to accept 'George' joining him, and a plausible back story. And how was that person going to lure Thierry to a spot where James could make an accurate, non-fatal, yet disabling shot?

"We need plans for the block, and the layout of the office within it. Vantage points in nearby buildings with a view of as much of the office as possible," said Valla, answering much of her question.

Enya saw Alison smile, it would appear the General was back onboard.

"I can get you all that," said Kairns, "but it's useless unless you have someone you can trust that Thierry doesn't recognise."

Enya realised that was a problem. Thierry would recognise Kairns, Glenn, James, herself, probably Chris, and definitely anyone Valla could come up with... or would he? He wouldn't know all the naval personnel, they rarely had a need to come to Weddell City.

"Who's the XO on the Coulter?" she asked.

She saw Valla stop typing on her laptop.

"Binh Mitchell," Valla paused, "He's the right age, he can certainly bluff his way around Progress, been with us from the start before we banned most shoreside visits."

"They'd have to volunteer. This is not within the navy's remit," cautioned Kairns.

"I interviewed Binh, he'll be up for it," said Valla, "I'll call the Coulter."

Enya heard a printer start up somewhere near the whiteboard at the back of the room.

"This'll be the plans," said Kairns.

The hubbub began again, this time over the noise of the printer.

Anatoli had seen the airport handlers take Eric's body away, and he'd intended to lock up and go home. Maybe have a drink, go to bed, even though he knew he'd not be sleeping. It seemed like that would be the sensible thing to do. But as he played with his keys at the foot of the jet's steps, he realised it wasn't what he wanted to do.

What he wanted to do was get the fuck out of Weddell City. As far as was safe, possibly further. He'd never felt so reckless, so loose about what to do next. As a pilot, he planned; he posted flight plans, he checked the weather, he checked the jet. He always made sure.

But having a plan hadn't saved Eric. They'd dragged him out of the tunnel and he'd still been alive, but... Anatoli's mind faltered, he could rationalise all the failings, the little steps on the way to Eric's death, but he still couldn't take himself out of those steps. His memory of Eric's face as Eric thrust the antidotes at him, came at him again. The cool determination against his own panicked thoughts.

He climbed back up the steps. Once in the cockpit he called for a fuel line. Maybe he'd head for Polar Station, persuade someone to let him use a gel bed. Or something more hedonistic, the Ice Cabin near Melchior. He had a look at the weather and let it decide for him, posting the flight plan. The tower asked him for his flying time so far. He lied. Told them he'd started in Slessor Station. They okayed it.

He felt giddy with the idea, but once he was in the air the old senses kicked in and he just flew. The weather had pointed him at the Ice Cabin, and he was on his way. He still wasn't sure what he'd do when he got there, but at least it wasn't Weddell City, it wasn't near the politics, the Navy, Intelligence or Anti-corruption. And if it had Greens, they better be drinking, he thought.

Chapter Thirty Four - Excitation

Chris was leaning over the jigsaw of printed sheets that showed the layout of the Planetary Cooperation Group's office block and its neighbour. He and James were trying to work out where the best views were, when his phone buzzed. He left James with his ruler and pencil and moved outside the room.

He was surprised to hear Chick the charter pilot. She sounded surprised herself.

"I didn't know whether to call or not."

"Oh?" he asked, wondering where this was going.

"I saw Anatoli, he posted a flight to Melchior, somewhere called the Ice Cabin. He'd have had to lie about his hours to post another flight. I don't want him to get into trouble, but he didn't look right."

"Ah. Thanks Chick, you've not got him in trouble, quite the opposite. Could I ask a favour?"

"Sure."

She sounded genuine, she always had, it was one of the things he'd liked about her when they'd been introduced by a mutual friend.

"When you can, will you go up and check he's all right? The Team will pay."

"It won't be for another six hours, but I can do that."

"Thanks, Chick, and, can you only call me? I don't want to worry Enya."

"Sure. See you around Chris."

He hung up and went back in the room. Nobody had noticed him go or come except James.

"I've got a few spots I can reach," James was saying, "all from the same place, if he goes into this room here..."

Chris saw James point to a long room, probably a meeting room that had an almost exact match in the office block opposite.

"Maybe we give Binh a map, or something that will need a big table to roll out?" he suggested.

"Yeah, that could work, the lights would be on too. I'd prefer a visual confirmation, I don't want to make any mistakes based on thermal imaging alone."

Chris recalled the bus driver in Vostok that James had thought was the UN special forces guy, and the fake Freddie in Denam prison. He understood why James had developed a need to know it was the right person. Neither of those were James' fault but Chris knew how hard it could be to live with mistakes that had cost people their lives.

He had decided early on, the job absolved him of unforeseen mistakes, and he didn't spend time on the few he'd made, not least because he sensed it was a hole down which he could lose himself. He knew not everyone could manage that.

Chris heard the door open, looking up he saw someone who could only be Binh Mitchell walk in. The Executive Officer of the MS Coulter was heading towards Valla, who'd also looked up when the door had opened.

Chris saw a short man, high cheekbones, narrow eyes, with a stocky frame, rather than the slightness you might expect, and Chris watched how he approached Valla. It could tell you a lot about a person. Binh didn't look awed, deferential but perfectly confident in his right to be in the room and Chris thought he'd be fine with what they were going to ask him to do. He was more confident about the plan now, even before Binh spoke.

He was about to turn back to the office block layouts when he noticed Enya gesturing him over. He hoped it wasn't something about Anatoli, but he was sure he'd have noticed that in her expression.

"Ray's called, there's fresh information from Perry Coia's phone, it proves Rafael didn't hire Isadora. It might be what we need to get our 'George' close to him. I bet Thierry would have suspicions about who hired Isadora. I know I do."

"That's good," he said, "James says Binh should take something that needs to be examined in the room he's picked, we're thinking something that needs rolled out."

"If we make it a micro-file, it would need the meeting room projector. Thierry won't be able to resist the chance to broadcast the information once he's checked it out."

Enya's phone buzzed and Chris saw her check the number. He thought he saw brief disappointment as she answered.

"Nikau."

Chris watched Enya's face move into familiar hawk-like calculation. Whatever Nikau was telling her had captured her entire focus. He was glad, it meant she wouldn't worry about Anatoli for a while.

He saw her put the phone down and motion to him to move to a quieter corner of the room.

"Nikau has had people watching Mariko recently, he was suspicious she was hiding something and he was right. Now he's got evidence Mariko hired Isadora, making it look like it was Rafael. I need to go over there now, with you and Glenn."

Chris recalled the meeting where doubts were first aired about President Mariko, at the time he'd treated them as feasible but unlikely. But he knew Nikau didn't make mistakes, he was the Torres' fixer, first for Valla's father then for Valla, and he always made sure.

"Are you going to tell the rest?"

"I don't know. I'm concerned about Valla. She's taken a bit of persuading to go along with taking Thierry out quietly, if she knows about Mariko she might get in our way. But we should keep Kairns in the loop."

"And we're just going to leave? Expect her not to notice?" he said, looking round the room.

He could see Valla bent over the office plans with Binh and James. Kairns was on the phone in a corner near to them. Alison and Glenn were talking together. Despite his question they could probably walk out now without too much trouble. He took Enya's arm, felt a brief resistance till she noticed the situation. Together they left the room.

Outside in the lobby he texted Glenn, while Enya was texting Kairns. He nodded to Enya and they headed down to the car park. As soon as their car was free of the building both their phones chimed with a solar alert.

"Shit," he said, automatically apologising as soon as he'd sworn.

He could see Enya's face, looking determined in the orange light of the radar. The energy saving had kicked in and it was entirely dark outside save for a few lights shining out from offices higher up. He turned for the Senate.

"No," said Enya, "She's not going to be there. Nikau said she was at home."

"Well, unless she's got access to VLF, she's not going to be alerted to us coming now."

"Might I remind you neither do we," said Enya, "there's no way to call for back up."

"Let's hope it's a false alarm," he said without any conviction.

He swung away and headed past the Senate for the nearby residential district. Diplomats and politicians mostly lived near to the Senate, in one of three luxury apartment blocks off Murcheson Road. Square footage was always a premium in the AFS, and most of these apartments could house two or three apartments from elsewhere.

He knew there would be CCTV, and it would still be working. If they drove into the car park of Mariko's block they'd be seen, and recognised. He knew Enya also preferred arriving on foot in these situations. He scouted ahead on the radar and found a sheltered service area for an adjacent office block.

"This do you?" he asked Enya.

Enya was leaning forward to check the radar, pointing at the middle block.

"That's hers," she said, "Top floor. This'll have to do."

He stopped the car and the lights went out. Momentarily savouring the total darkness, he pulled his visor down and saw Enya's pale blue suit and yellow face out the corner of his eye. He zipped up and prepared himself for the blast of freezing air on his exposed cheeks.

As a boy he had loved the dark and the coldness. It seemed so adventurous, so open to possibilities. He was always disappointed the feeling quickly evaporated once it was illuminated either by white light or infrared. He felt the old tingle of excitement as they stepped out into the black.

The wind was light but he already knew from the car readout the temperature was minus twelve. The walk was no problem at that value and he recalled when a winter temperature was usually minus twenty something, even in the city. There was no doubt things were changing and he wondered again about some of the things Thierry Vonne had said in interviews.

It was easy to see how the man could hold an audience, he was very charismatic, but Chris had studied environmental science. He knew Thierry over simplified a lot and missed out anything inconvenient. Yet if you didn't know, and it was only your experience of warmer winters, you'd be daft not to sign up to Thierry's vision.

He hoped James would be successful. Whatever he and Enya managed with Mariko, it was more important he felt, that Thierry was neutralised as a political force. He had no idea what Enya was going to do. She was famously tight with information and plans, but having worked alongside her for eight years, he was certain she had no plan. Which made him more excited somehow. The possibilities lay not in the dark but in the unknown mind of his boss.

They entered the service door at the side of the building: a benefit of the Team being universal access. The area was still covered by CCTV of course and Mariko's people would have minutes to prepare for them. He wondered what they'd do.

They headed for the service lift and he saw Enya punch up the floor below the penthouse apartments. She was clearly expecting resistance of some sort. He understood now why she'd wanted Glenn along with them. He'd told Glenn what they were doing but at that point had expected Mariko to be at the Senate. If Glenn was following he was more than minutes behind them.

James and Kairns had headed out to the office block opposite the Planetary Cooperation Group's. In about twenty minutes, Binh would arrive by taxi as agreed.

They entered the meeting room, leaving the lights off, and James headed to the window to set up. When it was work, he never experienced the tingling nerves that came with competitions. The seriousness seemed to be enough to absorb the adrenalin and channel him into a heightened state.

He could hear every rustle of Kairns' clothing, the soft crunch of the carpet in the room. As he looked through his scope on thermal imaging, he could see the wafts of yellow in the meeting room from the ducted-air heating, and he could even make out the faintest yellow edge to the room door.

"That's him going in," said Kairns.

James concentrated on being calm, and let time flow without any extra encouragement.

Binh Mitchell stepped out of the taxi. He had the fake ID showing him as George Tan, tailor, Progress City. He had Thierry's mobile number from Renner's phone. He had the file that would need the projector in the meeting room to view it. He had his civilian weapon, and a nagging feeling this could still go horribly wrong.

He recognised the feeling as an old friend, shook its hand and put it to one side. He knew it seldom went wrong, and this was just the way his mind prepared for action.

A second solar alert pinged across the AFS, heralding the imminent arrival of an M8 class, coronal mass ejection; a polar orbit satellite succumbed to the onslaught of high energy particles in the CME as they wreaked havoc with its circuitry before it completed shutdown. On the ground all non-essential systems were shutting down to protect the energy grids. There needed to be somewhere power surges could go, and the networks were designed to spread the extra energy. But it could still go wrong.

Chapter Thirty Five - Burning

Enya and Chris had reached the penthouse floor. She saw Chris carefully push the stairwell door open without moving forward into the corridor. A shot rang out. The door closed almost shut, she could see Chris had caught it with his foot. Given the shot she thought it was a risk.

"This is the Anti-corruption Team. Drop your weapons," he shouted through the crack.

A further shot pinged off the door. She could tell it was either another shooter or the original guy had moved. She gestured two fingers and saw Chris nod. They'd had their warning and just like at Melchior, it seemed some people didn't recognise their authority. It would be their mistake.

She crouched down as Chris pushed the door with more force than before. She aimed for where she thought the last shot had come from, and tried to take a look down the corridor while Chris also fired up the corridor at the likely first shooter.

She could see at least three shapes, two in the corridor one at an end door. She thought Chris had hit his target, as she rolled back into the stairwell landing and the door closed.

"You got a hit. Did you see the guy at the door? That must be her apartment."

"I think they'll fall back to there. You ready to go out?"

"Yes. Let's do this."

She let Chris push the door open again and rolled across the corridor, finding scant cover in a doorway opposite the stairwell door. There had been no shots this time. Chris was right. He was standing now in the stairwell doorway, and together they moved up the corridor.

"What's that noise?" she asked.

There was rhythmic thumping, and the sound of an engine.

"Helicopter?"

"Shit. She can't get away. There could be civil war."

They'd reached the apartment door. Chris crashed through the door, and she followed.

Her immediate perception was a big open plan space. There were shots coming at them from across the room. She dived for the couch that had it's back to the door, joining Chris behind it. Bits of stuffing and cloth flew up from the top of the couch.

"We could be pinned down for a while," she said, thinking about how to speed things up.

"There's only two now, maybe the injured guy's gone with her?"

She was looking through her visor across to the kitchen area, and saw the faint lines of yellow indicating a doorway. She pointed towards it. Chris was nodding.

"I'll cover you," he said.

She took a deep breath and ran. Splinters of wooden floor and chips of plaster sprayed themselves around her. She couldn't make out Chris' shots in the general noise, but he was clearly making it difficult enough.

It wasn't till she reached the door that she felt the dull ache in her shoulder. She reached back and felt the wetness. Ahead of her was a flight of steps, presumably leading to the roof. She ran up them, her breath more jagged as the motion jarred her shoulder. She could still hear the helicopter. She wondered what Mariko was waiting for?

She pushed the door and felt the icy blast across her cheekbones. A shot entered through the gap and ricocheted off the stairwell wall. She guessed they couldn't see her, but could see the heat escaping when the door opened. She heard the bottom door open and turned to aim.

The helicopter noise changed, preparing to take off. She ignored it, and concentrated on the opening door. She saw a hand move slowly into sight, signing: she breathed out.

"It's taking off," she shouted down, seeing the thermal image of Chris running up the stairs.

"You're hit," he said.

"We've got to stop her," she said. Mariko was more important than her shoulder.

"We'll have to wait till they're free of the buildings, those things don't come down nice."

"We've no choice," she agreed.

It was as if they were convincing themselves of the only obvious course of action. Enya knew Arne Dale's apartment was near the top of the next block. There was no shooting till they knew the helicopter couldn't hit anything residential.

The sound of the helicopter suggested it was moving away from the building now. She pushed the door open and tried to see where it was heading. All of a sudden there was a flash of light. Not just a single light, but as if all the blocks had everything switched on, the roof lights, apartment lights, everything. Her visor image distorted then went black. She took it off. It was just was black. She could hear the whump of the helicopter blades but not it's engines. She hoped to god it was far enough away.

The whumping got more distant and seemed to be slowing. It was the only noise she could hear. In the pitch dark she strained to discern what was going on.

"What the fuck just happened?" asked Chris from somewhere to her left.

"I don't know. A power surge?"

"But it should have been absorbed."

Before she could answer she heard the crash of metal on ice; screeching and scraping noises. The helicopter burst into flames, making a bright yellow glow, on what she thought was Murcheson Road.

She could hear sirens, already triggered by the energy grid failure. There would be no survivors from the helicopter. Poor soul, she thought, the pilot just doing what he was paid to do. And she caught her breath. She hadn't heard from Anatoli since they'd landed. That wasn't usual. Where was he?

She stumbled round and tried to find the door. Her shoulder now a deep burning pain.

"Boss, reset your visor."

Yes, of course, what was she thinking. She stopped and pressed the reset button. It flickered back to life and she could see Chris and the door.

"I've got to find Anatoli."

"He's okay," said Chris.

"Where? Why's he not called?"

She thought her visor was playing up again as the image went fuzzy, then she became aware her legs were bending. It went black again.

Chris watched Enya crumple, rushing to catch her as he realised what was happening. He dragged her towards the stairwell door. It opened and he tried to hold Enya and aim. A figure came out the doorway with hands up.

"Chris?"

It was Glenn.

"Enya's been hit. I think she's lost some blood."

"What happened?" asked Glenn as he came forward to lift Enya's legs.

"I don't know. Some sort of power surge, must have been local and the grid just failed. And it affected the chopper. Went down over on Murcheson."

Together they were carrying Enya into Mariko's apartment. Chris saw Glenn try a light switch on and off a few times without success.

"We need to pack her shoulder and get her to the hospital," he said as they lay her on the couch.

"The lift'll be out, you ready for ten flights?"

Chris had finished using what he'd found lying on the couch to put pressure on Enya's shoulder.

"No, but nevermind," he said as they lifted Enya again and headed for the service stairs.

James had cut a small hole in the glass, just like Tanya had in the empty building in Vostok. He'd had time since then to come to terms with shooting Toni the driver, mistaking him for the UN marine, but the resonances still echoed down his life. He'd visited Vostok since then, searching for Anatoli and Tanya. It was another layer covering up some of his guilt. Now he had a chance to cover more. Taking Thierry Vonne out, without killing him, without allowing him to become a martyr to his cause, was the right thing to do.

He lay down on the table they'd dragged to the window. The wind whistled through the small gap left around his rifle's muzzle. He saw the lights come on in the meeting room as Binh entered first. James was relieved to see Binh could resist looking across towards his building. Too often people gave the game away with a careless glance.

He could see Thierry come in next, his suit shrugged to his waist. Thierry did look across at his building. James felt seen, but he knew it was impossible. Thierry was naturally on edge, he'd be looking everywhere. And right on cue, he saw Thierry check under the meeting room table.

The projector kicked into life. It was now or never, since James knew there was no real information on the file and it wouldn't take long for Thierry to see that.

He breathed in and held the breath. He had the top of Thierry's right arm in his cross hairs. He squeezed and fired. Through the scope, he saw the glass fracture around the bullet hole. There would be a noise, but it would be too late for Thierry to react. He saw the blood spread through the shirt.

"Binh has him," said Kairns.

Suddenly the lights in the room went out, and so did the projector. James' scope flickered and went black, he checked his visor. Also dead. He pressed the resets, saw them both wink back to life.

"Was that a power surge?"

"Must be," said Kairns, "I can't see either of them."

"Shit," said James, who could.

He saw Thierry, his arm covered in red now across the neck of Binh's pale blue body and orange exposed face. Thierry's other arm had a pale blue, gun shape to Binh's head. James breathed in and took the shot.

He watched Thierry's gun arm convulse, and Binh push the arm off. He saw the heat flash down the gun's barrel.

"He's missed. Binh's gone for the gun. We need to get up there," said Kairns.

"That's a lot of stairs. You mean, I have to."

"No, you stay here, eyes on that room till Thierry's in handcuffs. I've a team waiting at the bottom of the building."

James saw Kairns approach the window and a series of light flashes began from Kairns' torch reflecting on the glass. He saw answering light flashes from the street below. He had to hand it to Kairns, he knew how to plan an operation. Well, nearly; he recalled the sniper at the airport who hit Isadora. Unknown unknowns and all that.

He continued to watch through his scope. Binh had managed to get Thierry on his knees but, with a shot to both shoulders, it was impossible to make him raise his arms to his head. He saw the door open and Kairns' men enter. He rolled off the table and went to the bag with the glass repair kit. Hearing the sirens, he wondered what carnage the power surge had caused elsewhere, it sounded serious.

Chapter Thirty Six - The Mercy of Strangers

Alison saw the two agents standing outside the room. Kairns had told her not to let Valla know where she was going, and they eyed her suspiciously. She doubted they could mistake her for Senator Valentina Torres, but they were clearly on their toes for any attempt on the prisoner.

"I have permission from Regional Controller Kairns," she said, showing them the paper pass. Everything had reverted to old school till the grid could be rebooted. The agent nearest her nodded.

"Negotiator," he said opening the door.

She went inside and saw Thierry Vonne sitting, bandaged up, at an interrogation table. He wasn't restrained. She felt it was a fair gamble, he'd intended to go out in a blaze of glory, the only danger he posed was to himself since Renner had died.

"I'm the State Negotiator, Alison Strang. I don't think we've ever met," she said sitting opposite him.

She watched his face: he'd looked up briefly when she'd entered but he'd stared at the table since then, and grunted in reply. It was more than she'd expected. He was a smart man, used to using charm and persuasion, but she knew the events of the last few hours would have caused a major reappraisal of his interactions with people.

He was going to be feeling powerless and trapped, he'd try to shutdown all interactions till he could regain his confidence. She couldn't let him do that and the grunt told her she had less time than she'd anticipated.

"Senator Vonne, why did you order the murder of Persimon Coia?"

She saw an imperceptible twitch at the word murder. It was a chink in the defence he'd mounted. A conscience she could work with, psychopaths were worse. She relaxed slightly.

She saw him look up from the table. He looked like he was still doing calculations, but seemed to have recognised Alison was as neutral a person as he was going to come across. She knew self-preservation kicked in stronger after a near death experience or a reprieve from an expected death. Thierry's wounds wouldn't have killed him but coupled with his martyrdom plan she felt she had an edge to prise open the chink.

"I came by information she was part of a plan to poison somewhere in the AFS. It would've given Mariko an excuse to proscribe all Green activists or supporters. Ask Valentina Torres what it was like when they proscribed the Resistance."

"I was here when it was proscribed. I understand some of that. But who gave you the information? We believe Green activists have been manipulated both by internal and external forces to the AFS."

She held out an olive branch, but if his information pointed at Mariko it was academic. Alison had heard about the helicopter crash just before coming down to the interrogation suites. However, it was worth uncovering as much as possible about what had happened. The usual AFS thing was to move on, but just because President Mariko Neish was dead didn't mean that other players were safe now, as far as she was concerned, and she knew Enya Zhao and her Team would feel the same. It was also certain, Senator Valentina Torres wanted the full truth, if only to direct her revenge at those who were left standing.

"It was anonymous, from a burner phone. We tried to trace it back, all we could get was it had come from the Progress Massif, probably Kunlun but we couldn't pinpoint it. We had no contacts in Kunlun, Rafael Dupont had infiltrated it completely."

Alison hadn't gone to Kunlun, and she didn't have all the information from the Team about what had happened there either. She was annoyed, she'd have liked to probe this point further, Thierry probably knew things he didn't even realise he knew.

She paused in her thoughts. Mariko Neish was from Kunlun, she remembered it was her father amongst others who'd died in the Innonnox Mine. Mariko had held Gordon Murcheson responsible but maybe Freddie Tran too. Mariko would never have wanted anything to happen to her home town. Could she have been the leak to Thierry? Two birds with one stone?

"Why did you risk your position, the first openly Green senator?"

She was genuinely perplexed and curious about how Thierry had rationalised it all.

"I don't believe in the Code, some people don't deserve to live if they put the planet in danger. I expected Blackie to wait at Kwazi Station, but he was never good at forward planning."

She saw him lean forward, careful of his shoulders and continue, "I regret the death of my friend, but he died for the cause."

Alison could tell Thierry was coming back together, as a result of her questioning, as much as anything else. She had to choose her next few questions carefully; very soon she wouldn't be able to trust his answers.

"President Neish is dead, the power surge took out her helicopter. If you have anything else to tell me, this is your last chance. I can't promise treason won't be on the list of charges."

It was her last offer and she could see in his face he was well aware of it. He looked like he was weighing it up. Did he think enough of himself as a saviour of the planet to keep going, or would he slip back to the idea of martyrdom?

"We heard a rumour Mariko had a gang contact in Kunlun. We couldn't substantiate it. I considered it plausible but we didn't realise the importance of the rumour till it was too late. Some relation of Frederika Tran was as close as we got."

That was it. All she was going to get from him. She could see his body language had already changed: he'd made his mind up about the questions that had previously been hanging over him.

"Thank you, Senator Vonne. Your cooperation will be taken into consideration."

She stood up and took one last look at him. There was no mistaking the self righteousness of his posture now.

She entered the meeting room they'd been operating from.

"I need to know everything that happened in Kunlun from everyone who was there. As soon as possible," she said to the room.

Glenn looked up.

"That's going to be difficult," he said, "Enya's been taken to hospital with loss of blood and gunshot to the shoulder, and Anatoli's at the Ice Cabin resort."

"Shit," she said, "you leave the room for an interrogation and this is what happens. Is Enya okay? What's Anatoli doing up there?"

"Yes, Enya's going to be fine. What did you get from Thierry?"

"Everything I could. He's not going to give us anything more. Shouldn't he be in hospital too?"

"Clean through, and first aid at the scene," said James, "he's not in any danger. The bullet lodged in Enya and hit a vein, bit more complicated."

"Oh, okay," she said, anatomy and firearms were not areas she knew much about, but she trusted James to not take risks with a prisoner, Unlike Thierry, James believed in the Code.

"We think Anatoli isn't dealing well with the death of Eric," said Chris, "I've asked Chick to get up there as soon as possible and keep an eye on him. I mean, what kind of trouble could he get into at the Ice Cabin?"

She watched Chris follow that thought to its answer. Debauchery was a byword for the Ice Cabin resort, an expensive spa retreat south of Melchior City at the north of the Torres Peninsula as it broke into the Torres Islands.

"Shit," said Chris, "I hadn't really thought about that."

"Well, there's nothing we can do about that right now," she said, "So you three are going to tell me everything you know about what happened in Kunlun."

Anatoli was sitting at the bar, at least that's what he was calling his grip on the rail running along the edge which steadied him. Without it, he reckoned, he'd be sitting on the floor, in a less coherent fashion. He knew he should go to his room, but he was concerned about trying to stand up.

He'd been drinking since he'd arrived two hours ago, and he knew he could hold his liquor. For a while, he'd had his suspicions his drink had been spiked, but he couldn't be sure, he was also certain his drink had never been out of his sight. It was confusing. Maybe he *had* been going at it a bit faster than normal. There was definitely something wrong however, and it was making him wary about the idea of getting off the bar stool. He looked over at the bartender, who appeared slightly out of focus. Anatoli shut one eye and the bartender looked better.

"I think... I think I might need some help."

He saw the bartender nod in what he hoped was understanding, and then he felt someone supporting him off the bar stool from behind. Anatoli gave himself up to the mercy of strangers and closed his eyes.

"Thanks."

Chick Ewing was waiting for the solar alert all clear in the pilot lounge of Weddell City airport. She'd had a decent nap and was on her third coffee, just over five hours since she'd talked to Chris and agreed to head up to the Ice Cabin resort. She was musing on whether the heavily hinted at permanent position with the Anti-corruption Team was something she wanted to take up.

It would be regular income which she desperately needed, but she was about to head up to 'keep an eye' on the previous incumbent who appeared to have gone off the rails, which made it sound like it had a few downsides.

She'd heard more than a few things about Anatoli Dale, however. He didn't sound like he ever rode the rails in the first place. The illegal take off at Vostok, which he seemed to have brushed off without censure, and then landing at Mellor Station in the cross winds, singled him out as an extraordinary pilot.

And Chris had been pretty open that the reason she would be offered the position was so Anatoli could marry Enya Zhao, the scary lady in charge of the Team, and, of course, there was the scary lady in question. Though Chick liked it when her clients were straight forward, she wondered what it would be like in every interaction?

Her phone buzzed across the table, echoing the other buzzings and alarms in the lounge. The all clear had finally come through. She hurried out to her jet, prepped for take off.

Chapter Thirty Seven - Seasoned Veterans

The barman nodded to the man at the back table as the two doormen carried Anatoli Dale, son of Senator Arne Dale out of the room. He'd recognised his target the moment he'd walked into the bar. Sons of senators were often up at Hielo Cabana, the Ice Cabin, for a bit of rest and respite from being on their best behaviour in Weddell City. Sometimes they asked for some 'respite', but even if they didn't, he'd end up with photographic evidence they had indulged anyway.

The doormen were taking Mr Dale to the room all set up for this photographic evidence. The all clear had buzzed its way around the room almost as soon as Mr Dale had been lifted off his chair. He never thought anything of that, but the TV flickered back into life with a breaking story that caught his attention.

There'd been a total blackout in Weddell City centre, a helicopter had gone down too. How the other half live, he thought. Helicopters were supposed to be grounded during a solar alert, like everything else. He bet Mr Dale had broken a few rules in his time too. Privileged arseholes. Still without them his income would be considerably reduced. They always paid up, either the sons, and in some cases the daughters, or their parents did.

He'd given Mr Dale a hefty dose, the first didn't seem to have had any effect. It wouldn't work if it looked like he was drugged, so he'd have to wait till he came round a bit, but there was no harm in setting the scene. He'd get Candy in, she was a bouncy blonde, just his type, he thought.

Chris put a call through to the Melchior Police department as soon as the all clear sounded. He knew it took two and a half hours to get up to Melchior and the police would take less time to find Anatoli than Chick, but she was still a good back up plan. It had been a bigger than forecast CME, there could be smaller ones behind it that would still interfere with his ability to communicate with up there. Better to have someone he could trust on the ground.

He told the officer they needed to find Anatoli and where he might be. They seemed reticent till he pointed out this was not some errant posh boy gone on the run. Once he was sure they'd grasped the situation he hung up. He was glad Chick would be around to make sure they continued to treat it seriously.

Enya was in surgery and he was waiting in the hospital to find out how long they would keep her in for. Ideally Anatoli would be able to get to the hospital. He didn't think things would go well for Anatoli if he wasn't back in time for her getting out. Though, he could understand what might have driven Anatoli to the outer reaches of the AFS.

Like James, Anatoli was a planner, and they never coped well when plans went wrong, especially if they thought it was their fault. He wondered if he should ask Alison how to approach Anatoli.

He was a fixer, he adapted his plan on the move, and he didn't want Enya hurt further. The death of Eric had done enough already.

The Melchior Police helicopter landed at the Ice Cabin helipad and a three man team piled out, running for the rooftop entrance. The agent in Weddell City had pulled no punches on who this Anatoli guy was and why finding him was a priority. Plus, they'd been keeping an eye on goings on in the Ice Cabin for a while, never quite managing to pin anything down to anybody, this sounded like it gave them the excuse to turn the place upside down and see what fell out of where.

The main resort building was only three floors, dropping to two floors on the two wings that stretched out in a curve from the main functions area. Two of his team went into the arms and he stayed in the main area heading for reception. As he appeared at the foot of the public staircase to the entrance lobby, he could see the few guests there looked startled. He was all in black, bulletproof vest, sub-machine gun held low to his chest, so he felt that was understandable.

What *he* was looking for was the faces of those who wanted to run having seen him, the word 'POLICE' emblazoned in easy to read letters across the top of his chest and his back.

The receptionist looked suspicious, not actively involved in any wrong doing but definitely under orders to keep an eye out. He saw her eyes dart to the bar area. He ran into it in time to see the bartender making a run for a back door.

"Got a runner from the bar. Keep searching. I think we're onto something," he called across the radio mike hung securely from his ear.

"Heading to the first floor on left-side wing, nothing so far."

"I'm just at the second floor, right-side wing, got some heavies outside a room door. Looks interesting."

He heard his team report back as he scrambled behind the bar to the back door. Outside, it was black. The shadow of the building cut out the lights from the front and it seemed the back area lighting was out or the bartender had had time to disable it. He brought his visor down, he didn't like them, but they were useful in the winter. Fiddling with the settings till he got thermal, he spotted a heat signature behind a large square object.

"Come out with your hands up," he said.

He saw the heat signature thin as whoever it was, tried to get more behind the object. He fired a warning shot just wide of the heat signature.

He saw a hand go up and the figure come out of the cover.

"Hands on head. Over here, nice and slow."

He fished his handcuffs out with his free hand.

"Turn around, bring your arms behind."

He slapped the hand cuffs on and hauled the figure towards the back door.

He could see the heavies were armed, and had called on his colleague to come over as soon as they'd finished their search of the left-side wing. He heard the footsteps on the stairs behind him, and he gestured for her to move cautiously to get a view of the corridor.

Across from the stair door there was no cover so they'd have to caution and be ready to fire if they were to stand a chance. In his experience most gang members did not drop their weapons preferring to go down in a blaze of glory. He had wondered why, till he'd caught a popular crime show, where miraculously nobody ever got killed or seriously wounded in gunfights. It began to make sense after that.

"Ready?"

"Yes."

He stood out into the corridor, aiming at the guy furthest down the corridor. He knew she'd be taking the nearer.

"Melchior Police, drop your weapons," he shouted.

To his surprise they did.

"Everything. Hands on heads, on your knees."

He approached them slowly, watching as they dropped to their knees with their hands clasped across their heads. Seasoned veterans of this manoeuvre, he thought.

When they'd dropped the guns, his colleague had moved into the corridor herself and he nodded at her to cuff the heavies while he went to the door they'd been guarding. It was unlocked.

Opening the door he heard a woman squeal and entering the room properly, saw the cameras, the lighting, the buxom blonde with nothing on and the prone figure of someone who looked a lot like the guy they were looking for.

"Police. Everyone down on your knees, hands on your heads, nobody touches anything else."

He went towards the guy laid out on the bed, he still had some clothing on, but his survival suit was crumpled on the floor, he searched through the pockets, finding the ID and confirming that this was indeed Anatoli Dale. It was an added bonus they had the blackmail gang they'd been trying to nail for two years now.

He cuffed the cameraman, and the woman once she'd put some clothing on. He checked Anatoli Dale's pulse, it was slow. He called for the local first aider and then let the boss know they had the gang.

He couldn't trust the security at the Ice Cabin so he called for reinforcements from Melchior and got the gang together in the lobby where they could be overseen. One of his team was with Mr Dale and the first aider as they tried to work out what he'd been given and bring him round. The bartender had refused to say anything. He reckoned, having heard the words Anti-corruption Team in the earlier phone call, that his refusal would backfire on the bartender, and he wasn't pushing the bartender too hard to talk.

About an hour and a half later a young woman entered the lobby. She looked flustered but also unconcerned by the cuffed gang sitting on the floor. He wondered who she was, and if she was something to do with the people back in Weddell City.

"Shit," she said.

It was an odd way of confirming his suspicions but it did.

"Is Anatoli okay?"

"You are?"

"Chick Ewing, charter pilot for the Anti-corruption Team. I'm here to pick up Anatoli and bring him back to Weddell City. What happened?"

"May I see some ID?"

"Oh, yes. Sorry, here you go. I don't have any official charter pilot thingie because I've only this moment taken over from Anatoli. But this proves who I am, and you can call Chris Saraband on the Team if you need more."

He wondered afresh at her apparent lack of concern; it seemed a part of her personality rather than any kind of foreknowledge now.

"He's in Room 207, he's been drugged but the first aider is trying to bring him round."

"Ah, thanks," she said.

He watched her run for the stairs and disappear up them and almost immediately saw his reinforcements appear round the same corner, having come from the helipad.

The lead one nodded back after the woman and he shook his head.

"This is everyone, though I'm sure there's a mastermind somewhere behind them. They don't exactly strike me as the enterprising sort themselves."

He saw the blonde pouting, and shook his head again.

Chick came through the open door of Room 207 to find a police officer walking Anatoli up and down in the room while the first aider was busy looking up information with her phone.

She went to look at Anatoli. His pupils were dilated. She felt his pulse and it was worryingly slow. His lips were pale.

"He needs the hospital now," she said, "it's only twenty four hours or so after he's inhaled Sarin, used antidotes, then he's not slept properly, he's drunk alcohol and been drugged. We won't know a thing about how to revive him from all of that. He needs blood tests and drips and stuff we don't have."

She nodded at the policewoman.

"Help me carry him up to the helipad. I can bring your suspects in by jet. But he needs hospital now."

Valla had left the Intelligence Agency when Kairns and James had headed out to the office block. She'd noticed then, that Enya and Chris were missing but she couldn't remember when they'd left the room.

She'd been at home when the CME had hit. Her apartment block had shielding above the minimum standard, but it crashed anyway as the grid overloaded. There was a few minutes in the total dark before the emergency lights came on with the auxiliary power supply. She knew to stay indoors and off the roads, so she and Martin had made the most of the enforced gloom by lighting candles and going to bed.

When the all clear came through she heard the TV snap back on and when she made out the reporter's breathless tone she got up to see why.

"Shit. I have to go to the Intelligence Agency. I'm sorry darling."

Martin had followed her through from the bedroom and was nodding at her.

"Sounds like it. Take care."

Chapter Thirty Eight - Family

Chris took the phone call from Chick in the Intelligence Agency lobby. He'd been told to go home by the hospital as they were keeping Enya in and not making a decision till much later. Hearing Anatoli was also in hospital he rolled his eyes, thanked Chick and asked her to let him know when they'd sorted Anatoli out. Though he knew it was more than dodgy substances in the blood that was wrong with Anatoli.

He'd not gone home, because he wanted to speak to Alison, and she'd said she was going to stay at the Intelligence Agency. He opened the door and, despite the best efforts of the building's air conditioning, the familiar waft of stale coffee and exhaled stress greeted him. There'd been too much of this lately, he thought.

He could see Alison lying across a few chairs at the back of the room while Glenn and James looked up and waved him over to where they were sitting at the near end of the table.

"What's the latest?" asked Glenn.

"Anatoli alive, in hospital, Enya alive, in hospital. I think that's a win," he said.

"Hospital?" asked James, looking concerned.

"Drugged by some blackmail gang at the Ice Cabin. Think Enya might follow that bunch all the way to the top," he said, "I was thinking, Alison should speak to Anatoli before Enya does. Not that our Dear Leader doesn't know her own man, but I don't think Anatoli is quite himself right now."

"I agree," said Glenn, "I'll let Alison know when she wakes up. You look shattered, you should go get some sleep yourself."

Chris looked at his watch, it was five in the morning, he'd been awake for nearly twenty four hours. He was past tired. He looked back at Glenn and James who'd also been up for the same amount of time. They all looked like shit, he thought.

"Yeah, maybe. Is there any chance of fresh coffee in the Agency?"

He saw Glenn smile in understanding and get up to go find whoever was in charge of coffee.

Anatoli became aware of beeping. More beeping than he expected in a hotel room. He opened his eyes and it was too dark to see. The beeping seemed to be coming from behind him. He tried to stretch over to find a bedside light but something was attached to the back of his hand. Fresh and more alarming beeping began. The door opened and the light was dazzling, hurting his eyes.

Before he closed his eyes he'd seen enough to know he was in hospital. He didn't think he'd panicked, but was aware there'd been an increase in the pace of certain of the beeps.

What had happened to him? He tried to remember. His last memory was the bartender. His stomach was sinking. Clearly he *had* been drinking something that had been spiked. How could he have been so stupid?

The nurse who'd opened the door was at the side of the bed, fussing and telling him to lie back, checking the drip into the back of his hand. He succumbed.

The door opened again and he instinctively shut his eyes this time. He hoped whatever was going on with them was temporary and didn't want to do any permanent damage. He heard the nurse's uniform swish towards the door and a quick whispered conversation. The door closed and he heard a familiar voice.

"Got to hand it to you Anatoli, the doctors said they were surprised you could function at all with what you'd been given."

"Chick. You know the rumours, I can drink most pilots under the table. Clearly, I have a remarkable constitution."

"Yes. That's what they said. You've got light sensitivity because of everything that was running around in your blood. They told me it's temporary. Did you know they had to chemically sober you up first? Before they could find out what the bartender used?"

He followed her voice around the foot of the bed, till she was on his right.

"Chick."

"Yes?"

"Too much information."

"Oh, sorry. It was fascinating, I didn't know you could sober people up like that. Wouldn't it be great if you could buy that at a pharmacy?"

"Chick. Why are you here?"

"Ah."

He could tell from the reduction in her effervescence it wasn't good news.

He had one thought.

"Enya. She's all right?" he asked with concern.

Shit. He'd been so desperate to get away from Weddell City he hadn't even called her. What else could have happened since then?

"Well," she started, "I'll work my way in to the bad news. First, President Neish is dead. A helicopter crash. There was a CME, bigger than forecast. Hit the whole of Weddell City centre and took out the helicopter."

"Who was flying? Everything should have been grounded."

"You and I both know there's ways round that. It was Kaysim, he never did care about the alerts."

"What does this have to do with Enya?"

He couldn't cope if she'd been on the helicopter, why was Chick padding this out?

"She's alive, took a bullet to her shoulder and had to go in to surgery. They were trying to arrest the President."

"Fucking hell, lead with that sort of shit next time."

The beeping increased again.

"Oh, okay. There'll be a *next* time?"

"Probably. You still want to be the Team's charter?"

"They asked to make me permanent. I think I'm going to say yes."

"Good."

He'd run out of energy now he knew Enya was safe.

"Can I stay here?"

"Sure. Why?"

"Chris told me to bring you back as soon as I could, and the chairs in the waiting room are tortuous, but this one reclines."

He could hear the motors in the chair at his right hand side. There was something reassuring about the Team still looking out for him. He let himself sink back to sleep.

Valla had arrived at the Intelligence Agency and headed straight for Kairns' office. The Agency also had auxiliary power and military grade shielding. Valla felt some things would need to be beefed up elsewhere in light of the power surge's effects. And who would order that, now Mariko Neish was ash and bone on Murcheson?

The Senate would need to convene, but not in person. Right now, however, the AFS had simply fallen back on the Code and the rugged individualism that characterised its inhabitants. There was something to be said for not getting too civilised, she thought.

Kairns had been awake, though she noticed the smells of recent sleep as she entered his office, and the crumpled blanket on the daybed.

"What are we going to do about all of this?" she asked.

She saw him look askance at her.

"What do you mean? We?"

She realised there were layers she'd not even considered to her question. 'We' could be the Navy and the Intelligence Agency, or it could equally have meant the Torres Family. She wasn't entirely sure what she *had* intended now she thought about it.

"Well, right now, you and me. The police are busy with basic law and order out there, the political order is more our responsibility. Some of Mariko's people are going to make trouble. You can guarantee there's conspiracy theories sweeping the social networks already."

"I've alerted agents to monitor the networks, we've put out a reminder to the news and current affairs media of their investigative responsibilities. We can't be too heavy handed or it'll look like we do have something to hide."

"Good. I can get enough senators to call for a senate session online, the sooner that happens the better. I think."

"Will they open a fresh election?"

"It's an option. They might go for another interim presidency, till summer."

She saw Kairns was looking at her with his worst possible poker face.

"No. Absolutely not," she said.

"You should stand. Properly this time, Valentina."

"I have other responsibilities."

She waved in the general direction of the sea, but she knew she wasn't fooling Kairns that it was the navy she was worried about.

"Veronica will be fine."

She saw he was playing with her.

"We need someone to fix more than the legislature," he said, "the pressure from Greens is only going to get worse and we'll lose the AFS' hard won independence if they get involved. There's too many outsiders invested in the Green movement. It's just a different kind of Global as far as I'm concerned."

"I'll think about it."

"Do think about it, Valentina. Don't fob me off."

Shit, he was good enough at seeing through other people's poker faces.

"You know the Anti-corruption Team is still downstairs. Why don't you go stir them up. Leave me to get on with things," he said.

"Are you dismissing me?"

She was seeing a whole new facet to Kairns. She wondered how cocky he'd get with her.

"No, I really do need to get on with stuff. And you need to be directing people to do other stuff. This is what you do in emergencies."

He looked as genuine as she thought he could manage. Over twenty years of working in Intelligence had worn away most of the genuine faces he could pull, she realised.

The smell in the meeting room wasn't an improvement on Kairns' office. She saw Alison stretching at the back of the room and Chris and Glenn standing next to what smelt like fresh coffee. James was stretched out over five chairs asleep but not looking comfortable, his lankiness causing his feet to hang off the end chair.

"Good, you're all awake," she said, loud enough to rouse James.

"Valla," said Glenn, "you're looking all General-like, What's up?"

"Agent Murcheson, there's work to be done. There's evidence to be collected from Mariko Neish's apartment. Nikau Burns to be interviewed. I understand from Agent Kairns that Melchior Police has a blackmail gang in custody. Let's find out who's paid up and if they've been in positions that could be compromised. The question is more, what few things are down? Since most things seem to be up."

She turned to James, "You, go home and get some proper sleep, back here in five hours time."

She saw James grumble but head out the room nonetheless.

She looked at Chris and wondered if she should send him home too: he was looking defiantly back at her.

"No," he said, "I'm fine. And I'm waiting to hear about Anatoli anyway."

"Why?"

"He's in hospital in Melchior. He's why Melchior Police have a blackmail gang. Got Mickey-ed at the Ice Cabin. Apparently that, coupled with everything else, has given him temporary light sensitivity."

"The pair of them. I don't believe it. Right, Alison..."

She strode up to the back of the room where Alison had been stretching.

"We need to sort them out."

"I agree. I heard that Enya had set a date. It's a week and a half away. But she's been too busy trying to find out if Eric Jordan had family."

"I can find that out."

She fished her phone out and called the Citizenry Department. When she'd finished her call, she had an audience.

"Eric Jordan grew up at the same State Home as Enya. He's got no next of kin because he's an orphan."

"Then we're his family," said Chris.

"Another thing to be sorting out then."

"Not without Enya," he said.

"Fine."

She and Alison could organise the wedding though, she thought. And Anatoli.

Chapter Thirty Nine - Secrets

Enya was sitting up in the bed. They hadn't let her have a laptop so she was busy trying to conduct business on her phone. They were supposed to be making a decision to let her go home soon. That had been four hours ago. Nobody had come near her since.

She wondered where Anatoli was, and also why Chris hadn't turned up yet. In fact, she was feeling pretty abandoned at that moment, and suspicious about it too. She'd rattled off a few emails already and had been checking for replies. Nothing had been forthcoming. Something was definitely going on, and she was beginning to worry it had to do with Anatoli.

She looked up as the door opened. It was Chris. Finally. And he looked sheepish. Again she was reminded of what Ray McCarthy had called the Team members. She tried not to be annoyed with him, but she knew it was written in her eyes.

"Hi," he said warily, "They said you can go in half an hour once the paperwork's complete. They were too scared to come tell you. What have you been doing Enya?"

"Waiting," she said acidly.

"Ah," he paused, then said, "I have some news about Eric, Valla pulled some Senator magic and got the details on why there's no next of kin. He went to the same State Home that you did. It explains a lot."

She was taken aback at the information. Even with the weight of the Anti-corruption name behind her, she'd wondered why it had been so difficult to find out where Eric grew up, but those who grew up under State protection had their privacy protected. She'd benefited from the same protections. The State also highlighted those who had been successful, as role models. It was done in an anonymous way, but she knew Eric could easily have worked out who she was. He'd had that strong investigative streak she had so appreciated.

"I want to help you organise the funeral, we've agreed, *we* were his family," said Chris.

She looked at him, her sergeant from all those years ago, and once again felt she'd been right to trust to her gut instinct. Even Eric had been the right choice. It had been her fault it had gone sour. She should have noticed sooner.

"Okay, but first you tell me where Anatoli is," she said.

She could see Chris was apprehensive, and wondered what part of the story was making him feel that way.

"So," he started, "Anatoli is in hospital in Melchior."

She saw he'd paused but she didn't rise to the bait, forcing him to continue.

"I'm not entirely sure why he was up at the Ice Cabin, but he fell foul of a blackmail gang, who spiked his drink. But, Chick was up there as soon as she could. She made sure he got to hospital. The police only knew about the spiked drink, not the Sarin or the antidotes."

She saw him looking at her, trying to figure out what she was thinking, but she had her very best playing-poker-with-Valla face on.

He's developed a temporary light sensitivity," he said.

"What?"

The idea that something would interfere with Anatoli's ability to fly broke through her silence. She knew how much that meant to him. His eyesight was key to keeping his licence.

"Temporary. Because of the chemical mix."

"Who's this blackmail gang? I want to get up there and interview them myself. Maybe I should take Alison."

She mused on how soon she could travel up. There were still things here in Weddell City to finish, not least Thierry Vonne.

"I think," said Chris, "Valla and Alison were talking about going up tomorrow. You have time."

The door opened and a nurse thrust some papers at Chris, retreating as quickly as possible.

"Right," she said, "Lets go."

Unfortunately, all her active bustling had to dissipate, since it took Chris' help to get into her suit. This was clearly how things were going to be for a while.

Valla and Alison followed the other disembarking passengers along the path through Melchior airport. They'd arrived on the evening flight, that made a connection with the weekly flight to Tierra Del Fuego.

"This is the route that Anatoli and Gary want to start their airship business with," said Alison, making as close to small talk as she thought Valla could cope with.

"That makes sense. I'd go for an Aotearoan route after that," said Valla.

Alison could see Valla's strategic mind working on the best routes to develop, and was thankful she was behaving just like her old self.

Chick was waiting for them after baggage, Valla had something to pick up but Alison had a set of clothes at her house so had travelled light.

"He's got shades, which the doctors have said he has to wear for a fortnight but they've said he's okay to be driven. Not to fly. Not for the next few days," said Chick, sounding very like she was reporting to some senior staff.

"Hi, Chick," said Alison," Thanks for doing this."

"Oh, I'm happy to. I was worried when I saw him post the flight. Chris told me I was right to call. I'm quite excited. They asked me to be the permanent pilot for the Team."

Alison could hear in her tone just how excited she was. She reckoned Chick must be only about four or five years older than Gary, her infectious energy reminded her of her son.

"I have a taxi waiting outside," said Chick, "It's still cold but *nothing* like Weddell City."

Alison heard the wonder, it was such an endearing feature of most natives.

There was no delay at the hospital since Anatoli's discharge papers had already been done, and he was bundled into the back with her and Chick. Valla was sitting up with the taxi driver.

The car wound its way up the mountain till Alison saw the deeper shadows of her house appear. There were already lights on, and she knew the local housekeeper would have provisions in for them.

She dashed on ahead to dim the lighting in the hallway and to set some candles in the living room, then she waved them inside. She saw Anatoli wave back at the taxi driver as it turned away.

"I love the shades," she said as he came inside. "Raybans, are they vintage?"

"Aviators, a present from my dad when I got my licence. I always kept them in the jet."

"Very..." said Valla, wryly.

Alison watched as Valla expertly manoeuvre Chick towards the kitchen.

"We'll make something to eat and drink."

She saw Anatoli had sat on the sofa and so she perched opposite, on the armchair. The coal fire between them, had a few flickering purple flames as it got started. There was no heat from it yet. A cold start.

"Anatoli. What are you doing here?"

She had decided against going in gently, he'd had time to think, lying in the hospital, it was time to filter those thoughts so only the useful ones were left in his head.

She saw him look at her, the understanding dawning. He looked relieved.

"I ask myself the same thing, now. It made a kind of sense then. I was just so tired of all the intrigue and worrying about why people were doing the things they were."

"You mean Eric?"

"I suppose I do."

"We found out he grew up at the same State Home as Enya. We think, unknown to anyone, she'd been a big part of his life for a while."

"Oh shit," he said.

"Anatoli, you can't be responsible for other people's actions. You've nothing to feel guilty about. Nothing you did was to hurt him on purpose. He chose to do the things he did."

"But there were things I didn't do that could have helped him."

"Probably not at the right time, though. It took a while for even Eric to realise. Ray told me he was genuinely shocked, when she suggested he was infatuated with Enya."

"You're right, as usual. But what will Enya say? I wasn't there for her when she got shot."

"You're not supposed to be permanently on standby, she's not a jet hire."

She heard him laugh then and knew she'd got through. The door from the kitchen opened at the same time.

"Laughter? Isn't there some saying about it being medicine? If it's not from Sun Tzu I don't keep it in my head," said Valla, " And he has nothing to say on laughter. Which is a pity, when you think about it."

"Who's Sun Tzu?" asked Chick.

Alison saw Anatoli shake his head in a warning to Chick, while Valla was putting the tray with snacks and a flask of coffee down.

"Charlotte, let me introduce you to The Art of War."

Alison saw that Valla was deep in an inside pocket of her shrugged down survival suit, the wrinkles making it difficult to access. Eventually she pulled out a small book, and handed it to Chick.

"Thank you, I shall read it tonight."

"You can keep it. I'll get another copy," said Valla.

Alison leant across to the table, picking up an empty plate and asked Anatoli what he wanted put on it: the general conversation descended into a food discussion.

The sun came through the window casting a golden glow around the room. In the winter it was never too early and Alison liked to keep the curtains open if she was at the house. She'd given Anatoli a south-west facing room so he wouldn't be blinded but she'd made sure Chick and Valla had north east facing rooms. Alison could hear Chick's animated appreciation from her bed.

She got up, dressed and went down to stir the fire and put more coal on. It felt normal; the daylight, the fire, the frost outside across the garden. Today they'd be planning the wedding. Nobody had told Anatoli yet, and she was looking forward to that moment.

Enya saw James, Chris and Glenn at the airport departure gate for the Melchior morning flight. She grew suspicious. They were up to something. She saw James was without his Vanta-black case, which meant it wasn't job related either. They were all checking in hold luggage. She hadn't okayed any holidays. She headed over.

"What are you lot up to?"

"Boss. Nothing," said Chris.

She knew the other two had let him answer because she gave Chris the least amount of grief, usually. She turned on Glenn. The Murchesons had a guilty look she'd begun to recognise. She could tell he was trying his best not to give anything away. James was the softest target, he was completely unable to bluff, she looked at him next.

"Ah. It wasn't my idea. I just agreed with it," he blurted out.

She saw Chris nudge him.

"My lips are sealed," said James.

And she knew then, even if they couldn't keep secret that they had a secret, they weren't going to tell her what it was.

"Suit yourselves. I'll find out soon enough."

She saw Glenn smile and it was mildly infuriating, but she was heading up to meet Anatoli and nothing could put her in a bad mood over that.

Chapter Forty - Thoughts

Thierry Vonne felt cheated somehow. He'd worked himself up to a martyr's death, been arrested and now they weren't even going to charge him with treason.

Aiding and abetting murder, perverting the course of justice, these were the least of his crimes. He'd be out of prison in under fifteen years, a disgraced former senator. His political career was over, his best friend was dead and he wasn't even sure he had influence in the Green movement anymore. He knew he'd committed treason. They should shoot him and get it over with, his life was meaningless now anyway.

Rafael Dupont was going to get shot, they were happy to charge him with treason. He'd no doubt the evidence against Rafael's numerous charges was insurmountable, even if Rafael had been able to afford Nancy Carter. He couldn't now, not since his backers had mysteriously vanished leaving him impoverished. Thierry wasn't surprised. Rats from a sinking ship, he thought. They'd simply regroup around some other weasel.

The guy Rafael had been working with, Karl Leyden was being sent back to the UN, a number of states had outstanding warrants, so there was reportedly horse-trading going on for who got him first. He reckoned Valentina Torres would be making the most out of that.

He was sitting on his bed in Weddell City Police cells, thinking about how he'd ended up at this point. The book he was trying to read was open in his lap but he knew he'd have to reread at least the last five pages since his thoughts had intruded again.

They'd set a date for his trial and he'd opted not to pay the bail, so they were sending him to wait on remand, in Denam prison. He closed the book as he heard footsteps out in the corridor heading towards his cell.

Alison had been waiting for them all at the airport. Enya knew then they were all in on something to do with her. This was no coincidence. It was only at that point she looked at her watch and properly took notice of the date. It was the seventh of August. It was only four days till the date she had told the Team she would marry Anatoli; back in Kunlun, around the table, before it all kicked off.

Shit. She allowed herself an expletive. This was what they were all up to. But she had nothing planned, no dress, no registrar, no venue, no invitations. Then, she recalled not seeing Valla about in the last two days. Valla loved to organise. She wasn't sure she wanted a Valla inspired wedding though. Still, she had a few days to reign the worst excesses in.

"I know what you're up to," she said as she got in the car.

"I never doubted that you would, Detective Zhao," replied Alison.

"Who have you invited?"

"You want to veto our list? You'll have to take that up with the General."

"I might and I will."

In the end she'd accepted they'd made a good guest list, but she put that entirely down to Anatoli being involved. It was the morning of the tenth and there was one more dress fitting. She nuzzled in against the back of Anatoli who was still asleep. He stirred.

"I know you're awake," she said.

They hadn't talked about why Anatoli had flown to the Ice Cabin, she knew it would come out from him when he was ready, but whatever had happened since then seemed to have got him back to his normal self. She suspected she had Alison to thank for some of that.

Anatoli was waiting at the foot of Alison's grand wooden staircase. It was something that was unthinkable in any UN state. Anatoli knew it had been smuggled into the AFS by the previous owner.

To calm his nerves he stared at the dragon finial where the staircase flared out and met the equally wooden, hall floor. There was a creak above him and he looked up, adjusting his sunglasses as he did so. He saw her come down. She looked to him, like she always did; serious and playful, petite but still filling the room with her presence; she was a wonderful union of opposites. He had to admit that she looked fabulous in the dress. To him she always did, but yeah, he was impressed.

He took her arm as she reached the floor and they went into the living room. The fire was roaring and the guests were spread out around the room. He saw Ray, Kairns, a few pilots he'd kept in touch with from the early days, there were faces in uniform he guessed were people Enya knew. His parents were sitting on the couch where only a few days ago he'd sat with Alison. He smiled at them, his mother was already dabbing at her eyes. The registrar was positioned in front of a closed curtained window, and they'd put a small table next to him. Anatoli saw more paperwork on it than he'd expected.

The ceremony went by in a blur, the most he could remember about it afterwards was them agreeing not to burden the state with offspring and various other needs. To begin with he'd found the questions amusing and it had only been the tightening grip of Enya's hand which had saved him from an out of character fit of the giggles. There were cheers when he kissed her at the end.

He felt he had finally come home somehow and was worried he might join his mum in a few tears, but when he'd turned from Enya to face the rest of them he saw that James, Glenn and Chris had whipped out sunglasses and were now smiling mischievously back at him. He went straight to wondering how Enya was going to take that.

He looked round to see and saw she too was wearing sunglasses.

"Very funny," he said through the fit of giggles, returned for a second chance.

"Food is in the kitchen, please come on through," announced Alison.

Most guests headed off towards the back of the house and Anatoli and Enya were left in relative peace with his parents. His mother was still dabbing at her eyes and his father was smiling in a way Anatoli hadn't seen for a long time.

"I'm glad to see you're going to settle down a bit, son," said his father.

"I'm still going to be flying, but not as much charter work. Gary and I are almost ready to start on the airship."

"Ah yes, the young man Alison introduced as her son. It was nice to finally meet him," said his father, now turning to look at Enya still on his arm, "And you my dear, look wonderful."

"Arne, Paloma," said Enya, "thank you so much for coming at short notice, it's not quite how I thought it would be, but I'm pleased with how it is."

"Well then, it's perfect," said his mother.

"Let's eat before there's nothing left," Aantoli said, and taking his mother on his other arm he moved with them towards the kitchen.

Two days later Chick had arrived with the remains of Eric Jordan. She'd declined Anatoli's wedding invitation, although it had been a hard decision to make. They were all nice people, but she didn't want to get caught up in their personal comings and goings.

The jar of remains she now had in her hands at Alison's door only served to remind her how much danger existed in their line of work and how much pain could result from it. She'd barely known Eric Jordan before he'd died in Kunlun, and she realised she'd prefer to keep it that way with the rest of them, just in case.

They were standing in Alison's garden, the soil was still frozen but Glenn had said he'd used a hand-screw excavator and she could see a neat cylindrical hole. Enya was now holding the jar.

"This was Eric Jordan, an exceptional officer, a friend when I had few, who died in the line of duty and saved lives with his actions. He will be missed, and not forgotten by his family."

Chick saw Enya kneel onto the ground and drop the jar into the hole, the metal of the jar scuffed against the edge of the hole. She saw Anatoli help Enya get back up.

She watched as Chris, James and Glenn dropped loose earth into the hole until it was filled, then Anatoli brought the stone over. It was a large, polished, garnet schist pebble. The stone that had inspired the AFS' flag, and it had the Weddell City Police crest carved into it while underneath the crest, his name, Eric Jordan, was carved with the two dates that now represented his life. She thought from her brief knowledge of Eric that he'd have appreciated the sentiment of the stone.

She'd noticed he'd been only a few months older than her, and that had an impact on her. You grew up fast in the AFS, it was true, but you didn't always last long either. She thought about all the instability that might follow behind the loss of President Neish and realised she was now amongst some of the people whose job it was to eliminate any threat to the AFS. It was, she had to admit, slightly exhilarating as well as slightly dangerous. She couldn't wait to get started.

Valla was running through the pre-flight checks when she heard Martin come into the cockpit.

"Hi, won't be long."

"Valla."

She could hear he had his XO voice on, she was about to get some unsolicited advice.

"Yes," she said warily and stopped at a safe place in the checking procedure.

"You should run for President."

She moved round in the seat to look him in the eye.

"You've been talking to Kairns. I'll sort him out later."

"I brought it up. *He* agreed with me. I think you'd be a great President."

"Of course I would. I was. But that doesn't mean I have to do it again."

"I'm not the only one who thinks that you do have to do it. It's you who can get things done, and done in the right way. Not underhand..."

"Let me cut you off right now. I haven't always been this Angel of Democracy you seem to have in your head," she sighed, "Look, do we have to talk about this just now? I'm going to miss our slot if I'm not careful."

"I have you at a disadvantage, I had to make a play for the idea while I could. Think about it, please?"

"Why's everyone saying that?"

"Because."

He was leaning towards her with his twinkling eyes, snatching a peck on her cheek, and she forgave him instantly.

"Go, get strapped in and feed Kairns some peanuts, that'll keep him quiet."

She turned back to the instrument panel and carried on where she'd left off. It was only when she'd reached cruising altitude that she allowed herself to go over what had been said to her at Enya and Anatoli's wedding.

Kairns and Martin were not the only people asking her to 'think about it'. Arne had spoken to her, going so far as to offer to nominate her. One of Enya's police friends, someone she recognised from the ranks of Moss activists, had also asked in passing if she'd 'thought about it'. They'd said how much it had been a topic of discussion amongst the Moss activists and in a positive way. They all deserved at least a 'good think' from her.

Ray McCarthy	Detective Inspector with Progress Police
Pat Gallway	Green activist
Enya Zhao	Head of Anti-corruption Team
James Wylie	Team member, sharpshooter, Olympic competitor
Glenn Murcheson	Team member, grandson of Gordon Murcheson
Chris Saraband	Team member, Enya's sergeant from Police time
Eric Jordan	Team member recruited from Weddell City Police
Anatoli Dale	Team charter pilot, Enya's fiance, son of Arne Dale
Thierry Vonne	Junior Lomonosov Senator, Green activist
Rafael Dupont	Senior Moss Senator
Steve Jung	Green activist
Karl Leyden	Green activist, author of Manifesto for a Green World
Valentina Torres	Senior Torres Senator, Defence Portfolio Holder
Veronica Tambor	Junior Larsen Senator, deputy to Valentina
Isadora Ley	eco-assassin, aka Enid Decourcey
George Tan	Green activist, owner of survival suit shop in Progress
Sheena Ricci	Progress Police pathologist
Colin Rosko	Green Contact in Progress, owner of Confessional bar
Gordon Murcheson	ex-President of AFS, Glenn's grandfather
Adil Choudrey	Green activist, receptionist at Juniper Hotel, Progress
Martin Kostov	Executive Officer of MS Mercer, partner of Valentina
Alison Strang	State Negotiator, partner of Glenn
Roy, Philippe Mousad, Poul -	ice scientists at Mellor Station
Daniel Ektov	assassinated senator, Glenn's maternal grandfather
Jonathan Blackbird Renner -	Thierry Vonne's friend
Maddy Clearbright	AFS Green Network Coordinator
Dante Castillero	Senior Lomonosov Senator, head of Legal Review
Kairns	Regional Controller of Intelligence Agency
Nikau Burns	State Negotiator
Mariko Neish	President of AFS, Senior Lomonosov Senator
Gary Strang	Alison's son
Lukas Brandt	Green activist
Persimon Coia	Green activist, chemist
River Sampson	Senior Lomonosov Senator
Victoria Beauchamp	Lomonosov investigator
Liam Kelly	Captain of MS Alvarez, AFS navy ship
Ian Khan	Captain of MS Coulter, AFS navy ship
Nicola Larsen	Executive Officer, MS Alvarez
Binh Mitchell	Executive Officer, MS Coulter
Jim McAndrew	Mayor of Kunlun
Yang Lau	gang boss in Kunlun
Freddie Tran	gang boss, ex-Resistance member
Jean Mirales	inventor of Larsen SASER
Chick Ewing	charter pilot, first name Charlotte
Cassie Galados	Green activist Kunlun, first name Cassiopiea
Reuben Ektov	Mine owner Kunlun, Glenn's cousin
Evan Redbarn	Green activist Kunlun
Arne Dale	Senior Glencor Senator, Anatoli's father

DID3304599

L - #0129 - 270422 - C0 - 216/140/23 - PB - DID3304599